FOUR CORNERS

A Novel by **Diane Freund**

MacAdam/Cage Publishing
155 Sansome Street, Suite 620
San Francisco, CA 94104
www.macadamcage.com

Library of Congress Cataloging-in-Publication Data

Freund, Diane, 1944 —
    Four Corners / by Diane Freund.
      p.   cm.
    ISBN: 0-9673701-8-3 (alk. paper)
      1. Girls — Fiction. 2. Problem families — Fiction. I. Title.

PS3606.R48 F68 2001
813'.3 — dc21   2001037046

Manufactured in the United States of America.

10 9 8 7 6 5 4 3 2 1

Book design by Dorothy Carico Smith.

FOUR CORNERS

A Novel by **Diane Freund**

MacAdam/Cage Publishing

San Francisco ◆ Denver

For Donna, Kathy, Steve, Heidi, and Jason
— my children

I was ten the summer we drove our mother crazy. My father wrapped her up in a flannel blanket and put her in the car. She sat rocking back and forth as though she still held our baby brother Kevin in her arms when instead Emily held him. Em had just turned eleven, old enough to hold him.

Usually my father drove with the window rolled down and his arm on the ledge even though my mother knew a boy who'd done this on the school bus and had his arm torn off when the bus came too close to a telephone pole. But on the trip to the hospital my father kept both hands on the steering wheel, holding on tightly as though he expected the car to start rocking back and forth too. I sat behind my father between Emily and David. Toby stood on the hump, one hand on the seat back, and the other twirling my mother's long matted hair around his index finger the way he used to when she nursed him. I had to keep a close eye on Toby because he was jealous of Kevin although we'd had him for six months already. But Toby had been the baby for three years and every chance he got he'd climb into Kevin's crib or playpen and yank the bottle from his mouth. Sometimes he even bit Kevin, but that only happened if we left them alone in the same room.

When my father pulled into the emergency entrance, Toby shifted suddenly and lost his hold on our mother's hair. Before he could right himself, two doctors came to the car door and opened it carefully, helping our mother to her feet. Then they took her away. We had to wait in the car, but for several seconds we could still see her, swaying and rocking, down the empty corridor in her lilac housedress and her bare feet. I had the sensation then that we were moving backward, the way I lost track of movement when we were stopped alongside a bus and it began to move before we did. It made me sick to my stomach.

It was not quite night when my father came back out alone. By then the car was thick with heat and tears and sour milk. David's face was deep red where Emily had slapped him and my arm had three bracelets of Indian burns. I'd put a pillow on Toby's head and sat on it until he almost suffocated. We'd fought silently and just as silently drove home, David in the front seat holding Toby, smiling, my father squinting as if peering into the sun, though it had set some time before. Kevin lay on the back seat with his eyes stuck open. The same thing had happened to a doll I had, and the only way to fix it, my mother said, was to take its head off. When she did, the rubber bands that connected the head to the neck snapped and its eyes bulged out. That was how my mother's eyes looked in the car. And Kevin's. I looked down at him and tried to get him to close his eyes by closing mine.

It was August 10, 1953, David's twelfth birthday, but we didn't celebrate it. We would, my father said, when my mother came home. Without her, there'd be nothing to celebrate our father told us that night as we sat shivering in the summer heat around the kitchen table. We knew that was true. It was our mother who baked the cake, who knew exactly where the candles were, who knew to add the extra candle for good luck. My father was always surprised when he came home and there was a birthday to celebrate. When will she come home, we wondered. Our father didn't know. What he did know was that our mother needed a good long rest. I pictured this as another one of the extended naps she had begun taking since we'd started summer vacation. For the time being we all had to pitch in and help. David, because he was the oldest, would be in charge. David got up then and went to the refrigerator and brought out a bottle of milk. "I'll make some cocoa," he said and reached into the pantry for the can of Hershey's. Just where the top of his head brushed against the wood-work, my mother's thumbprint was imbedded in the paint. My father liked to tease her about it. He said that's where she kept us all, under that thumb. We were under her heart, she corrected. Under her skin was more like it, Merle said.

Merle was our aunt. She came up several days later with her daughter Joan, to take care of the goddamn bunch of nuts she knew we were. Merle told us this, Em and me, two mornings later as she stood brushing our hair and drinking a beer, for courage, she said, in the face of the rat's nest before her.

She'd left Uncle and Wayne, Joan's older brother, behind in the Bronx, she said, to come to this frigging sorry excuse for a Shangri-La because we had finally succeeded in driving her sister crazy. And it would behoove us to learn, and she would beat the bejeezus out of us if we didn't, to take care of our own damn selves and leave our mother the hell alone. She said this with one eye squinted shut, holding a cigarette between her fingers as if it were a dart she was planning to throw at us.

Emily said it was the rat that drove our mother crazy and not us. The one that had gotten into the baby's crib the week before. Our mother had found it there. We'd seen rats around the house before even though my father had plugged up all the holes with the tops from cans of Maxwell House coffee, and even though he'd stuffed steel wool in the holes where the drains went into the floor. One had gotten into my parents' bedroom when my mother was taking a nap, but that one didn't drive her crazy. It was the one that got into the crib and had rabies.

"Are rabies rat babies?" I asked my sister. Em said no. Then she pressed her thumbnail into my skin twice to make a cross.

"That's what rat bites look like, Rainey. That's what our baby brother could have been covered with." She told me this when we lay sweltering on top of our sheets a few nights after Merle arrived. Joan was pressed in between us, her slip up above her waist, looking at the hair that was just starting to grow between her legs.

"It's called a pussy," Joan said. Just then Merle shouted up for her to take a bath and Joan said she had. "A PTA bath," she whispered to us, "pussy, tits, and ass." I had never heard those words before and the shock of them instantly cooled our room, a room that was so unbearably hot — it swarmed with heat and smelled stale as the attic — that the slightest movement made my skin sting. I was utterly awed by Joan and studied her carefully. She was thirteen, but not much bigger than Emily. We hadn't seen her in two years, not since we left the Bronx so that our mother could sleep at night without worrying about rats getting at us. Joan wouldn't have anything to do with us then, even though when we were leaving Merle told her to take a good long look at us because it might be the last chance she had. Merle said she'd be damned if she'd follow her sister to the country where people still wiped their behinds with corn husks and papered their walls with pages from the Sears and Roebuck Catalogue. And she hadn't followed our mother. But the rats had.

Joan was wild, anyone could see that, the kind of girl my mother would say was bold. She was the kind of girl who would walk into a house without knocking, who wouldn't say thank you no matter what she was given, and who called adults by their first name. In fact she called my father Andy, and he seemed to shrink when she did. She sat in his chair at the head of the table. The first time she did it my father

circled the table for several seconds before David gave up his seat to
him. My father didn't know what to make of Joan and neither did we.
Emily was mostly mad at her for coming, but I sensed an ally. I was
on her side from the start and so lay staring at her body, the wonders
of it, the blueprint of veins at her temples, the pale yellow of her eyelashes and the darker hairs on her pussy. They were the same color as
the copper filament in the light bulb pinging above our heads. She
had two soft mushrooms she called her tits. I looked at my chest for
the first time. I had two flat pink stars on my chest with nipples that
sank in like the knuckles on my baby brother's hands. He had sucked
our mother dry, Merle said. We all had. And that included our father.

"If you want to see another pussy, look up Merle's skirt. She
doesn't wear underwear," Joan said. She called her mother by her first
name too. So did we.

"Your mother's crazy," Emily said.

"But not like yours," Joan said, putting her two middle fingers in her
mouth to suck on. She didn't care that we saw her do this. She didn't care
if we thought her mother was crazy either, but I could see Em starting
to get mad about ours. She sat up for a minute, put some of her hair
inside her mouth, and then plastered it to the side of her face as
though it were a rat's tail.

"Let's see how you like sleeping next to a rat all night," Em said
and lay back down next to Joan. Seconds later we heard scuttling in
the walls.

"Rats," Em said. Joan stopped sucking long enough to listen.

"Squirrels," she countered.

"Rats," Em insisted. She could tell by the sound.

"I'm not afraid of rats, not like you," Joan said matter-of-factly. I
could see that Emily was striving to find something to scare Joan with,

something that would silence her once and for all.

"I hope a rat crawls up your pussy," she whispered at last and yanked the light chain so hard that she almost pulled the fixture out of the ceiling.

"Wiseass," Joan hissed into the dark.

I lay awake with my legs crossed and listened to the crickets, their steady *chirrup* sounded like the noise the scissors made when my mother trimmed the yards of white satin that she bought to make my dress for First Holy Communion. Usually I wore Em's clothes, the ones she grew out of, but not this time. This time my mother wanted me to have everything new. She knew what it felt like to wear hand-me-downs and so had taken me with her to buy the fabric, though I wouldn't receive Communion until the following June. It was so new that it seemed like something freshly born. Three yards. Three yards would be perfect, she said. It was too early to buy my shoes. I grew out of shoes before I had a chance to wear them out. But she bought me socks, white nylon socks with a lace ruffle, and these were wrapped in paper the same color blue that the cotton in the box in the bathroom was wrapped in. Those socks were on a shelf in my mother's closet. The satin was on the sewing machine cabinet waiting for her to begin. From where I lay in my bed I could see the fabric shimmer.

Outside, lightning burst sporadically across the sky like ghostly white chicken's feet. I thought then of my mother's white feet, how she'd forgotten her shoes when she went to the hospital, how when we followed her out to the car she didn't remind us of our shoes, didn't tell us the story of lockjaw, how our chins would rust shut if we stepped on an old nail.

Later that night I dreamed the first dream I would ever remember. My mother was standing in the dining room, in front of the bay window that looked out on the lilac bush. She had been looking for something. I'd watched her go from room to room, window to window, fingering each panel of curtain. I thought she was looking for me and tried to make myself bigger by pulling in my stomach and sticking out my chest, but she still couldn't see me. *Ah, there you are*, she said finally, but not to me. She was staring out the window at the lilac bush. Instead of roots it had feet. Her white feet. And they were making a squishing noise, like the sound our shoes made when we'd been in puddles.

I woke to that noise. Only it wasn't my mother's feet making it, just Joan sucking on her fingers, harder and harder, as the thunder shook the house and loosened the plaster from the lath and sent it scuttling down the walls. At least I'd hoped it was plaster and not the rat that had driven my mother crazy.

I didn't see her go crazy. David had. He kept what happened a secret, though knowing exactly what happened was very important to me. I knew some of the things that could drive her crazy. Living in the city could. Polio could. Seeing one of us in an iron lung would drive her insane, she said. Also being locked in could. I had an earlier, confused memory of standing on the porch once and looking in at my mother squatting in a corner sobbing in the summer kitchen, her shoulders hard and white as the porcelain doorknob that had come off in her hand. I couldn't hear what she was moaning. She was as distant as those mothers at Mass on Sundays who sat in the Crying Room, holding their screaming babies behind the thick plate of glass. I'd seen the ushers take mothers in there, put their hands on women's elbows, help them up the aisle, then shut them in. Once our own mother had been one of those women. If we missed her all we had to do was turn around my father said. We turned then, the four of us and looked at our mother. There she was, behind the glass, her face as twisted as Kevin's. Our mother couldn't sit in there. Being closed in the Crying Room drove her crazy quicker than anything else.

Lying alongside my sister and Joan, I was still hoping that being crazy lasted only a few days. When I tried to picture my mother I felt the hair rise, then fall on my arms. For a moment I heard nothing, and nothing but gloom was visible along the edges of the room. It was as though suddenly my bedroom was like my parents', empty as winter, but then I heard noise in the wall again. The hair resurrected on my arms. I turned and shook Em. She opened one eye.

"Tell me a joke, Em," I whispered. "Tell me a joke." But Em didn't move. Instead Joan sat straight up though she looked as if she were still asleep. "Say lettuce and spell 'cup'," she said.

"Let us c.u.p.," I said.

"Okay," Joan said, "but not here in the bed."

It was David who peed the bed even though Merle said she'd tie his pecker up in knots and make him scrub his own pissy sheets if he didn't cut it out. Emily told Merle what our mother said about David's bedwetting, that it was not to be discussed. When Emily told Merle this she just said "hah" and blew smoke from her nose. Em squinted her eyes at Merle but it didn't help. Merle called David the piss clam after that and made him keep a chamber pot under his bed until his room stunk. But he still wet the bed.

Joan didn't mind David's pissy sheets. Sometimes when I woke in the night she'd be gone and I'd hear her in David's room. I could see them through the doorway, Joan curled next to David sucking her fingers while he read *Tom Mix* out loud to her because she had trouble reading. Before Joan came, Emily was his favorite. This had never really bothered me, but now in the face of such chaos and loss I wasn't willing to share anyone. I meant to claim whoever I could. The next time I saw David reading to Joan, I got up from my bed and asked to use his chamber pot. Joan paused long enough to take her fingers from her mouth then told me to go piss up a rope. David laughed. Joan was the only one who could make him. Despite this, I pulled down my underpants and squatted to pee. When I did, David took out his sling-shot and snapped the rubber band against my bare behind. The crack was so sudden and so sharp that I screamed. Merle was up the steps and in the room before I could move, and she was slapping us all for scaring the living bejeezus out of her and for waking the baby whose wails rose and mingled with mine. Merle told Joan to stay out of David's bed if she knew what was good for her and yanked her by her hair. But I was the only one who cried and not because of the pain. As soon as Merle left I turned my back on David.

"Piss clam," I said to him. This time Joan laughed and came back to bed with me and Em. In order to cheer me up she said she had a boyfriend in the Bronx who was fifteen years old. *Eye-talian*. We had no idea what this meant, but we did know about older boys. Em and I had had our share of trouble with one. Harold Birdseye.

Harold was fifteen years old and lived up the road from us. His father was an Indian. His mother was one too, but she was dead. She'd died when their house burned to the ground the year before, and Harold almost died too but instead he seemed to have melted. His body was badly burned, but his face was the worst. The fire had flat-tened his nose and burned his forehead all the way up to his hairline. He had no eyebrows. We were not to stare at him, so we never did. We tried not to even look at him. And he wouldn't look at us. Instead whenever he came near us he looked at the ground. His skin was still tight and red. Inside his skull his brains had fried up, Em said, which was why he was so mean. My mother said we were to ignore him, ignore his threats. He wouldn't dare to hurt us. Besides, her heart went out to him. She knew what it felt like to be motherless.

Our hearts didn't go out to him. At least mine didn't, not when he inched his horse nearer and nearer to us, until we could smell the heat rising off Shadow's coat and see each one of his grass-stained teeth. Not when he tried to trample us to death every morning on our way to school.

For most of the summer we'd avoided Harold. But the day Merle had to start smoking again because we'd driven her to it, our luck ran out. Em and I tried to get out of going to the store for her cigarettes until Merle warned us that we better get moving while we could still move. Joan was happy to go. Where she lived in the Bronx there was a store on every corner. Where we lived it seemed like Harold was on every corner.

Em and I kept watch for him without saying a word. I checked the field and fallow land and Em watched the orchard. It was she who saw him first. Her whole body went tight. Then I saw him. He was riding Shadow along the stand of poplars that bordered our property. Joan was down in the ditch searching for bottles she could return for deposits, so she didn't see Harold or his horse. I knew Shadow. I'd fed him grass, careful to keep my hand pressed flat while he ate from it. I'd given him lumps of sugar, and apples too, when he was pastured in our field all the while Harold was in the hospital. But when Harold came home and reclaimed him, I kept my distance.

Harold's trick was to ride up to us at a gallop as if he meant to lasso us. Then he'd stop short and slowly inch the horse's rump toward us until we jumped in the ditch. He did this wordlessly, and we were wordless too because we knew he had a rifle. Not with him, but at his house, and we had to pass that house everyday, and when he wasn't on Shadow, he was waiting for us at his window. Then we could see the gun plain as day.

Em and I were used to Harold's routine. We didn't hesitate. We didn't waste any time. As soon as we saw him coming we jumped in the ditch, splashing Joan. She stood there picking her scabs and eating them, the color fading from her face while she watched Harold, as if the two-thirds water that she told us our bodies consisted of was slowly draining out of her open sores. Harold had already turned the horse and was about to ride off when he saw Joan. She looked at us and then back at Harold for a long moment, then slowly climbed back onto the road. In one hand she held an empty soda bottle. Harold stayed still for a minute eyeing that soda bottle, and in that minute I thought, miraculously, that he was going to gallop away. But then he turned the horse's rump toward Joan. She didn't move. Shadow edged nearer. I watched his hooves. They looked like they were hinges and bent backward as he came forward. From the ditch I could see each iron-rimmed hoof. Joan's feet were bare and looked as thin as the porcelain cups my mother kept on the top shelf of the hutch. My own feet started to move, but Joan stood her ground. Harold kicked Shadow and pulled on the reins; the horse snorted and moved closer brushing against Joan, and when he did Joan made her move. I thought she hit Shadow with the bottle she held, but she didn't. She bit him, sank her teeth into his side hard and quick. It sounded like Shadow screamed when he reared but it was Harold, the first sound I'd ever heard him make. He landed on his back. "Redskin," Joan sneered. "You lousy redskin. Go back to your tepee." Harold stared straight at Joan. He had no eyebrows. His forehead was as red as the hot water bottle that Merle had hung from the bathtub faucet. I had never been this close to Harold and backed away quickly. Not Joan. She stood staring down at him for a moment shaking her head at the sight of him, then she jumped back into the ditch where she found a dirty Coca-Cola bottle worth two cents.

We might have been in trouble, Joan said afterward, if the lousy sonsabitch's horse didn't spook and knock the wind out of Harold. That gave us enough time to get away from him.

I was sorry that she'd done this and said so, said I was afraid of what he'd do to us. "Don't worry," she said, "now you have me." This was precarious at best — Joan's loyalty wavered — but she was who we had right then. She was tangible. I turned to look back once at our house riding the heave of the hill, every window open and sheets and spreads hanging like long white tongues from our bedroom windows, exhorting us all to get the hell to the store for those cigarettes right now or else risk being tied to a tree and shot, with socks stuck in our goddamn mouths. Shot. That's right. And not by crazy Harold either.

"When we get home I'll ask Merle to take us to the lake," Joan said by way of consolation after I told her that Harold would probably shoot us when we passed his house. She simply shrugged her shoulders as though that was the price we'd have to pay. Our lives were worth about as much as the deposit on the soda bottle as far as I was concerned. Emily simply stood there in the ditch shivering. Joan was disgusted with us both. Cowards, yellow bellies, sissies. She called us every name she could think of, but said that she'd still ask her mother to take us swimming even though earlier Merle warned Joan that if she asked to go to the lake one more time, she was going to kick Joan so hard she'd land in the middle of it.

I knew then that it was all right to be afraid around Joan. She understood being scared. She could be mean, but if she saw that we were really afraid, she could be kind. For the first time since she came to live with us, she put an arm around each of our shoulders and walked us past Harold's house straight to Moe's store where she stole each of us a piece of gum.

Moe's was the only store we had in Four Corners. The store, the post office, and Willy's Garage made up three of the four corners. The last corner stood empty, Merle said, because the town had run out of ideas. Eleven houses lined the road, six on one side and five on the other. All were white, and most had porch swings, though only one had shutters. Down the road was the school house, and farther along was the old roadhouse where my father tended bar. He worked days, nights and weekends. We never knew when he was going to be home. This drove Merle crazy because she could never count on using the car and she sure as hell wasn't walking the two miles to Moe's. That's what we were for.

Mr. and Mrs. Moe lived above the store, but we'd never been inside their apartment. Mrs. Moe was kind and fat. When she walked she shifted her weight from one side to the other like a skater. She couldn't take the steps anymore so it was Mr. Moe we did business with.

When we arrived he wasn't in the store. We had to call up the steps for him to come downstairs to sell us the cigarettes. Joan said he must have been sitting upstairs bare-assed naked because when he came down the steps he was adjusting his suspenders and zippering his fly. She didn't steal anything until he was there. He called her Blondie and my sister and me, Marsy Doats and Doesy Doats. If I came in without my sister, he called me Sunny to tease me about my nickname, but Mrs. Moe, who was the postmistress, called me Lorraine Dougherty. Whenever she did, I felt as though she'd just put a stamp on my forehead.

All the while Joan was moving through the dark store, Mr. Moe stood winking at Em and me.

"Don't light up now till you're out of sight of the store, or the missus'll kill me. And you too," he said, handing us the pack of Lucky Strikes. After we promised we wouldn't, he let us pick a candy out of the penny candy bin. Joan had already stolen a candy bar and stuck it in her underwear so we wouldn't ask to share. By the time we left the store the day was nearly flattened by the heat. All along the roadside stalks of grass were doubled over in misery, the Queen Anne's lace felt starched, the black-eyed Susans collapsed against one another, the hollyhocks were withered. What hadn't folded under the weight of heat stood parched and dried to razor sharpness and ready to cut our legs. There was no sign of Harold. All around us the land lay flat and still as my heart. There was not a tree high enough to offer shade the entire two miles home. Joan's feet were bitten and bleeding by the time we got there. Crusted blood, like tiny red canals, had hardened between her toes. Pickers stuck to the sash of her dress, her face was bright pink, Em's too, because they were both so fair. Even their scalps had reddened. Before she went inside with the cigarettes, Joan put her head under the pump. It was an old rusted pump that took three pumps before the water came up and spilled down the spout. It smelled of ice and iron and made my feet ache where it emptied on the ground, but Joan kept her head under the spout until her face went from pink to bright red. When Merle saw us leaning against the porch, she said we looked like we'd just finished a forced march. My father had just gotten up. He slept in the day bed in the alcove in the dining room because he couldn't bear to sleep in his own bed without my mother. Their bedroom was just as she'd left it, their sheets crumpled and caught up in places, frozen as my mother's smile.

"Christ, Merle," he said when he saw us, "you better take them for a swim before they collapse."

"I should be so lucky," Merle said and rolled her eyes behind my father's back as he left the room. Swimming was one of the things she hated to do, especially in Lake Minerva because it was fed by cold springs. But my father could make her do things she hated, he could make us all do things we hated to do because he was missing my mother so much.

"The water's colder than a well digger's ass," she warned us as she yanked on her strapless bathing suit. She put it on in the kitchen, right in front of the stove, without taking off her dress. It was periwinkle blue with huge splashy white water lilies over each breast, over her belly button, and on each cheek of her behind. One was perfectly centered over her pussy. Then she grabbed her hairbrush and gave her hair five hard pulling strokes, put some lipstick on, grabbed her perfume from her purse and sprayed herself all over, then once between her legs. "You never know who you're going to meet," she said.

"Merle," Joan warned.

"Merle, what?" her mother challenged. Then she ripped her red hair from the hairbrush, dropped it into the trash, slung Kevin on her hip, her purse on her shoulder, and kicked open the screen door far enough to let her out and keep us in.

On the way to the lake she stopped and bought two bottles of Rheingold though she and Jesus Christ Almighty both knew this wouldn't be enough to get her through the next few hours. And God help our asses if she got one grain of sand up hers.

I liked to watch her drive. She tucked her skirt between her legs so they could get tan and she balanced a beer on the lower rim of the steering wheel and never spilled a drop. She smoked, drank, and honked back whenever truck drivers looked down at her legs. Her toenails, fingernails, and hair were bright red. Believe it or not, she said, she was one of the few redheads who could wear red. I believed it with all my heart.

For most of the afternoon Merle lay splayed on the blanket as though our shoes were holding down every corner of her instead of the corners of the blanket. Kevin lay beside her trying to grab the water lilies on her suit. Toby sat near the water's edge pinching ants. We stayed close to the shore trying to learn the dead man's float, a feat our father assured us would save our lives if we ever got too tired to swim. We tried to teach this to Joan, who stood up to her neck in the water yet made no move to try it because it hadn't saved the man who it was named for.

We stayed in the water until our ears ached and then staggered out and onto our towels. Joan wouldn't come out though she had turned completely blue except for her lips, which were the same dusky purple as night crawlers. She stayed far enough out in the water so Merle couldn't see this. But Merle wasn't looking at her. She was looking at Emily and me as we sat shivering on the towel next to her.

"You have your mother's eyes," she said to Emily suddenly, possessively, as though Em had plucked them from our mother's head. The word *mother* stopped my heart. I hadn't thought of her in days. At night, yes, when I was alone and the sky turned inexplicably white for an instant after the blue and before the black, then I thought of her saying softly, *There's no use crying over spilled milk*. I pictured her wetting a tissue to clean up any remaining broken glass from the floor because she knew of a girl who'd stepped on a shard that her mother had overlooked and it went into her bloodstream and straight to her heart. Now, standing in front of Merle, the word *mother* became that shard of glass, sailing slowly up my legs, through all the body parts

Joan had shown us, working its way, silent and sharp, to my heart. I started to shiver. I could see cars appear, disappear, then reappear on the ridge behind Merle's head. Any one of those cars could take me to my mother, and at that moment I couldn't for the life of me understand why they would not. Then Merle turned to me, her eyes fat and green.

"You have your father's eyes, Rainey." For some reason, I started to sob.

"Oh, for crying out loud," Merle said and reached down to pick up the baby. When she did, Toby leaned over and smacked him on the forehead with his shovel. For a moment it seemed as though the baby was gulping in his pain. We were all momentarily silent, watching to see if he would stop breathing. He had started to hold his breath whenever he got mad or hurt. Sometimes he held it so long he turned dark blue, but this time he'd turned the same color as Joan's lips. I thought his heart had stopped but Merle said no. She said he just needed his ass whacked, Toby too, but she didn't hit either one of them. Instead she just flipped Kevin over onto his belly until he started screaming. She stood up then, flicked her cigarette into the water and waved Joan in just as a truck pulled off the lake road and into the parking lot. For a moment Merle stood absolutely still, holding her breath like Kevin had, but then she let it out. It was Mr. Birdseye, Harold's father. Then it was our turn to stand perfectly still. We thought he'd followed us here to tell on Joan. We knew how he felt about Harold. But it wasn't us he'd come to see. He just wanted to let Merle know if she needed anything she could call on him. "Eddie Birdseye," he said extending his hand. Merle took his hand but didn't give her name. She just stared at him and smiled the way she smiled at the truck drivers. Two cameras hung around Eddie's neck, and he brought one, then the other up to his eye and pointed them at her. She threw her head back and laughed and then moved closer to him. They spoke for a few minutes, their heads leaning into each other the way the tops of the pines that surrounded us did when the wind took them. Toby couldn't stand it anymore and started to chant Merle's name. For some reason he loved Merle, but she ignored him until he stuck his head between her legs. Then he got a whack, even though we heard Mr. Birdseye say that he envied Toby's position. When he turned away he was laughing.

He began to walk toward the lake clicking pictures as he went. Several of his photographs had been made into postcards. These were the ones he took from an airplane. He called them Birdseye Views. He had also taken pictures of David, hoping to convince some magazines in Manhattan to use them in ads, but so far there'd been no takers.

When he finished taking pictures of the water, he came back toward us briefly. I smiled all the while he took his pictures just in case, but the only one of us girls that he photographed was Joan, who'd come out of the water and just scowled at him.

We all watched him walk back to his truck as Merle began to gather up the towels, the baby slung on her hip. She had two of the fingers of her right hand stuck into the brown beer bottles. With her free hand she brushed the sand off her legs. It was time for us to leave. But she didn't move. She just kept staring after Eddie Birdseye.

Joan said that she was keeping an eye out for Uncle. She still had the lump on her head where he'd hit her with the telephone. She'd better watch herself or she'd get another lump. Em said she was glad we didn't have a phone, but before Joan could respond, Merle said we better get our asses in the car or she was going to leave the bunch of us to the mosquitoes who'd be more than glad to suck every last drop of blood from us. Then we'd know how she felt.

"Why did Uncle hit Merle?" Em asked later that night when we were in bed.

"Rouge," Joan said. "He hit her for wearing rouge."

Merle kept the rouge in a cigar box that we were forbidden to touch. She said the box contained her natural beauty. Merle used eyebrow pencil too, one with the word Maybelline embossed elaborately in gold along one side. She sharpened it with the potato peeler every morning because she'd shaved her eyebrows off when she was young and needed to draw them on each morning. Once you used a razor, she said, there was no turning back.

"He hid behind the door and choked her too because she said she was going to California," Joan continued, looking straight at the bedroom wall as though she could see the fight played out there. "After he hit her, he picked her up by the neck and held her against the wall." Given what we knew of Merle, this didn't seem at all possible to us, though Joan insisted it was the truth. Part of it. There was other stuff, but we were too young to hear it. We were babies. Em said we weren't, but Joan just stuck her fingers in her mouth and began to hum. When Em insisted we weren't babies, Joan stuck her fingers in her ears and began to sing as loudly as she dared, *Lady of Spain, I adore you, pull down your pants, I'll explore you*, until Merle appeared in the doorway. I thought she was going to slap Joan but she acted as though she hadn't heard her. She was going out she said, up to the roadhouse to have a beer. Joan was old enough to keep an eye on the five of us. Kevin started to wail from his crib, Toby did too. Joan said that she wasn't old enough. Merle said that was too damn bad. There were a lot of things she wasn't old enough to do when she was Joan's age, but that never stopped anybody from practicing on her.

Merle had on her opal necklace, the one she kept in her purse, the one that would crack if we dared even touch it because none of us were born in October. She seemed glittery, like the stone, and nervous, as though she too might crack if we touched her. Her hair sparkled in the light from the hall. She had pinned it up, and I could see the long neck that Uncle had nearly broken and the splash of freckles and moles that seemed to shift and jump under the light. She wore a plain white blouse, freshly starched, and a loose black skirt cinched at the waist, every bit as tightly, I imagined, as Uncle's hand around her throat. Joan burst into tears when Merle turned to leave. Em and I lay stiff and silent in the face of this. It was the first time we'd ever seen her cry.

"Oh for Chrissake," Merle said and leaned back into the room. "It's only up the goddamn road." Joan continued to sob.

"Knock it off," Merle yelled as she headed down the hall, "or I'll stay out the whole frigging night."

"Now who's the baby?" Em said. Then she put her hands over Joan's mouth and told her to stop, stop, or she was going to tickle her to death, like the girl whose brother tied her to a bedpost and tickled her until she died of laughing. We lay then in silence.

Thunder began to roll toward us from some storm that was still far off. It had been a season of rain, but this would end soon. When the lightning finally struck, I imagined myself going from room to room closing windows. In truth I was too afraid to leave the bed.

"Em," I said at last to my sister, "do you think our mother will be home soon?" Em shrugged, turned to the wall and began to peel the wallpaper, pulling some plaster off with it.

"Do you think so?" I asked turning to Joan.

"Your mother," Joan blurted out. "Your mother. I don't give a good goddamn about your mother." This filled me with such despair I couldn't move, couldn't turn from Joan, though this is what I wanted to do. Later when I heard a car in the driveway, I awoke. Joan turned and sighed. Em pressed nearer the wall. The storm had subsided, or passed, or gone deeper, as though the night had covered over the dark bulbs of thunder, the white roots of lightning; the clouds had thinned and the sky was thick with stars, stars as small as seeds the storm had sown to silently propagate the new season, season without rain, season without my mother.

CHAPTER TWO

In the last clear days of summer, days that draped and swayed like the sheets Merle had forgotten on the line, it seemed that we were always in the house, the one place where we were least welcome. Outside in the orchard, the Seckel pear trees had begun to drop their fruit and the yard was rife with the smell of rotting fruit and the sound of yellow jackets. On these mornings Merle sat drinking tea and reading the paper, usually the Sunday edition of *The New York Daily News*. She especially loved a section called, "A Justice Story," which invariably featured the murder of a woman by either her lover or husband. After she finished reading, sometimes whole sections to us, she turned her teacup upside down on the saucer, twirled it around counterclockwise three times and read her leaves. As often as not there was the shape of a cross in the cup, which she interpreted as Uncle's death. The lousy bastard.

By late afternoon Merle was still in her slip. She had already, or her voice had, forced us outside several times but we had just as insistently worked our way back in. At five o'clock she set up the ironing board and pulled a beer and one of her blouses from the refrigerator. She kept them there, damp and rolled thick as dough on the bottom shelf. As she ironed, the steam and yeasty smell of starch mingled with the sour smell of the oilcloth on the table, the acrid smell of her cigarette left burning on the porcelain sink, and the smell of fermenting fruit. If I closed my eyes it could have been my mother standing there baking bread, or canning pears. Then I never wanted to leave the room. I'd stay and watch Merle peel the blouse off the board like piecrust and put it on, molding the sleeves to her arms and crimping the collar. When she put on her lipstick Em's mouth opened too, and Joan's eyes followed her mother's hand. We watched her in silence making her so nervous she'd tell us to get the hell outside. Then we watched her from the porch, brushing her hair until it rose red as a sailor's warning. When she was finished she'd come outside and sit in one of the two Adirondack chairs on the front lawn until the kitchen cooled off enough to cook. If my father came home there'd be a hot meal, if not, we'd have sandwiches, mayonnaise, apple butter, anything we wanted. If we complained that we were still hungry, as Joan often did, Merle would remind us that when she was thirteen years old she only weighed fifty pounds. That's what living with aunts and uncles did to a child.

Home to her, she said, was the third drawer of a deal dresser in various aunts' houses. And they ran their dirty little fingers through her things anytime they wanted. And the uncles were worse. Oh she could tell us plenty about uncles. She'd rather be tied to a randy old goat with shit hanging off its ass than find herself alone in the room with her uncles. Especially Ira, the one with the webbed hand. That old fart was still alive.

Another beer and we might find out more. I sat perfectly still pulsing with an anticipation of knowledge that I was totally unprepared for, and therefore doubly thrilled to hear. It was there, on the front lawn of a summer thick with beer and bitterness that we gave as good as we got. We plied her with beer, Joan and I, and she plied us with stories. Emily wouldn't stay to hear any of this. Like David she was spending more and more time alone. But Joan and I were mesmerized.

We were the sneaks, Merle said, because we got a hold of the medical book, *The Pictorial Medical Guide*, written by forty specialists.

Joan read it to us each night. What she couldn't make out, she made up, but we didn't know this, not until Emily asked Merle if a woman got pregnant when a man spit in her mouth. Jesus, Mary and Joseph, Merle said, though as one name, Jesus MaryAnn Joseph. After Joan brought her the book Merle cut all the pages out that dealt with sex. And if she heard one more word on the subject she might start cutting out some goddamned tongues.

But then she would forget about her threat and tell us about the uncles, about Ira and what he could do with that one hand. Plenty. We'd be surprised. But she wasn't. We were never to let a man touch anything on our bodies that we could cover with two fingers. This made me dizzy with images, especially of my private parts that looked very much like two fingers pressed together.

Our bodies were everything and the only things we had, Merle said, which was why any man from the age of two on up wasn't to be trusted. Men were dead set on getting a piece of our asses.

The most important thing was not to be in a room alone with one of them, Merle said. If we ever found ourselves in this situation her only advice to us would be to start screaming right away because we could be damn sure we'd be screaming before long.

"Never sit on their laps, even if there's a dozen people in the room. *Especially* if there are a dozen people in the room." Never put our hands in the pockets of their trousers if they said they had something in there for us. We might get a whole lot more than we bargained for. She addressed this remark to Joan, whom she called Bottle Betty because she was always looking for bottles to return for money.

And it would be much worse when our private parts began to grow. Joan pressed her knees together in the face of this news. And several days later while I was playing near the ditch I looked down and saw two bumps under my shirt. They were only the clasps of my overalls but I thought they were tits. I fell headlong into the ditch, trying to outrun them.

Nothing a man did surprised Merle. Look what her own father had done to her and to our mother after their mother died. And to their baby brother whom he had left to die in a foundling home. Deserted them all so he could chase a skirt. We weren't to trust men, even our own goddamned fathers. And don't say we weren't warned.

Twice a week my father made the one hundred twenty mile round trip to see my mother. When he got home we'd all be waiting in the kitchen. He was always surprised to see us still up, forgetting, it seemed, what importance we attached to our mother's absence, so keen was his sense of personal loss. Then he'd say that our mother was doing fine, getting fat and sassy. We'd have to wait until the next night to get the truth from Merle and this information would be parceled out according to her mood, a mood determined by what my father would tell her in the morning, for she would have to wait too, though it was in her, at least in her eyes, to drag the words from his mouth right there and then. These mornings she'd be up long before us reading the paper my father had brought back with him, her legs crossed, her right foot moving up and down impatiently, a fresh pot of coffee perking just as impatiently, against the glass eye of the coffee pot. I might find Merle and my father in deep conversation when I came down the stairway, or more often than not, both of them silent, Merle at the sink scraping the dishes fiercely, the fork against the plate making a shrill scolding sound, a tone she'd never take with my father. And he sitting with his shoulders hunched and tight as clenched fists raised against her, but smiling his hard smile, his teeth locked shut against the avalanche of angry words he was prepared, but too well-mannered, to use.

Though Merle wanted to be the first to hear about my mother it sometimes happened that one of us would be up before her. On the last day of our summer vacation, I was up at dawn. Pockets of fog still lay across the fields like swatches of gray flannel. The fields looked as though they were still in their pajamas. I was still in mine. But my father was dressed. I had come upon him unawares and watched him for several minutes. He was alone in the kitchen on a gray chair and his feet, the only part of him uncovered, were bare and wrapped around the rungs. I stood watching how he buttered his bread with thick slabs, then folded the bread in two and dipped it in his coffee. This was his favorite breakfast, fresh bread and coffee, and part of his meal was the newspaper he kept propped against a can of Carnation evaporated milk. If I disturbed him I knew how he would freeze, how he'd hold his bread, poised in midair, how he would be slightly impatient at my presence because he was a private man. I also knew that he would try very hard to pretend he wasn't. He would try to find something funny to say to mask his impatience. I was anxious about disturbing him, remembering nights when my mother would send one of us in to wake him from a nap and no matter how softly we crept into the room, or how light our touch on his arm, he literally sprang from the sofa at the merest pressure of one of our hands and stood wild-eyed and disoriented for several seconds, until he came back to us and we, equally startled, came back to him.

But this morning, as the fog slowly dissipated he sensed my presence, perhaps because he was preparing for Merle, and turned and found me deep in the shadow of the stairwell. He patted the chair next to him and laid the newspaper down. On the front page was a picture of two little girls who were sound asleep. The headlines called them, *The Sleeping Beauties*. When my father saw me looking at them he said

I was a sleeping beauty too, even though I was awake.

"You are awake, aren't you?" he teased, because I was staring at the picture, especially at the mother of the girls who leaned over them protectively. I knew not to ask about my mother, not directly, that never worked, so I asked about the sleeping girls instead. He said they had fallen asleep several days before and the doctors couldn't figure out why. They started to wake up every afternoon, but then, mysteriously, fell back to sleep. I could imagine what Merle would say about that.

"But this wouldn't happen to you," my father said and winked. This because I was the lightest of sleepers, and occasionally wandered in a twilight state through the house late at night. One night he had watched me slather mayonnaise on a half dozen pieces of bread then carry them to my room where I found them the next morning, stale and curled next to my bed.

"Maybe it would be good if it happened to Kevin," I offered. He'd started waking up in the middle of the night and was inconsolable.

"Kevin's easy to get back to sleep though," my father said. "The trick is to take him for a ride in the car. But when you were a baby, I used to have to get under your crib and lift the mattress up and down to get you to sleep. You liked to be rocked." It was because I'd been a Navy baby, he said, I'd been born when he was on a ship. He liked to be rocked too and that's where I'd gotten it from.

"I didn't see you until you were six months old. You were scared of me. At first. That's why I had to hide under the crib. If you saw me it was no good."

"Where was Mom?" I asked.

"She was in bed right next to you. We kept your crib in our room. Your mother couldn't keep her eyes off you."

"Because of the rats?" I asked.

"Good Lord, no. Don't worry about the rats, Rainey. Forget about the rats. I've got the rat problem solved."

"Like hell," Merle said, shuffling into the room. " Unless what I'm hearing at night is leprechauns scratching their little green asses." For a moment my father paused, his hand holding the bread above his coffee, the steam already melting the butter. Merle hadn't painted on her eyebrows yet and looked like a picture of the man in the moon, all her features concentrated in the center of her face.

Then my father stiffened. His teeth were hard and white, locked against any further conversation. And that was enough to stop Merle. She slid into the seat next to me and picked up the paper. She read the paper the way she read tea leaves, with as much scrutiny as comment. "Christ," she said at last, looking over the front page with the picture of the sleeping sisters, "whatever it is, I hope it's contagious."

Three nights later as we sat on the steps watching the sun dissolve along the horizon, Mr. Birdseye pulled into our driveway. For the first time since Merle had been with us she told us to get inside instead of out. This infuriated Joan. She claimed that she could smell fire on Mr. Birdseye. She could smell burned flesh a mile away she said. She believed that he'd set fire to his house purposely, though we knew better, knew that his wife had fallen asleep with a cigarette.

Merle was smoking hers and using the cap of her beer for an ashtray. Merle called Mr. Birdseye, Eddie, and he called her Miss Rheingold and said she should enter the contest the beer company was sponsoring. We'd seen the poster with the pictures of the twelve finalists on it propped up in the window where my father worked. All of the women were redheaded, like Merle. Merle said why not, she was a good advertisement for their product. That was not all she was a good advertisement for, Eddie said, and then handed her the picture he'd taken of her when we were at the lake. Only he wanted it back. Merle glanced at it and laughed, knocking the ashes from her cigarette onto her skirt. She had her legs spread and her skirt was looped like a hammock between her knees. But she didn't notice the ash, she was just smiling and looking out across the field.

In every room in the house someone was usually sleeping, my father, Toby, or as now, Kevin, so we were quiet by habit, and without revealing it to one another, hung on every word Merle uttered. Some rose, some fell and some seemed to land in her beer bottle, lost to us. Eddie had asked about my mother. He had some proofs of David he wanted my father to bring her. Merle said, "Better not." Then we heard "Bess" my mother's name and pressed our faces to the screen.

Merle had said it and immediately waved her hand in the air as though she couldn't stand to have it said in front of her.

"She should have used rat poison," Merle said.

"Bess would never put down poison with the kids," Eddie said. "I'd tried to talk her into getting a cat, but she was afraid it would suck the breath from the baby." That would be a nice change since the baby had sucked the life from her sister, Merle countered.

"Kiddies and kitties don't mix," Eddie laughed. His speech was punctuated by sharp intakes of breath. We peeked out the window to see why but he only sat there, his black hair nearly blue in the fading light, his skin reddish brown, the same color the sun created as it singed the wild sedge in the western fields.

"Neither do kiddies and I," Merle said. And she laughed. Her voice had taken on a teasing sound.

"You don't mean that," Eddie said.

"You don't know what I mean," Merle said and handed him her beer. "Not all women are like Bess. Look at that mother in the

Queens, drugging her kids. It was either her or them, that's what it comes down to." Eddie looked confused.

"The Sleeping Beauties. The little sisters. It was in the newspaper, the front page. Here's a picture of the mother touching her little girls' faces, and the doctors are shaking their heads. It's a big mystery why they are wide-awake one minute and sound asleep the next. Then the mother takes out a hairbrush and begins to brush her girls' hair. What the doctors don't know is that she's got Phenobarbital in her purse, too. As soon as they step out of the room, out comes the dropper. She was pregnant with her sixth kid in as many years. *She* was the one who wanted to climb in that bed and go to sleep. But she couldn't. There were all those other kids at home. So she gave them the drugs, but it was like she was drugged herself. She was addicted to putting her kids to sleep. Not a bad habit. I'd like to get a hold of some Phenobarbital myself. It'd make my life a lot easier around here."

Eddie just shook his head and looked at the buttons on Merle's blouse.

Joan and I looked at each other. Joan said she wasn't going to eat anything Merle cooked, but then we were afraid that she could put it in our milk. We made a pact. I would eat and Joan would watch to see if I got sleepy. If I did, she'd make me some cocoa. But if she ate and got sleepy, I was to make her coffee.

"They sent her up where Bess is," Merle continued. "For observation. Maybe Bess'll learn something from her. God knows she wouldn't take my advice. I'd shoot these little bastards." Then Merle shouted over her shoulder for Joan to get her a beer.

Joan didn't move. She was sitting beside me in the dark practicing turning the pages of a magazine with her toes, imitating an armless woman who came to their apartment in the Bronx. She sold Fuller

Brushes and could demonstrate all the products, even open the boxes the brushes came in, with her toes. The only problem, Joan said, was that she had to sit down to do it.

"Get off your ass and get your own damned beer," Joan whispered, and as if on cue we heard the porch stairs creak. We immediately fled upstairs.

"You better get up there," Merle shouted after us. And then, "Sneaks."

Joan hated to be called that. "She's going to get it," she said. But I didn't know by whom. "My father," Joan said, her nose flaring, then she whispered, "whore bitch" to herself, and flung herself on the bed. She was sucking her fingers so hard I was afraid she was going to swallow them. She had her right leg up in the air and was trying to catch the balled chain that hung from the light with her toes. My heart was racing. We heard Merle say, "Drop it," and Joan automatically dropped her leg. But Merle wasn't talking to us. We could hear her throaty laugh, the bitter edge that meant that she knew a lot more than she cared to reveal about her sister. She could tell Eddie plenty. Oh boy could she.

Three weeks into September, weeks when we had to pass Harold's house on our way to school with the fear of being shot to death always with us, Uncle drove up from the Bronx with Wayne in an old panel truck filled with rotten fruit and followed by a swarm of bees. When he pulled up in front of our house Merle wouldn't go outside and neither would we, not even when the bees, in unison, settled quickly on the roof of the truck. It was Sunday and my father had taken the car to go visit my mother. He wouldn't be home for hours. From inside the house we could see Uncle looking for our car. When he was certain that it was gone he got out. He was wearing a large fringy straw hat with the word MAUI stitched in red across the crown, and an Hawaiian shirt. I thought if we were lucky he might be stung to death before he could reach our door. But he knew bees. He'd been supplying greengrocers with fruit for years. He opened the back doors of the truck and the queen bee flew out from a bushel basket of soft peaches and straight to the branch of our Seckel pear tree. The swarm immediately engulfed the branch like a miniature tornado with dozens of stragglers flying in frenzied circles. Merle was wearing her white nylon slip but had put on one of my father's flannel shirts against the morning chill. She had her hands tucked deep inside the sleeves and was staring hard at Uncle. He started to lift baskets of apples and bushels of potatoes from the back of the truck with quick sure movements. Merle just shook her head from side to side, but her shoulders drooped a bit. Or so it seemed to me. I was expecting much more from her. I had expected she'd keep us safe from him. Hadn't she told us he had reason to fear her? Hadn't she thrown a pot of coffee at him, scalding him so badly that Joan could hear him screaming as he ran down five flights of stairs? And there was more. Hadn't she thrown him down a flight of steps and when he lay unconscious on the landing she'd run down and kicked that bastard until he fell down the next flight of steps, and the next? And what about his chest? The triangle scar she'd left when she'd pressed a hot iron into it? All those acts of courage and revenge had come to this? Locking the door and turning away? But I had forgotten about the shotgun my father kept in the rafters in the basement.

For the first hour Merle stared out the window. But the sun was the only thing that pushed its way through the torn blinds. It must have had the same power as the evil eye because before long Merle couldn't bear the force of it. She jumped up from the chair and went about her business, taking out a loaf of bread and hacking slices off for oven toast, boiling water for tea, the steam rising high enough to set a strip of flypaper twirling merrily above our heads. Merle held the knife in her hand, low to her waist and tested the blade with her thumb. A fly with its wings stuck fast buzzed one long, one short. May Day, May Day.

Outside Uncle stood and stared at the house wiping the sweat off his face with a blue bandanna. He was fat and soft like the fruit he sold. He was turning redder by the minute. He was also the main reason why we didn't go into the city to visit Merle anymore. It only gave him an excuse to drink, my mother had said, and once he was drunk he got surly. Joan watched him with narrowed eyes. "He's drunk," she announced to her mother. They pulled close for an instant and peered at him through the blinds. Just then Merle's dog, Clover, a black cocker spaniel, jumped out of the truck. Uncle grabbed her collar and looked back toward the house. I was afraid he was going to choke Clover but he reached in the truck with his free hand and brought out a length of clothesline and tied her to the back bumper before she could run to Merle. He hesitated for a minute before hefting himself back in the truck. Wayne, who'd been sitting still as a mummy in the front seat, rocked uneasily from his father's weight. He wouldn't look at the house. But Clover did. She sat patiently watching us as we pressed against the screen and when any one of us moved, she stood up in futile anticipation of her release.

Merle said Uncle could sit there until he rotted. Just ignore him, she said, though she kept her eye to the window. She had a beer in one hand and a cup of tea in the other.

We saw Uncle light a cigar, suck on it as if he meant to swallow it whole, then exhale and watch as the smoke escaped out the window. All through the long morning he sat smoking and drinking from a leather flask. The truck was reflected in our milk glasses, in the windows, in one another's eyes, in our very hearts. Mine at least. We stared at the truck and when we grew bored we stared at the drooping swarm of bees. Merle said she ought to call a beekeeper, except she couldn't. We had no phone. The bees had settled in as surely as Uncle. Merle said they'd swarmed because the hive produced two queens. She said it was a freak of nature, just like that SOB sitting outside in the truck.

"Gravity keeps them there," David said importantly. We followed his voice. "The same force that keeps us from falling off the planet." I loved David when he made sense of things. But he got on Merle's nerves. She said maybe it was gravity that kept him from falling from his high horse, but what kept those bees where they were was their determination to get a piece of the queen's ass. Just like what everyone wanted from hers. She was cooking for us, nonetheless. All morning long, oatmeal, eggs, biscuits and ham, anything we could conjure up just to keep us there with her. She even dragged the playpen into the kitchen and sat Kevin in it, propping pillows behind him so that he could sit up and be apprised of the situation at hand. For the rest of the morning we sat playing cards at the table, Slap Jack mostly, Merle's favorite. She beat us one by one, hitting the jack with such stinging force her hand was useless by noon. Poor losers she called us. We could go ahead and cry our eyes out but our tears would be nothing compared to what we were going to shed if Uncle took it into his head to kick the door down. Without her right hand we were defenseless.

After lunch we heard the truck door open. Wayne got out with a bowl and came across the grass to the pump and got some water for Clover. Merle made no move toward him. Finally we heard the motor start up and saw Uncle shift the truck into first gear and start to pull away with Clover tied to the back, as though he'd forgotten her. At first Clover just sat but when she started to be dragged up the road she began to run, her ears blown inside out from the exhaust. Uncle drove slowly at first then faster and faster until she couldn't keep up. We could see her through the plumes of dirt, see that she was being dragged again, though when Uncle slowed to turn around she tried frantically to get back on all fours. That's when we knew he was doing this on purpose.

"Bastard," Merle shouted through the screen and ran to the corner hutch, grabbed a handful of cartridges from an old cigar box my father kept on the top shelf, then ran down the cellar steps and reached for the shotgun that was wedged between the crosspieces in the rafters near the coal furnace. As she did, the gun slipped loose and the butt came down hard on her head, before falling on the dirt floor. For a second it looked as if she might fall as well as she staggered toward where we stood on the cellar steps. But then she righted herself and picked up the gun and waving it told us to get the hell out of her way unless we wanted to be shot to hell and back too. We ran back up into the kitchen taking the steps two at a time. We could hear her cock the gun. It made a sickening crack, like the sound of a bone snapping. We clung to each other as she pushed by us in the kitchen. She was out the door in a flash, running across the grass, the gun pressed into her shoulder. Uncle tried to brake the truck when he saw her but it was too late. She had him in her sights and squeezed the trigger. The bullet hit the windshield dead center, shattering it. Glass exploded in every direction, flying, flashing, then clattering back onto the roof and hood of the truck. Some shards landed on the lid of the mailbox one of us had left open and lay like crystal teeth on a metal tongue.

The sound of the shot was so monumental it seemed foolish to follow it up with another but Merle seemed determined to do just that. She aimed the gun straight at Uncle, centering it between MAUI and a splash of red hibiscus that twined across his shirt. That stopped Uncle.

"Bitch," he screamed. "Bitch. Bitch. Bitch." He was beating the steering wheel with the palm of his hand. Emily was beside me balling her skirt up in a knot. Joan was eerily silent, her pale skin gone completely white, like the moon slowly fading in the morning sky. David could have been imbedded in the pantry door, like my mother's thumbprint, he pressed so hard against it. My own body felt like it had taken the force of the bullet. It was still reverberating. The sound of the shot rang in my ears, echoed for several seconds and then stopped. After that I couldn't hear anything. I felt as though someone had blown air into my ears. There were circles of red in front of my eyes wherever I looked and I could feel my teeth chattering. It was several seconds before I realized that I had my hands over my ears and my eyes clenched shut. When I opened them nothing had changed. Outside in the road Uncle revved the engine harder and harder.

"Just try it, you son of a bitching bastard, just try it," Merle screamed. She was choking with rage. But Uncle didn't move. Wayne was nowhere to be seen. He could have been splattered with blood, dead in the back of the truck between the baskets of peaches and apples for all I knew. The fields across from us lay unperturbed, as though nothing at all extraordinary had just taken place. Birds that had been launched from the power line, resettled themselves easily, and the bees, blown like scatter shot, closed ranks once more over their queen.

Just then Clover let out a long low howl of protest. She was covered with dirt and lay panting near the rear tires, the stub of her tail making tiny fan shapes in the dust. Merle looked over to where she lay, hesitated, raised the gun and her chin once more, looked back at Uncle, then at Clover, sighed, then lowered the gun and went to her. When it looked safe Uncle got out of the truck and went around to the back and stood over Merle as she untied the rope and lifted Clover up and walked toward the house, holding her close to her face. Uncle followed anxiously behind carrying the gun. Wayne had risen, as if from the dead, from the floor of the truck. We scattered as they approached the house.

"Was that a joke?" Emily asked as we ran up to our rooms. She was so confused and distraught she almost ran straight into the closed door. Joan said no but she could tell us something funny.

"Just think about this," she said. "If Wayne or I had been tied to the bumper it wouldn't have worked." Then she laughed, a short bitter laugh and collapsed on the bed.

When my father came home that night Uncle went outside to greet him.

"Hawaya, hawaya, hawaya," he said, reaching out his hand and pointing to his Hawaiian shirt. He was carrying his ukulele. It seemed to me such a child's toy especially against his girth. He'd been inside in the kitchen, where Clover lay in a box by the stove, singing "Danny Boy" to her over and over again, until he'd broken down in tears, and we, despite are best efforts, had too.

"Well, lad," Uncle said, and put his hand on my father's shoulder. "How was the sojourn?" The tears were still standing in his eyes. My father said the trip was fine, the car ran fine and my mother was getting sassier everyday. He rushed the conversation because he didn't want to see any tears. Then he asked Uncle how he was.

"Fair to maudlin," Uncle answered. Nothing was said about the gun or the windshield. Who would dare?

After this Joan refused to talk to her parents. She was angry with her mother for taking her father back.

"Listen, sister," Merle said, "I can play that game too." She could be as cold as ice, she said. She wouldn't talk to Joan even when Joan relented or forgot and tried to talk to her.

Uncle and Merle moved into my parents' bedroom that night and after a week it seemed that they had always been there. More than once, seeing them sitting on the bed, Merle in her slip and Uncle in his boxer shorts, his privates hanging out one side, the same soft brown as the sour apples we smashed on the road, I'd have the uneasy feeling that somehow they were now my parents. Whatever transpired between them, flashes of anger or fists, seemed, after a time, completely ordinary responses to me. Only once since Uncle arrived had I seen Merle angry enough to do some real harm, and that was after

Eddie Birdseye had dropped by to get David for a shoot and Uncle had come at her threateningly saying she was hot to trot, wasn't she. Merle was ironing and only had to hold up the iron and Uncle backed down. He called her Calamity Jane and this always made her smile. Sometimes, and this astonished me, she even ran her hand over his back when she passed by his chair. I couldn't believe she could bear to touch him.

After a week their bedroom smelled like the old carpet in the bar at the roadhouse where my father spent more and more time. Uncle said he didn't blame him. He had the best job in town.

When my father wasn't at work he was out on the roof laying shingles. Sometimes when I saw him climbing up the ladder, I had the feeling that he was going to keep on going. I was glad then for gravity, for anything that would keep him from falling off the face of the earth. He was still silent on the subject of my mother though once or twice I'd caught some bits of things he said to Merle. Joan said she heard him say that they were trying shock treatment, but we were unsure what that meant and we couldn't find it in the medical book. We thought that it meant scaring her but one night when Merle was drunk she said it meant shooting her head full of electric shocks. And if that's what it took to land in the lap of luxury like my mother had, Merle said she'd be more than happy to stick her head in a goddamn light socket. This was after my father brought home a picture of my mother he'd taken for us on one of his visits. She was surrounded by trees and paths and benches, and looked like she'd just had her hair done. She was smiling the same smile she used if I disturbed her when she was reading, her eyes momentarily blank as if she couldn't quite place me. My father said not to pay any attention to what Merle said when she was drinking though I knew this was the very best time for gathering information. He said to believe nothing of what we heard and half of what we saw. And I took this to mean that we were to see only half shapes the way I imagined he did because his left iris had been sheared in half when he was hit by shrapnel during the war. But despite my best efforts, I was never able to see Merle other than larger than life.

October came and Uncle set up a roadside stand on the barren corner across from Moe's store. He sold apples and cider and pumpkins. Even honey. He was often gone during the week scouring the countryside for the best price for produce. Wayne had to watch the stand after school. He was a strange and lonesome boy. I often saw him walking up the railroad tracks that ran alongside the river, shoulders hunched against the sun, the rain, the wind. No one liked him in school and even when he was home it seemed he didn't belong to us. He talked to Joan sometimes, pulling her into the summer kitchen where he slept on a cot near the backdoor. When he came to the table to eat, he rarely sat, and if his parents asked him a question, he repeated it, stalling for time to better gauge the answer they wanted. At night, if I was up late enough I could sometimes hear him singing. He had a beautiful voice, like his father, though if Uncle heard him he'd bang on the wall until he stopped. He had beautiful eyes too with dark lashes that seemed to be drawn, irresistibly, to his cheeks. I knew that he was my mother's favorite. She encouraged him to keep on singing and she practiced scales with him whenever she saw him. She had tried to talk Merle into getting him private lessons, but she couldn't, even if she had the money, not with Uncle. He was jealous of his own son. I suppose if my mother had been there he would not have become friends with Harold Birdseye. She would have discouraged it, but instead Merle told him she'd break every bone in his body if he took up with Harold, and so he did.

They were the same age. Fifteen. An age that spoke of hardness, silence, cruelty, spitting and a perfect balance between sneering tolerance and intolerance. I was terrified of boys this age and understood, when I saw them together, what Merle meant about never wanting to be alone in a room with any of her uncles. It was in me to wish that Harold had been burned to death along with his mother. It was in me to wish that Uncle had tied Wayne to the bumper of his car and dragged his bare ass up and down the street. Fear made me hateful. I was growing alarmingly mean, especially to my little brother.

Kevin still woke up at night, and sometimes, if I was awake I'd ask to go with my father on the ride to get him to sleep. He lay Kevin on the backseat, blankets tucked around him to keep from rolling off the seat. I always sat near my father, watching for the Zooks' farm and the trestle bridge where the ivy climbed and swayed and seemed to swing us up, then over the river. Beyond that, beyond the Caution sign and the sting of tires on the metal grid, was the hard road and a night so deeply dark it seemed bottomless. One night we drove for hours, along the river, in silence, almost to Rome, where Uncle went to buy apples. Kevin was long since asleep, his brow still furrowed above the bridge of his nose. Earlier I had been mean to him, picking him up by his feet and whirling him around in the dark as he slept, until I took his breath away. Then I laid him back down and for a moment his eyes fluttered, then closed as he sank back to sleep, and when he did I picked him up again and did the same thing. My father had caught me and made me come with him for a ride. For a talk. He wanted to know if I'd done this before, if this was the reason Kevin woke at night. "But it couldn't be," he said to himself. "You're a good girl," he added, but this again more to himself than to me.

I hoped for this goodness. And I hoped too that Kevin would

think what I had done to him was only a bad dream, like the one I'd had.

In my dream my mother came into the kitchen where I was standing. I was still a baby. I didn't know where she ended and I began. A storm had come up from out of the blue. *Out of the blue*, my mother repeated, and because she said it twice I knew she was afraid. Outside it wasn't blue at all but fiercely gray. The hollyhock bush looked as though it was a giant peacock tied by its feet to the ground. I said this. She shook her head no. *Holly hawks*, she smiled, explained, *it's because they're holly hawks*. One panel of curtains flickered, went out like a flame, as my mother closed the window. She turned and left the room. I followed her by her sounds as she stepped to each of the three windows in the dining room. I could hear the *tap*, *tap* of the iron weights inside each sash, and the rustle of glass. *Stay away from the windows*, she warned and her voice sounded like the roar of seashell, a sound so far away from its source it seemed a wail. I listened for her, to her, her steps on the stairs, the muted sound of windows being shut in the bedrooms overhead. Outside the wind picked up and pitted grains of sand against the house. The hollyhock lunged back and forth. I was completely still, only listening, waiting for her, when the first bolt of lightning struck and a miniature bolt shot out from the outlet near the kitchen floor. It was then I saw my mother. She was carrying the oil lamp. The wick was a flat white worm, swimming in the oil. She placed the lamp on the table, lifted the chimney, struck a match and lit the wick. Her hair was long and red, and in the lamplight glowed bright as the flame. She turned then and took my hand and when she did I saw her face. It was covered with tiny lightning bolts, broken arcs and needle-sized forks. I couldn't move. I could only stare. She cocked her head to me. *Oh these*, she said at last, laughing softly. I woke instantly as though thrown from the dream by my mother.

Sitting in the car next to my father I wanted to tell him this, though I couldn't have put it into words. My father patted my leg and said again that I was a good girl. He drove on through the night as though in search of this simple goodness. He drove as though it might rise as strongly and surely as the hope he held for all of his children.

When my father carried me up the stairs and laid me down next to Joan, I moved toward her and she moved away. If I stretched my arm, and I did, I could reach her hand. Once I had it in mine, I could sleep because I knew that if I had another bad dream I wouldn't go into it alone. I would bring Joan with me.

CHAPTER FOUR

My sister Emily was in a state of grace and so stood outside on the sidewalk, dangerously close to the road. We were waiting for Merle to pick us up after Mass. Emily had made it from Sunday to Sunday without sinning and was feeling especially proud that she hadn't had to go to confession before she received Communion. She said that if, at that very moment, she was struck by a car she would immediately ascend into heaven because she had just received Holy Communion.

"I wouldn't even care if I died," she said. I said I wouldn't care if I died either.

"Rainey," Em said, "if you were killed, you'd go to purgatory probably because you're definitely not in a state of grace." Then she looked down at the sidewalk, the crack in it, as though that was the way into purgatory. I said I still didn't care. She wasn't going anywhere without me. Em looked at me for a minute, began to say something, but decided against it. Just then Merle came roaring down the street, lipstick in hand, looking straight into the rearview mirror as she brought the tube to her mouth. I instinctively stepped back from the curb. Em stood her ground.

When we got home Merle ran from the car to the house holding the Sunday *News* over her head though the swarm of bees hadn't moved off the branch and there was no activity suggesting that it would. But Merle was allergic to bees. She'd fall over dead, she said, if one landed on her. Just the sound of them was enough to make her faint, though the tealeaves showed that a bee sting wouldn't be the death of her. We would. We were worse than that swarm outside, at least they were productive, and at least they settled down at night. But we wouldn't sit down unless she glued our asses to the chair.

In truth all she had to do was snap her fingers and we all sat down, chairs or not, right where we were. But it would be Emily who'd get up first. Merle said this was because my mother tripped over David's tricycle when she was pregnant for Em and went into labor. She was literally born on wheels, two months before she was due, she was that much in a hurry. And still was.

Emily never stayed around long enough to listen to Merle. She was too busy flitting around. Her movements were like our father's, sudden and quick. She could have the table cleared and the dishes washed, dried, and put away before the coffee perked. But she had our mother's beauty, her delicate features, her fair skin and true green eyes, the kind that stayed green no matter what color she wore. Merle said that these were the rarest green. "Mine are fickle," she'd say, pleased with herself. Emily also had our mother's fragility. The mere weight of her clothing sometimes seemed enough to bring her down. It was easy to imagine her sleeping in a shoebox on top of sterile cotton for the first weeks of her life, my parents too fearful even to pick her up. She did not like to be touched anyway, and cried if she was, my mother said. As soon as she could walk, she ran, ran away from anyone who tried to grab her. I, on the other hand, would go into a trance at the touch of a hand.

It was only when Emily was alone that she was able to sit still and so when we got home from Mass, she went outside to watch the bees, certain that she wouldn't be disturbed.

"Get a load of Martyr Mary," Merle said when she saw Em near the bees. Merle was setting down rattraps, as big as roller skates, behind the stove and refrigerator. She was all dressed up, wearing a dress that I loved. It was dotted swiss, with a full skirt, caught at the waist by a wide belt that looked like two red hands. She was going to see our mother, driving in with my father after they dropped Kevin and Toby off at the Moes'. I could tell that my father didn't approve of this. He kept telling Merle what it was a good idea not to say. It was a good idea not to mention us, for starters.

Joan was tipping her chair all the way back, teetering close to the cast-iron stove even though she'd been warned that one of these days she'd split her head open and all her brains would spill out. If she had any brains. Joan was trying to see if she could pick up her toast from her plate with her toes. Merle told her to cut it out, then turned back to my father.

"What the hell am I supposed to talk about then? What am I supposed to do? Shrug my shoulders when Bess asks me about the kids?"

"She probably won't ask," my father said softly. I was shocked to hear this. Merle, sitting directly under my mother's painted thumbprint, threw back her head and laughed.

"In a pig's ass she won't, Andy." At that moment I loved Merle. My father just smiled his smile that meant he was angry and looked at her as though he might have to ask her to leave the table. Then he looked over to where I sat before turning back to Merle. He frowned and shook his head at her. But that didn't stop her.

"Don't tell me what I can and can't say to my sister. That's all I'm saying," Merle said. "We've been through some harder times than this together. Harder than you'll ever know." For a moment she raised her chin like she did when she was daring Uncle to just lay one hand on her. But my father had already pushed back from the table and wore that let's-change-the-subject look on his face. He was patting his pockets. "Keys. Money. Glasses. Glasses?" he said, then left the room to go look for them.

"Go ahead, walk away," Merle said to his back. She was looking out the window, stirring the pitcher of cream instead of her tea.

"You think you have her all to yourself don't you now? Well, wait. Just you wait." She threw down her spoon, opened her purse and grabbed two bottles of beer from the refrigerator and stuck them inside it.

"That's what your father always wanted," Merle said to me. "He wants your mother all to himself. The selfish bastard. He's always been jealous of me. But I'll tell you something, if push came to shove, she'd side with me." Push came to shove often enough in our house and so I believed Merle. I looked her straight in the eye, risking the slap I might get for this. But she wasn't looking at me. She was looking at Joan.

"What in the hell are you doing?"

Joan held the toast between two of her toes. She almost had it to her mouth.

"Maybe we should cut her goddamn arms off," Uncle said pulling on his pants as he came into the room. "Maybe then we'd get some work out of her." Wayne was right behind him pretending to suck on his fingers to make his sister mad. Joan wavered a minute, her left foot wrapped around the table leg for balance, then she dropped the toast. Clover made a dash for it. Joan just closed her eyes and put her fingers in her mouth and began to suck. She was still leaning backward but she had her toes on the floor. Uncle reached across the table and slapped her hand from her mouth.

"Stop it, goddamn it," he yelled, but turned to Merle. "Tell her to stop it, for crying out loud. I hate that noise."

"Don't get him started," Merle warned. That meant don't get him started drinking. But it was too late. He was already unscrewing the leather flask he kept in his back pocket, tilting his head back, just like Joan.

"You had to start," Merle said and slammed her hand down on the table. Joan opened her eyes at the sound and when she did she fell over backward with an incredible crash.

"Now are you satisfied?" Merle asked. It was impossible to know who she was addressing.

"You're not hurt," Merle insisted looking down at her daughter.

"You didn't hit your head." Joan was silent, lying with her eyes closed as if she was unconscious. She lay there a long moment. When no one bent to her, she got up and ran out of the room. Behind her a thin trickle of blood was inching its way down her pale braids and onto her back.

"You're not hurt," Merle insisted again and turned her wrath on Uncle. I ran after Joan but she slammed the door in my face.

Within ten minutes the house was eerily silent. Merle, my father, and my baby brothers were gone. Uncle had gone to the stand cursing because Wayne had disappeared, and Joan had locked herself in the bathroom. I opened the back door and called to Emily. She came in blinking from the sun and smelling of fresh air and leaves. I told her our mother had forgotten about us and that Joan had split her frigging head open.

"She did not," Em replied to both my assertions. "And don't say swears." I'd forgotten she was in the state of grace.

"Where's Joan?" Em asked. I said that she was in the bathroom bleeding to death. Em just looked at me. We knew Joan wouldn't come out if we asked her to, we knew if we showed any sympathy that she might swing open the door and punch us in the shoulder, right in the muscle where it really hurt. This is what Wayne did to her. We knew he hurt her but she always said that it tickled. Em and I knew too that we'd have to wait for Joan to come to us so we set to making ourselves sandwiches. We decided we'd take Joan on a picnic to the river when she came out. We wouldn't mention that this was to make her feel better, only that we wanted to go once more before it got too cold, before Merle came back and said we'd better keep our goddamn asses away from that river. It was filled with slime and snakes and God only knew what else. It was a frigging death trap.

Em loved mustard and sugar after Communion. She made herself two sandwiches but ate the first one before she could find the wax paper. We made two for Joan as well. One mustard and sugar, and one apple butter, then sat down at the table near the window to wait while our fillings bled into the bread. Em's looked so soggy and yellow that she didn't know if she'd be able to eat it. I sat and stared at mine. By the time Joan came downstairs the apple butter had turned the bread rusty, the same color as the blood in her hair.

Em asked Joan if she knew that it was Indian Summer.

"For Chrissakes," Joan said. That meant she'd never heard of it. It was possible that in the Bronx Indian Summer did not exist. I myself had no idea what it meant. Em said that it was like Indian giving, something given to you for a short while before it was taken back. Joan asked Em if she knew what Indian wrestling was. Em shook her head.

"It's when two dogs get stuck together. Ass to ass."

Emily shook her head. In truth it did seem hard to believe, so hard to believe that I thought it might be true.

"Who said so?" Em wondered.

"Your father." My face went numb with this knowledge. If this was true, and it had to be if my father said it, I understood why Joan didn't want anything to do with Indians. Still, she'd come to the river, regardless of what the damn Indians up the road would do to us when we passed their house. I could only picture the worst scene. Indian wrestling. And so I stayed close to my sister. Joan walked a few feet ahead of us slashing at the weeds alongside the road with her bare hands. That's what she'd do if anyone laid a hand on her. Especially a redskin.

Em yelled to her that she shouldn't judge all Indians by Harold Birdseye. How would Joan feel if she saw her own mother burned to ashes right before her eyes? Joan said it would be fine with her, that she'd be happy to see her own mother burn in hell.

"I thought you didn't believe in heaven and hell," Em said. Joan was always deaf to anything Em said about religion.

"I believe in hell." I liked this about Joan, that she chose what she believed in.

Despite its present intensity, I knew that the sun was not to be taken seriously at this time of year. Just over its shoulder the wind raised the skin of the Finger Lakes up in goose bumps. We lived on a spit of land, threaded with rivers and creeks, between two of the Finger Lakes, Cayuga and Seneca, on the outskirts of a village similar to a dozen others that seemed to have been cast down from heaven like fallen angels. These villages sagged from neglect. Their front porches drooped like the overalls of the old men who sat on them. When the men died, the women lingered on, cloistered and brittle behind their dusty drapes. On Halloween they offered apples or pennies and held them out to us with hands that were so dry it felt as though they'd fall right off when we took their treats. I was glad that they couldn't hold us there.

From Eddie Birdseye's postcards the villages looked like stepping stones to the larger towns, towns with tree-lined squares, wooden churches, granite banks and red brick firehouses. Towns where you could be saved, even if you were a cat, by the fire department. Keansville was the nearest town that could be counted on for anything more than a laugh, Merle said, and it was their fire company that had responded to the fire at the Birdseye's house the year before. We re-created the scene every time we passed the river, what we heard the old men recount again and again in the dark corners of Moe's store when-ever the sight of Harold or Eddie ignited the memory.

That night the fire truck emptied the river. By morning the river rocks were as dry as the ones Eddie Birdseye had built his fireplace with. Or so Mr. Moe said. Regardless, that fireplace was the only thing left standing after all was said and done. It still was, standing like a swimmer posed for a dive, along the river's edge.

The night of the fire the neighbors wouldn't let Mr. Birdseye back in the house a second time even though he begged them to. He'd got-ten Harold out alive and that was all a body could ask of him. Or that he could ask of himself. They could see Mrs. Birdseye standing at the bedroom window, her long black braids on fire, the sky in flames behind her. Harold was running around with a wet towel wrapped around his face trying to keep the skin from melting off his face. He kept screaming, "Jump, Ma, jump," through his blistered lips. But she wouldn't. Then Mr. Birdseye began swinging at the men. Old man Zook was knocked out cold but the others held fast. And then she was gone, the old men said, the house with her, both simultaneously breaking free from whatever held them.

"The house damned near rolled into the river," Mr. Moe said, wresting the conclusion of the story from their mouths, as was his right. He'd been there. We'd wait, spellbound. "And then, I'll be damned what happened next," Mr. Moe said, rubbing his whiskers, as he pondered this mystery anew. "There wasn't a cloud in the sky, but

just when that house flew apart, there in that field over there," and
here he pointed to a shelf displaying an advertisement for Campbell's
soup, the mouths on the faces of the Campbell soup kids and ours
rounded in wonder, "a huge bolt of lightning, in the exact shape of a
fleeing woman, lit up the sky."

"Like a stick figure," one of the old men finished for him.

"Probably headed toward the happy hunting ground," Roger
Beasley Sr. said to break the silence.

"Or the roadhouse," Gideon Yetter said. "She liked her drink."

"Yep," the men said in unison, pushing back their chairs as if
they'd just finished Sunday dinner. But we knew there was more.

"She was more Indian than him. She looked it anyways," Roger
allowed.

"He's no Indian. He's Canuck," Gideon said.

"Nope," Mr. Moe said, as though he was being challenged, "that
bolt of lightning was her exact likeness." And that's when Eddie
Birdseye's voice had changed. That's when he started breathing in that
wheeze. Her death broke his spirit, broke his voice right in two. It was
her name under his every word. "Now I know it ain't my ears playing
tricks on me neither," Mr. Moe said, winding down. "It's her name,
plain as day, I-rene. Just you listen." And then he looked up over his
head and shouted, "Missus," demanding his wife materialize before
his eyes lest she take a notion to set herself and the whole lot of us on
fire.

Mrs. Moe came swaying up the dark aisle, the floorboards creaking in her wake. The men all looked up at her.

"That's what he needs," Gideon said. "A good woman."

"She's taken," Mr. Moe said possessively, and grabbed hold of her
plump arm as though he was going to take a bite of it.

We sang, *Irene, good night ight-ight,* whenever we came to the river, hoping to put Irene Birdseye's and our fears to rest before we entered the woods.

The woods were strewn with soggy mattresses, branches thrown across them like sleep-flung arms, and the path littered with discarded tires, their exposed threads white as the roots of violets we tore from the ground. Deeper into the woods the path gave way to brush and an occasional rusted can pitted with holes and scattered rifle casings which we gathered and hoarded in our pockets believing that if we dropped one it would explode. Faded *No Trespassing* signs, dry as butterfly specimens were nailed to the trees.

We were never far from the road in these woods and could hear the occasional whoosh of cars through the trees and the sharp squeal of brakes as they approached the bridge. I could even see the great yellow sign with that one word that I couldn't sound out or make sense of when I was younger: CAUTION. I'd once asked my father what it meant and he said, careful. But it didn't sound out to careful. My father spelled it out, c-a-r-e-f-u-l, and said I should remember it had the word *car* in it and the word *full.* It was a warning for cars to go slowly over the bridge if they were too full.

It had rained all week, the river was swollen, the ground sodden. We could hear the sudden plunk of frogs in the small pockets of water that stood in the bottomland but we hadn't seen one yet. Emily knelt down by the water and I did the same. Joan was looking around for bottles. The sun was hot, the water warm, the ground steamy. Gnats swarmed around my head and flew into my eyes.

"Why do they always fly into eyes?" I asked as Emily twirled the end of a tissue into a soft white toothpick. I was blinded by the gnat. My desire to blink was maddening.

"Because," Emily said, as she spread my lids wide and swabbed the corner of my eye, "they think your eye is a tiny pool of water they can swim in without drowning, or without frogs trying to eat them. We're giants to them."

"So is the one in my eye," I said. She lifted it out and held it up to me.

"There," she said, standing up. I sat by the water and watched the dragonflies dip down for a drink and the water spiders skim across the water. The gnats came back again and again, and I brushed them away. Not all of them aimed for my eyes. A swarm of them kept hovering in the vee between my legs. Joan said they were piss flies trying to get into my hole and if they did they'd go straight to my stomach and lay eggs there. I stood up quickly.

The gnats followed us through the woods, inches in front of our faces, until we reached the river. Then they suddenly disappeared. We made our way along the bank until we came to the railroad bridge. The train didn't run along this section of bridge anymore. Just the wind. It played through the corroded braces and girders, whistled through the cables and through the dried and creaking wooden planks and set the whole bridge to music. We swayed to the hum that rose off the rusted tracks and trembled in anticipation of a ghost train suddenly appearing from nowhere, us leaping off the bridge to the river below. I imagined our dresses parachuting us to the riverbank because I couldn't swim.

To test our bravery Joan insisted we eat our sandwiches in the middle of the bridge. Em didn't care because she was in a state of grace. But I wasn't. Joan said in the Bronx she lived across the street from the El. She spoke with food in her mouth and because of this I heard the word as hell. We wouldn't last more than ten seconds on the tracks of hell before we were flattened Joan said. In view of this I almost swallowed my sandwich whole.

Because we survived our lunch the only possible thing to do that was even more fearsome was to go swimming. At least this was how Joan saw it. We were forbidden to swim without an adult with us. To test our loyalty to Joan we would have to swim naked. Em and I both stared at the knot of bruise and blood on the back of Joan's head. We watched as she raised her dress above her head. This, I knew, was not a good idea. I thought immediately of all the things my father had said to Merle about good and bad ideas earlier. I was still angry with him for saying that we were not a good idea to talk about to our mother and didn't want to say that swimming was not a good idea because of this. But I wanted to distract Joan and Em from the idea of swimming. Joan was already in the water and Emily was stepping out of her slip and it seemed to me, out of her state of grace too. To delay this I asked again whether or not it was possible for our mother to forget us. I was standing by the water's edge, peeling bark off a twig and dropping it into the water.

"No," Em said, then, "why, have you forgotten her?" I said no, though sometimes I did forget about my mother and this made me itch, made me want to throw my dress off too and plunge into the water.

I knew my sister's body, knew that though her hair was dark, parts of the blonde baby hair still held on in pockets near her shoulders or in the soft cup between the dimples of her lower back. What I didn't know was that her perfectly pink and flat nipples had puffed up into soft and sudden tits.

I stared when she raised her slip over her head. But Emily must have forgotten about her tits because she didn't turn away. She slipped out of her cotton underwear and ran to the river's edge. Joan turned to wait for her. It seemed to me that both of them had pussies, tits and asses and because of this I only took off my shoes. I waded along the bank, leaning out carefully trying to catch a rope that the older boys had tied from a branch overhead. The bank was mossy and sharp with brush and broken bottles. The sun sailed in and out of clouds on its way, more rapidly than we imagined, to the western horizon. The bridge hummed above our heads. My sister floated, white as the birch log she'd thrown her dress on, under the shadow of the rope. She turned her head slowly from side to side and cupped her hands, the way my father had shown us, the way that worked for her but never for me. Joan was still walking in the water, feeling her way to the drop-off before being swallowed up and swept into the current. She had just given herself over to the force of the water when I heard a snap behind my back. Harold and Wayne had materialized from out of nowhere. *Out of the blue*, I heard my mother say. They looked at me, then at the clothing on the bank and beyond to the water, and my sister. Wayne gave a long wolf whistle. Harold laughed.

"Let's make them get out of the water," Wayne yelled loud enough for Em and Joan to hear. That betrayal could come from this quarter astounded me. I fully expected it from Harold, but not from family. Our parents always told us to stick up for one another. But Wayne was trying to impress Harold, trying to prove he was every bit as mean. The week before Harold had thrown his puppy against the barn and killed it. When Merle heard about it, she was outraged. She said his father ought to take him out in the woods and shoot him and put us all out of our misery. If he came within a yard of our house that's exactly what she planned to do. He gave her the creeps with that face of his, the way it was stretched into a grin. She'd be more than happy to wipe that look off his face.

"Out," Wayne yelled suddenly, jerking his thumb toward the trees behind him. He sounded exactly like Uncle. I looked at him. He looked at the ground, smiling down at the twigs that he was methodically breaking underfoot. Emily stood up, her braids like two ropes binding her to the river bottom. Only her shoulders were visible. There was something fixed in her expression. She shifted her eyes to look around her, look for something to protect herself with. But there was only water, water so thin and so suddenly clear that I could see through to her nakedness as easily as I could see the church babies in the Crying Room. When Em's eyes finally came back to the center of her face they were like the green stone eyes of the statues of saints in church.

"Out!" Wayne yelled again. Em stood frozen. Joan was several feet behind her and coming closer. I believed that she could save us all. I knew that she would, though I knew Harold was powerful. I looked at his hands. They looked as mighty as God's hands, hands that could raise the dead, could lift my sister from the water as easily as a twig if he wanted to. But he didn't move. He was as anchored to the ground as Em to the river bottom. It was Wayne who started toward the bank. He held a stick in his hand.

"See this," he said, looking straight at Em and snapping the branch, "this is your wrist." Joan had come up behind Em. She raised her thumb and pressed it to her pointer finger.

"See this," she said, making a small circle and holding it up to her brother, "this is your brain." Wayne threw the broken stick at her. Joan ducked under the water and disappeared. Em started to shake.

"Oh, is the baby cold? Does the baby need to dry off?" Wayne sneered. He looked around and saw Em's dress. He reached down for a rock and tied the dress around it then threw it to her. It started to sink. Wayne took another step. Em grabbed her dress as though it were

a life-line Wayne had thrown to her. She began to move forward, coming slowly but steadily into view. For the briefest instant I thought that
Wayne was pulling her out and turned to look at him. When I looked
back at my sister she had put the dress between her legs like a diaper.
Her hair was a black slash across her cheek. Though she was getting
nearer I could feel her move farther and farther away from me. From us.

"I'm telling my father," I yelled. "I'm telling." But Wayne knew I
wouldn't because you didn't tell on older kids, not if you had to live
with them. There were endless opportunities for retribution, places in
the barn where they could take you and hurt you.

"Go ahead, go to the nuthouse and get your damn father, and
your screwball mother, while you're at it," Wayne said, then spit on the
ground. I thought of how my mother loved Wayne. Harold gave him
a quick look then started to walk along the riverbank, trying to keep
track of Joan. She was being swept away by the current. Harold quick-
ened his pace, until he was running. The current carried Joan closer
and closer to the bridge. Only her head was above water. She wouldn't
look our way or call for help. I imagined she would set sail and con-
tinue to float down the whole length of the river once she passed
under the bridge.

I turned back to Wayne. He held another stick in his hand. I thought
he was going to throw it at me, but instead he lashed out at the world
around him. Emily was out of the water. Her new titties had turned completely inside out it seemed, gone below her flesh and disappeared. She
stood hunched over, the water from her dress streaming down her legs.

"You're pissing your pants," Wayne said, and Em was so confused
she pressed her hands between her legs and sank to the ground. Then
something hit the water beside me. It was Joan's dress. Wayne had
kicked it into the water. It floated on the surface for a few seconds

before it started to sink. When I looked for my cousin she was gone, as though she too had sunk as silently and completely as her dress.

"You raper," I screamed. I had no idea where this word came from but there it was, and there was Wayne, his face as purple as Harold's.

"My father will kill you," I vowed. Something in my voice had hardened into a pure edge of certainty. My father would kill him. Seeing Emily on her knees convinced me of this. It must have convinced Wayne too.

It seemed to me that the trees began to shake, and the sun, moving in and out of the clouds in long basting stitches like the ones my mother used to hem my sister's dresses, had reached the end of the sky and tied itself off in a hard orange knot. I had never felt such fury and such despair in all my life. It doubled me over.

Grief, that's how I learned grief. I walked straight into the river. I stood in water above my waist, my own dress billowing up. I was ready to pull it off, to lift it over my head so that I too would be naked and drown. It seemed the one thing that kept me from Em and Joan. I would have kept going, I was headed for the bridge I think, but suddenly Wayne grabbed me, pulled me out then pushed me down near my sister. We stared out at the river. It was flat. Joan was gone. Wayne was gone. Beyond the bridge Harold stood on the bank scanning the water. Across the river I could see docks and small boats, clearings where families picnicked, where we once picnicked. I could almost see us there when the wind picked up and smocked the water as neatly as the bodice on my dress, and the image vanished.

"Go to hell!" I yelled at Harold. I knew I had some power over him then. But he couldn't leave. The sun was setting, the sky was bright orange and the wind had picked up.

"She's drowned!" I screamed though my voice was thick with sobs.

"You killed her. You and Wayne killed Joan. You're going to burn in hell." He was looking out at the river, at the orange sky, the way the water shifted the light and shone on the place where Joan had disappeared. Then suddenly he tore himself away. It sounded as though his feet were roots being ripped from the ground and as he ran he swung at the branches that hung low on the path, at the trees shedding gold and red leaves, and at the early evening air that had come quickly upon us all. When he passed under the second trestle he stopped short. We heard a scream. Em and I grabbed one another. We thought Harold had gone crazy and was going to come back and drown both of us so we wouldn't tell. I looked toward the path. I saw some movement and held on to my sister more tightly. She refused to look. I could hear branches breaking underfoot. Someone was running. I was riveted to the spot. And then miraculously there was Joan in the middle of the path. Some twigs were stuck in her hair, her skin was bluish white, her chest was heaving, but she was safe.

I had never doubted that my sister was holy but I'd had my doubts about Joan. But now the golden down on her arms seemed a blessing to me, the dying sun suddenly gilded her like the statues in church, illuminated and resurrected her before our eyes. I ran to her and brought her back to us to where Em had crawled and sat hiding. We sat in the bushes with our arms around each other hoping that our clothes would dry.

"It's these," Joan said finally, bitterly, pressing her pink nipples flat against her chest. "It's these they wanted to see." Em dropped her head against her chest and began to gulp the air around her. Joan pressed her mouth against her shoulder and bit it. I knew then that if she could have reached her chest she would have bitten her nipples right off and I wouldn't have blamed her one damn bit.

CHAPTER FIVE

The day after Merle went to visit my mother she was unusually quiet. She padded about in her slip, a red sweater and a pair of Uncle's black socks, her knees spilling over the top of them like hot-cross buns. She'd started a fire in the wood burning stove and stood directly in front of it as if she were trying to bake herself. She was holding Kevin like a shield against her chest. Toby was still at the Moes'. He was sound asleep when my father went in to fetch him and Mrs. Moe said let him sleep. Kevin, of course, was wide-awake.

"I can't seem to get warm," she said to Uncle. The heat from the stove was pushing her hair up and down and the baby was lunging for it.

"Get some clothes on," Uncle said, "it's cold as a witch's tit." Then he said, throwing his voice like a ventriloquist, "or your tits," and looked around to see who said that. "It's useless as a witch's tit," Merle said distractedly. "That's the expression. Not, 'cold.' Useless."

"Yours too," Uncle said, throwing his voice again. Joan almost smiled. Her father was in a good mood because of all the fruit he'd sold over the weekend. He took out his money and laid it on the table and said, "How do you like them apples?"

Merle had her mouth pressed against Kevin's bald head. Her eyes looked red. "Ow," she said suddenly. Kevin had grabbed a hold of a mole on her neck and was trying to bring it to his mouth.

"He thinks it's a ninny," Uncle said laughing. "All your efforts will come to nothing, lad. Take it from me. You need your mama for that." Merle started blinking her eyes quickly, then turned around to face the stove and shifted Kevin to her hip. On the back of his neck was a red mark, the size of a thumb. My father said it was where the stork had pinched him when he dropped him down the chimney, but I was afraid it was from something mean I'd done to him. I reached out to touch his foot but Merle said "Don't" because I had a fever and might be contagious. She told me to put on something warm and get back in bed. But she didn't yell, she didn't even warn the others to get the hell to school before she put them in Catholic school where the nuns would set the boards under their feet on fire if they were even one minute late.

Uncle said he was off to Rome. He meant Rome, New York, to buy apples, but whenever he said it, he sounded as though he were off to Italy. He might just as well have been, Merle had remarked on several occasions, for the time it took him to return.

"Try to bring home something more than a snootful," Merle said to the stove.

I lay in bed most of the morning drifting in and out of sleep. I dreamed that my father took me to see my mother. We had to travel across a lake in a giant teaspoon, which would capsize if we moved one muscle. I woke up before we got to her. Every one of my joints ached. For one heart-clenching moment I thought I might have polio. I pictured myself encased in an iron lung, like the one Merle had threatened us with after she'd seen pictures of it in the newspaper. That iron lung showed a picture of a young girl with a mirror angled above her head. Merle pointed to her and to me. That's what she had to look at twenty-four hours a day. It wasn't a pretty sight. I reached for my pillow but it was gone. Joan had brought all the pillows down to the cellar so they'd be cool by the time we went to bed that night but my head was so hot I decided to go down and get mine.

When I stood up all my brains shifted from the back of my head to the front. If my mother were home she'd put me in her bed so she could keep a close eye on me. I could make all the demands I wanted but she would never lose patience. She'd sit me in a chair while she changed the bedding, smoothing down the folds of the sun-bleached sheets, as though their freshness was contagious and would spread to cure me. She'd keep a fresh pitcher of water by the bed at all times, and she'd come into the room and press her palm to my forehead, and the backs of her hands to my cheeks. If I were too hot she'd rub me down with alcohol, careful to expose only one limb at a time. There would be soup and toast and Jell-O though she herself couldn't eat a thing if there was a sick child in the house.

But nothing curbed Merle's appetite, and she wasn't concerned about mine, especially when I was sick because she thought most illnesses were just a ploy for attention. Staying home from school was equivalent to an invasion, and we were treated as enemies until we were well, and even then we were suspect for weeks afterward. I had learned to stay far from Merle. I would have been given the death sentence if she became sick — it was bad enough I gave her nightmares. I knew that if I wanted anything I'd better damn well get it myself. As I walked slowly down the steps, the weight of my feet on the stairs sent drum rolls of pain to my head. My eyes were sore. Even the hair on my head ached.

The kitchen was empty and, to my amazement, clean. All the dishes were done and the floor scrubbed. The mop lay against the sink, its head like a woman getting her hair shampooed. On the table two loaves of bread were rising in the hot sun. I tiptoed down the cellar steps to avoid jarring this scene or waking Kevin who was sprawled on his belly in the playpen, as though a stork had truly dropped him there. The cellar was cool and dank. Beads of moisture rolled down the rock walls and formed wet spots on the earthen floor. I could have been walking under the roots of trees it was so dark and rich. I felt the weight of the floorboards above my head and the shift and crumble of dirt as Merle, sounding lead-footed, made her way through the rooms. I'd thought she might be outside hanging up wash despite the bees. Anything was possible if the kitchen was any measure of impending change. But then I heard her climb the stairs. She'd forgotten I was home; I was sure of it because I heard her singing, something she never did in public, when I made my way back up the stairs. She was singing, *California here I come right back where I started from*, though her rendition sounded sad. I pulled my pillow to my chest and made my way back up to my bedroom. Merle hadn't latched the bathroom door and as I passed by the door I could see her stepping out of her slip and turning to fill the tub. It was a shock to see her naked, like slicing open skin and seeing bone, but it was also wondrous. I stayed and watched her because I hadn't meant to. If I had, I would have been far more nervous and probably would have revealed my presence.

She lay in the tub and waited until the bubbles enshrouded her. She seemed completely unaware of anything except the bottle of beer she held in her hand. I couldn't see her body except for her white shoulders, the round mound of each breast, the translucent tawny cloud around her nipples. When she moved, her freckles slid and wavered. Every few seconds I could see her pussy wet and dark, glistening where the hair held the bubbles. She had shut her eyes to all of this and looked as though she were asleep. But she wasn't. I could hear her humming. She must have soaked herself for a good fifteen minutes, then without moving anything except her foot, she pulled the chain to the plug. Still she didn't move. She lay perfectly still while the water dropped away, and as it did, it was as though she were rising up, as if her soft flesh was emerging from the hard white shell of the tub, rising warm and yeasty like the loaves of bread in the pans she set out to rise on the kitchen table.

The water fell away from her in increments, encircling her breasts, then her belly, momentarily, in silvery halos. The bubbles caught in the hair between her legs reflected myriad prisms of light that seemed as sanctified as the light streaming through the stained glass windows during Mass.

The window was open and I could see the water evaporating from her shoulders. Her skin was flushed and steamy, then suddenly chilled. She sat up and pulled a towel to her face then lay her head on her knees. It was then that I realized she was crying, silently, without will or effort, and this crying was more private to me than her nakedness. I suddenly felt deeply ashamed of myself and frightened for all of us. A loud beep and the sound of a truck in the driveway made us both jump. Merle stuck her head out the window. It was Eddie Birdseye. He came by to drop Toby off. He'd stopped by Moe's Store and thought he'd save the old man a trip. Besides, he yelled, he wanted to know how my mother was. Merle said she'd be right down and grabbed my father's robe from off the hook. She jumped back when she opened the door to me. "Jesus Christ," she said taking a swing at me, "you scared the piss out of me." She had in fact, scared the piss out of me.

I stood by the sink washing my pajama bottoms out. The smell of the soap, Fels Naphtha, made me gag. Merle used it to wash our mouths out, mine most recently when I said I saw David and Joan fucking in the barn. I had borrowed the word from Joan, though after my mouth was washed out, I decided to give it back to her. Merle ascertained that what David and Joan were doing was hardly more than showing parts, nothing much to brag about on either count, but God help them both if it happened again, and God help their not-so-private parts. I got my mouth washed out as much for the word as for tattling, a habit that neither scorn nor shunning, unfortunately, could break me of. Emily simply told everyone right off that I tattled, getting it out of the way along with the introductions. Joan threatened to pull my tongue out by the roots and stomp on it if I didn't stop. David told me the story of the boy who cried wolf. My father had already tried this, in both cases the moral to the story was lost on me because there weren't any wolves where we lived.

But then I heard a long wolf whistle, followed by Merle's teasing laugh. I went directly into David's room. It was above the kitchen and had a grate in the floor next to the bed so the heat from the wood stove could rise to the bedrooms. We had one too but it was under our bed. I could hear Toby running from the living room to the kitchen silently. I could picture his worried face as he checked to see that everything was as he left it. Merle said she'd completely forgotten about him.

"I don't believe that," Eddie said.

"You don't want to believe it, then. I didn't miss him."

"I don't believe that Merle," Eddie said again, sighing and sawing her name in two. My father said Mr. Birdseye refused to believe bad things about people. It was one of the things he liked about the man. Merle said she could name several things she liked about the man.

"Think what you want."

"I think you're pretty and I think you love these kids."

"I love my sister, and I think I'm pretty too," Merle shot back. "That's the only reason I'm here."

"Because of your looks? Well, I thank you for that."

"You know what I mean. I'm here for Bess."

"How is she?" There was a long pause. I could hear Merle going for another beer. Then she walked over to the steps.

"Rainey?" I heard her foot on the step. "Just checking," she said to Eddie. "She's a nosy little brat. You can't trust her." Lies, I wanted to shout, all lies.

"She wanders," Merle said. I thought she meant me. "Not physically. I mean you're talking to her one minute and she seems fine and then the next minute…well, she's talking crazy. Like a goddamn fool. I felt like slapping her. If it would have done any good, I would have." It was the beer that was making her talk. Somehow Eddie had caught on to this.

"You don't mean that," Eddie said, then, "not with that soft hand. Look how it fits in mine." I tried to look but could only see the top of the stove and their long shadows on the floor. Merle just went on, warming to the subject.

"She's wandering around in her childhood. It's like she can't find her way out of it. I don't know why in the name of hell she'd want to go back to that. It's not like it was the Garden of Eden. Well, come to think of it, it was. We were always being thrown out of someplace. Bess more than me."

"I can't imagine anyone wanting to throw either of you out," Eddie said. His voice was getting kind of smoky.

"You sound like Andy. He can't imagine that he's to blame for driving Bess nuts."

"Andy? Not Andy."

"Now you sound like Bess."

"You sound a little bit jealous."

"Hah," Merle said. "I know what I know. Why do you think her doctor wants to talk to me? But I'm not stupid. I don't want that creep crawling around in my brain, investigating my dreams. I told Bess just tell him you don't dream."

"Do you dream?" Eddie asked. I could tell he'd lost interest in my poor mother who was stuck inside her childhood. Merle knew it, too.

"Anytime you get me near a bed," Merle said.

"What do you dream about?"

"I dream of getting out of this hellhole. The only thing keeping me here is Bess."

"And your kids. You've got a beautiful daughter. She's a beautiful young girl. She could be a model. I wouldn't mind doing some proofs of her." Merle didn't answer. When anyone told our mother we were beautiful she said all her geese were swan. I pictured us all swimming in a pond. I tried to remember if Eddie Birdseye ever said we were beautiful, Em and I. David was all American. I wasn't sure if that meant beautiful. I hoped that I was beautiful. I hoped that if I was that someone would let me know.

"I could have been a model, myself," Merle said. "It's not like I didn't have offers."

"You could have made some money at it," Eddie agreed.

"By the time I was Joan's age, I was working full time at Woolworth's and giving every cent I made to the aunts. They'd hand me back carfare."

"I do the shots for free," Eddie said, "use them for stock photos. If I sold any you'd make some money and so would I. It's the same arrangement I have with Bess." Merle shook her head.

"I'm not Bess. Her kids are leeches. They suck the blood right out of her veins." I had seen leeches on David's leg once when he was swimming. They looked slick and black. And serious. Even after he'd gotten out of the water, those leeches held on.

"What the hell do they want? They're fed, they're dressed. I'm sup-posed to get down on my knees and play tiddledy winks with Typhoid Mary upstairs. Christ. That's all I need. If I get sick I'm out of here. I mean that. As far as I'm concerned, motherhood's what drives a woman nuts. Look at my sister. Every time she has a kid, she needs to move. You should have seen her when she lived in the Bronx. You know she lost two babies. One she carried to term. But she's got that disease monkeys have. R-H. That's why there are so many years between Rainey and Toby. It wasn't as though she was practicing birth control. God forbid. She'd get pregnant and immediately start pack-ing. She and Andy lived in this one tenement building on Tremont Avenue. Do you know that in the four years they lived there, she moved five times? Five times within the same building, and each apartment was a floor higher." Merle was shaking her head. I was shaking mine too; I'd never heard the stories of the lost babies.

"She was sent away then, too. This isn't the first time."

I couldn't remember my mother being gone before. I did remem-ber that Em and I were gone, though. We stayed with two old women who were my mother's aunts. They had to teach us manners, to not use the dishtowel to wipe our noses when we were drying the dishes, to pull back the bedspread before we sat on the bed. The two old aunts, Dorothy and Mildred, slept in the same bed. They spent a lot of time in that bed because if anything upset them, they said the thing to do was get into bed. They did get out of bed long enough to take us to the Empire State Building, where, if we leaned over the edge and fell, we would be as flattened as a penny left on a railroad track. We would be unrecognizable. Emily and I had to go to bed after this news.

"You'd think Andy would remember that. If she doesn't move

when she's pregnant she cracks up. The Bronx, Yonkers, Queens. Each time it's farther and farther north. If he gets her pregnant again we'll all be freezing our asses off at the Arctic Circle." Kevin was starting to fuss. "Here. Can you hold him a minute?" I heard the chair shift back and Eddie step forward.

"They're connected in her mind. Moving and bearing children. Andy acts like this is perfectly normal behavior. He keeps knocking her up. Nothing slows him down. I blame him for this. He never should have moved her out of the Bronx. She's always been afraid up here. For Chrissakes, we're city people."

"That's a market I've been trying to crack," Eddie said. "Manhattan. I've got some nice shots of David. All I have to do is sell them some pictures of him to use in ads. Then every time the picture appears, I get paid. And Bess and Andy get paid."

"Good," Merle said. "Let them make some money off the little bastard, instead of handing him money every time he asks for it."

I could hear Merle open the refrigerator then go to the stove. She was right under me. I could see the top of her head, she still had the bath towel wrapped around it though she hadn't washed her hair. I knew she liked the way she looked in a turban. She told us that, told us it was a definite plus. She was one of the few women who could get away with it because she had a perfect forehead. It didn't recede, or stick out like a shelf. And she didn't look like a monkey like some women who had widows' peaks, though she'd be more than happy with the peak if it guaranteed she'd be a widow. She was still in my father's robe, though it was hard to see if this was a plus or minus.

"Have you sold any pictures of David?" Merle asked.

"Not yet," Eddie admitted. "That's why I'd like to take some of Joan. Change my approach." Merle shook her head. "Talk to me when you make your first sale," Merle said in that voice she used with Uncle whenever he said there was money in apples. Name me one millionaire who started out selling apples, she'd say to him. But she didn't say this to Eddie. When the water began to boil she took the bottle out and handed it to Eddie. He was standing next to the stove with Kevin so far over his shoulder that it looked like the baby was hinged in the middle.

"Oh no, not me," Eddie said and handed Kevin back to Merle. As he did, Kevin clutched at the robe for safety and Merle's beautiful white titty appeared like an answer to a prayer. Both Eddie and Kevin reached for it at once. Merle gave a slow marveling laugh. I almost fell off the bed. Just then Toby ran into the room and punched Merle in the stomach for holding the baby.

"You," she said, "you little bastard, I would have left you in the street before I brought you home. Now get inside before I whack your ass." I must have shifted then because suddenly a handful of grit fell from the grate down onto Merle's bare shoulder. She looked straight up at me. She sure hoped the eyeful I thought I got was going to be worth the beating she knew I was going to get.

CHAPTER SIX

Laugh before breakfast, cry before dinner, Merle warned us the morning when my father told us that our mother was well enough to come home for one weekend. Not Thanksgiving because the doctors said it would be too much excitement for her. And not a weekend when Merle, Uncle, Joan and Wayne were there. Ten people in the house would be more than my mother could handle. Too many personalities to deal with. Egos is what my father meant, Merle said. Egos. What my father lacked in height he made up in ego. The word sizzled like her wet thumb on the hot iron as she pressed her favorite blouse, the red polished cotton with the stand-up collar. She picked scraps of lint off the blouse, and dropped them on the floor. Who the hell was my father? Napoleon? She peeled the blouse off the ironing board and held it as though it were a red flag and my father a bull.

But despite her anger, despite the fact that she fought him every inch of the way, on the first Saturday in December, Uncle got Merle into the front seat of the panel truck and Wayne and Joan into the back where they sat between empty bushel baskets and pumpkins, which rolled like their heads would roll if Merle heard one damn word from either of them. Then she cuffed them both in the head in advance of any complaints because she knew damn well that they'd start in as soon as the truck left the driveway. They were on their way to the Bronx to see Aunts Belle, Mildred, Dorothy, Gladys, Blanche, Emma, and Aggie, the "girls" as Uncle called them, the "ghouls" according to Merle, the seven sisters who had turned their backs on their youngest sister's children.

As soon as they left my father dragged the parlor chair into the kitchen. He put it in front of each window, then sat in it in order to view the world as my mother would see it. The world as she would see it was drawn up in icy puckers no matter where the chair was placed. It had already snowed, a spiteful snow of small account, followed by a sleet storm that had encased all the branches of the Seckel pear tree in icy sleeves. The land around our house was barren and uniformly brown, the trees all fingers, elbows, and knees.

My father had been up since dawn, giving the house a final cleaning. We were, by turns, to be on our best behavior or be ourselves. It seemed he couldn't make up his mind. We were not to overwhelm our mother in either case. She would be tired after the drive. It would be a good idea if we greeted her one at a time. It would also be a good idea if we didn't tell her anything sad. "Try and cheer her up," my father said with a smile. We smiled back at him. "Now that's the ticket," he said as he hurried out the door.

But all of this was forgotten when, eight endless hours later, my father pulled into the driveway. Our car was an old green and black Chevrolet with locks under both windows that looked like silver tears. For a moment it appeared as though he was alone. But then we saw our mother. She'd been lying down in the back seat. When my father opened the door and helped her out, her hair was disheveled, and in some places, standing straight up. She looked directly at us and then turned back, it seemed, to the safety of the car. My father lifted his hand above his head and signaled to us to get away from the window. With his free arm he gathered her to his side and walked her slowly up the sidewalk. He had grown used to seeing the changes in her, the extra weight, the cut and permed hair, the shadows under her eyes, the way her internal anguish had produced such incredible force that she'd nearly pushed her front teeth out of her mouth from grinding them all the time. But to us she looked completely changed. At the sight of her standing in the driveway Emily and I looked at each other and ran from the room.

We must have looked equally strange to her because she burst into tears when we came back into the room. "Look at you two gypsies," she said. We were both wearing red. For some reason Emily had her raincoat on and I was wearing Merle's sweater. Em was trying not to cry. David too, stretching his mouth so far open that it pulled his nose into a straight line. And then we were all in her arms hugging her, kissing her wet face, smelling her burned hair, holding on to what we knew of her, what was left of her, for dear life.

But it was Kevin she couldn't get enough of. He had changed the most and so she clung to him, turning his hands over in hers, fingering the lines in his palms, trying to find the line that would tell her exactly when he got his first tooth, or when he first sat up. He slept as though deflated against her chest. Finally she agreed to put him down but insisted that she be the one to put him in the crib. We wanted to follow her but my father shook his head no. Earlier we'd followed her right up the stairs and into the bathroom, and she had laughed, and gently pushed us from the room. We'd stood in the hallway talking to her through the door until she came out.

"Now leave your mother alone," my father said sounding just like Merle. But we couldn't. We crowded around her at the table while my father made coffee. Emily and David sat on either side of her. Toby stood solemnly beside her holding on to her skirt, his shoes on the wrong feet as though they were as bewildered by the advent of having my mother in the kitchen as he was. I sat across from her watching everyone jealously. My father brought a cup of coffee to the table and set it down in front of my mother.

"Oh, no coffee for me Andy," she said looking suddenly fearful, "if I drink coffee it makes me doubt myself." My father looked startled. "How about something to eat then?" he asked, sounding fearful himself. My mother shook her head. She had her purse open and was rummaging around in it for something. Her cigarettes. She turned and asked David if he had a light then said, "Oh no, you don't smoke." She laughed again and put her arm around him. He smiled down into his lap. We were making her nervous. She looked at my father beseechingly.

"He got me good last night," my father said looking at David. David continued to grin, just like he did in some of the pictures Eddie had taken of him.

"The old egg trick," my father continued. My mother looked completely confused though she was the one who'd started the whole thing the year before. The trick was to go to the refrigerator and pretend to take a fresh egg from the bowl and then to go behind the person you wanted to fool and knock the top of his head, then slowly, and this was the hard part, trickle your fingers down so it felt like the inside of the egg spilling over his hair. Only David had used a real egg. On our father. My father sat there foolishly, smiling that stretched smile of his, while we watched, both thrilled and aghast, as the yoke oozed down his cheek. When it hit the table he finally realized what had happened and leapt from the chair. David was already out the door, his bare feet barely hitting the ground. My father was right behind him. David was laughing, jumping over brown puddles, running as fast as he could. My father too, though he was not laughing. Laughter would never have given him the speed he needed to overtake David. He was angry. His feet hitting the ground sounded like a series of punches, a sickening *oof, oof, oof.* Em and I stood at the door holding it open. When my father reached David, Em put both hands over her eyes and started pushing at them as though she were going to shove them back into her skull. My father lifted David up by the waist then and turned him completely over. David's legs were still running, and then my father seemed to be laughing. David was yelling, *Dad, Dad, no Dad,* but my father did it anyway. Dropped him head first into one of the frozen puddles and held him there. It was the way he held David there that made me fear my father. I knew in some way it was what he'd like to do to all of us. I was afraid that in some ways he was much like Merle. But I didn't tell this part to my mother when it was my turn to add something to the story.

"It wasn't funny," was all I said. I still hadn't come back to trusting my father yet.

"Oh come on, sourpuss," he teased.

My mother had sat through all of this with her unlit cigarette in her mouth. When my father realized this, he struck a match against the bottom of his shoe with a flourish and brought the flame to her mouth. But she jumped back as though she was burned.

"I burned my tongue doing that," she said turning to us. Em held out a pack of matches to her, tentatively. My mother smiled and took them.

"When Belle put me on that train," she continued, slipping the cellophane off the package of cigarettes and using it for an ashtray.

"Speaking of trains…" my father interrupted looking at the clock as though at that very moment a train was spinning around the numbers instead of the second hand. But my mother was not to be deterred. She was staring hard at her hands as if the story were written there.

"I told her that if she left me on that train all alone, I'd strike a match and put it on my tongue. Belle said, *You go right ahead*. So I did. I don't know where I got that match, but I struck it on my shoe just as I'd seen Belle do it a hundred times before. I burned my tongue too. But she'd already turned away. Just left me. And then all those hours on the train to Chicago of all places." Here she paused and looked at us. We shook our heads, outraged. Chicago! Chicago of all places!

We had no idea what she was talking about.

"The sound the train made when it went through the tunnels. It's what thunder sounds like out here. Whenever it storms I think of trains. I was only five years old. But I never cried on the train. Except once, when the conductor read me a story. He said if I needed anything just to let him know. I said that I thought I might need to cry. He said well if you do be sure and let me know." My mother had begun to cry softly, wiping at her tears with the palm of her hands. Then she lifted up her face to ours, looked at each of us questioningly and said, "I called her Mama. I thought she was my mother. It was the second time I'd lost a mother."

My father, who'd been standing with his hand on her shoulder, said "Whoa, whoa, now slow down," as though he'd suddenly found himself astride a runaway horse.

The room was immediately permeated with a pervasive sadness. It seemed the kind of room you could bring any sorrow into, and so into the ensuing silence I brought the news that Joan and Emily had almost drowned because Wayne wanted to see them naked. And then, because of the look on my father's face, I began to rush the other things. How Merle had shot Uncle, how Joan split her head wide open, and finally, breathlessly, that Eddie Birdseye loved Merle, had pressed up against her in the kitchen one day when I was home sick and kissed her titty and how Merle said if she had half a brain and half a chance she'd leave us too, hop on a train to anywhere. To California.

"Oh Jesus," my father said. My mother had her legs crossed and was tapping her right foot against the floor steadily and as she did she lifted her left leg against the drawer in the side of the table where Emily hid the liver my mother used to cook for us when she was home. I'd forgotten about the secret drawer but it was on my mind to bring that up too, to bring the subject around to something we might laugh about, but by then my mother had started to swing her whole leg back and forth violently. This set the cups and saucers on the table rattling, and the milk in our glasses sloshing back and forth as if we suddenly found ourselves in the dining car of that train taking my mother to Chicago. My father reached over at last and pressed his hand down on my mother's knee. She stopped shaking her leg and turned to look at us all. Then she turned to my father.

"Andy," she said, "get me out of here."

CHAPTER SEVEN

I awoke into a day so gray it seemed a hundred years old. For the first several seconds I couldn't remember what was wrong, but then it came back to me. I wished that I could sit on my tongue the way Joan could sit on her fingers to keep from sucking them.

I knew Emily was mad at me. She'd slept facing the wall again, wearing an Ace Bandage around her breasts to keep them from growing. She was so quiet it could have been around her mouth. David was already up and downstairs someplace, probably practicing the story of the boy who cried wolf. I pulled the blankets up and put my pillow over my head but I could still hear my father as he started up the stairs. He opened the door to our bedroom slowly, came into the room, sat on the bed and lifted my pillow. I tried to pretend I was asleep. I could smell the starch in his shirt as he leaned over to tuck my hair behind my ear. I could hear my mother moving around in her bedroom, the slide of drawers, the drag of her slippers against the wooden floor, each sound grating against my heart. I opened my eyes. My father lifted his head. We were both listening to her.

"Rainey," my father whispered, "what are we going to do about you? When are you going to learn to think before you speak?" I didn't know, I honestly didn't know, and so I guessed. "When I receive Communion," I said. Somehow I hoped that the bread of Christ would be like the paste Merle said it was. Flour and water. To keep women's traps shut on the subject of divorce. My father smiled. "You're a good girl," he said. I knew he must have been angry with me and was now feeling sorry about it. I wanted to whisper that he was a good father too but I'd begun to cry.

"Don't cry," he said and with such despair that I immediately stopped.

He had to take my mother back a day earlier. There'd been a change of plans. We'd all have to go with him because Merle wasn't back. He knew she'd be disappointed that she hadn't seen her sister, but there was nothing he could do about that. I agreed with him. There was nothing he could do about my mother but there was plenty Merle would do to me when she found out I was to blame.

The bed lifted as my father rose. He walked to the door, turned, and hesitated. He had his shoulders held back, his head craned. Then he threw up his hands as if there was nothing more to be done about me and came back to the bed and hugged me, hugged Em, too.

"Now get dressed, both of you," he said and left, closing the door behind him. But the door didn't latch, and because nothing was plumb in the house, it opened back up. I could hear my parents' voices, seesawing at first, as one then the other spoke. I could hear Kevin cooing in his crib, hear the Andrew Sisters singing on radio in the kitchen, *I don't want her, you can have her, she's too fat for me*, hear Toby, the earliest riser, pushing marbles along the floor. Even David, I could just make out his voice as he carried my mother's suitcase back out to the car.

The suitcase would have to be tied on the roof because once we were all inside the car there was no room for it. I wished with all my heart that it could have been me tied to the roof. If it was true, as Merle asserted, that we had driven our mother crazy in August, and more and more I was coming to believe this, it was equally true that I was solely responsible for driving her crazy now. I understood at last what it was exactly that drove her crazy, drove her away from us. It wasn't the rats. It was sadness. This was why my father always tried to make my mother laugh.

He tried to make us laugh too as we sat in the car. My mother was looking out across the fields, not paying any attention at all to him. As we passed each house or farm she'd say the name, Yetter's, Zook's, Moe's, Meekle's, the way Toby would stiffen, point and shout: truck, car, cow, horse, alarmed as much by their appearance as by their inevitable disappearance.

"Stand up," my father yelled as we came to the trestle bridge. We leapt up, David so quickly that he hit his head on the roof of the car. This startled my mother. I saw my father take hold of her hand and rub her knuckle with his thumb. "It's just water under the bridge," he said, winking in the rearview mirror at us. I smiled at the back of his head. I could feel he was scared, too. I looked down at the water, the icy flash of sun on the cold, cold water, and started to shake. My father, sensing our grief, challenged us to say *black bug's blood* ten times in a row without jumbling the words, but we all remained silent, lost in our own thoughts, as lost as I suddenly understood our parents were.

We drove north along the river. It was early, the mist lay on the river like a woolen shawl. The river was high and swelled in huge arcing swirls, engulfing the trees. It looked as though they were walking on water. The land beyond the trees was a brown scribble of weeds. Here and there layers of fog hovered above the ground as though unable to come to rest.

"Miasma," my mother said looking at it. My father smiled. "That's what Ma said I had when I was little. But she meant asthma." Ma was really her grandmother. We saw her when we went to the Bronx. She couldn't stand up because she was so fat. She'd call us to her chair but I would pretend I didn't hear her. Toby simply screamed NO, but she was deaf and tried to grab him whenever he passed by. The last time we'd seen her was Easter and that time Toby had gotten so scared he swallowed a jellybean whole and nearly choked to death.

"I couldn't breathe," my mother said, "I remember that." My father was still smiling so it seemed that he was happy for this news.

An old man appeared through the mist, walking along the side of the road with a shredded burlap sack in his hand. Something struggled inside it.

David was watching my mother very carefully, studying the side of her face. Next to him lay Kevin. He was asleep but his eyelids drifted open from time to time, and just the crescents of his dark eyes were visible. A blurry blue still hung on the rims of his irises, like the wavy blue oil that leaked from the car. Emily was leaning against the door as though she planned to jump out at any moment. When the sleeve of her coat touched me she moved even closer to the door. Toby clung to her. She was his favorite, and she usually carried him everywhere though Merle said she was going to rupture herself one of these days. Suddenly Toby shouted, "Cow." There in a field were dozens of rust-colored cows, lying like piles of raked leaves against the fence. My father slowed for them so that Toby, who screamed, cow, cow, cow, could get a better look.

"Why don't you kids play cows and graveyards?" my father suggested. Usually this ended up with one of us in tears, and I was waiting for my mother to point this out. But she was silent. David said no, but after a few miles he spotted more cows and quickly counted them.

"Twenty-four," he said. "Whoever gets to one hundred first wins." But if we passed a graveyard, then all was lost. I had eagle eyes. That's what my father said, but they seemed to be of no use. David would start counting as soon as he saw a barn. Or so I said but no one paid attention to me.

"Eighty-four," David said after we passed the third herd in as many miles. I could just make out the steeple of the church in Keansburg. The church was on the outskirts of town and surrounded by a huge cemetery. If there were no more cows, then by the time we passed it, David would lose. He knew this too and began looking around, even looking out the back window as though he meant to count the last herd again.

"Six," my mother said. "There were six in one week." My father looked at her happily, beaming, because she'd come back to us. But she wasn't pointing at cows. She was pointing at some small weathered headstones surrounded by a low wrought iron fence on a small incline on the side of a hill. Below it were the cows. David punched the seat.

"I thought the mattresses were headstones," my mother said. My father's head was half turned, his expression turned too, but held momentarily between confusion and understanding, though always I felt he was compelled to smile at my mother. "The mattresses in the foundling home," my mother said. It was here that I started to smile too, hoping like my father, that our smiles might encourage, might elicit some wonderful story, something that would make us all smile.

"It was because my baby brother died. I have that memory," my mother said, snapping open her purse as though she kept it there. "I was only two years old and he was in the next crib. Crying and crying. But no one came. We were sick. My throat, something was wrapped around my throat. I couldn't breathe. When I woke up, the crib was empty. The mattress stood on end. And then Belle came and took me home. I remember the steps were wet, and there was a railing like that," she said. We looked to where she pointed at the iron fence around the graves. "And it was wet and gleaming like the patent leather Mary Janes Belle bought to take me home in. Belle still has those shoes, and my brother's booties."

My father, suddenly reminded of his own feet, pressed down on the accelerator. He seemed determined to drive her away from the fields and whatever was in them as fast as possible. We were nearly in the town by then, passing the church, and the house, where we had first lived when we moved from the Bronx.

"She won't part with the booties though," my mother said. "I wanted them for David." David acted surprised to hear his name, surprised to hear he'd lost something else that day.

It was a few weeks before Christmas, and on the sidewalk in front of the gas station stood a Santa Claus with a sack. Joan had long since disabused us of the notion that he was real, and so we just stared at him with contempt. He waved to us but only my father waved back. We were in the center of town now. The sky was a dark, dark gray. It would rain, not snow, nothing white could fall from that sky. I wasn't thinking of anything particularly, except for the booties. My mother had knit us all booties against the cold winters, every year we had new booties, we had booties everywhere, enough to make most people happy. More than enough to make up for that one pair that my mother wanted. I was thinking this and looking at all the storefronts, the Christmas displays, the reflections of people and traffic in the windows, as we made our way slowly through the streets, when suddenly I saw our reflection in the store windows. There we were, the suitcase lashed to the roof, my father staring straight ahead, my mother bracing her hand against the glove compartment, the five of us crammed into the back seat of the car, all of us wide-eyed and watching, watching it seemed, as our very lives were passing right before our eyes.

We drove on for miles past everything that was familiar to us. I stared out the window, then back at my mother's hair. She seemed as unfamiliar as the landscape. Her stories were strange to us, her appearance too. We could have been driving one of the farm wives we often saw at Moe's Store to the state hospital and not our own mother. That's what I told myself at least, so that two hours later, when we turned into the long tree-lined drive, I wouldn't cry when my father took my mother inside.

White Stone. That was the name of the hospital, though it was a gray stone building. It seemed too quiet to be a hospital. There were no ambulances. No one rushed in or rushed out. No one brought flowers or gifts. No one laughed or cried. Except us.

We waited in the car and when our father came back out, he drove us into town and bought us all lunch at a diner that looked exactly like a train to me. At first I thought he was going to put me on it and turn away, and I wouldn't have blamed him a bit. But he herded us all in and sat down beside us and seemed determined to stay. I was not sure how long David and Emily would remain mad at me, but my father seemed forgiving. He told us to order whatever we wanted from the sandwich list. David read the selections out loud. I ordered a BLT. We all had things we'd never eaten before, clubs and Reubens. Emily had a Monte Cristo. But my father had his usual, chipped beef on toast, which Merle privately called SOS. Shit on a shingle. When I saw him take a bite of it, my stomach turned. He asked for evaporated milk with his coffee, and the waitress smiled and put the whole can on the table. Flower and all she said, pointing to the red carnation on the label. We didn't know to smile at her yet. My father seemed so suddenly shy that we tucked our heads down to our chins too. Even Kevin. But later when the waitress put a plate of fries in front of him, he shook with such intense pleasure at the sight of them that David and Em had to smile.

"He's gonna do away with that right quick," the waitress said, and her voice sounded just as strange and comforting as the food she set before us. But when we left to go back to the hospital, most of the food was still on our plates. Emily had gotten tired or forgotten she was mad at me by then. She'd filled her coat pockets full of cubes of sugar and a handful of crackers and showed them to me. I knew it was stealing, but I was happy for it if it brought her back to me. I would have stolen the pies from the shelves in heaven to make her smile. Or to make my mother smile.

I would have done anything in the last moments we saw her to change the vision I would have of her as we pulled away from the hospital later in the day, a vision that I've kept, as close as Em kept Toby, when we looked back at her. The sun had set by then, and at some unseen command, all the lights came on at once in the hospital. But instead of illuminating the many faces that appeared at the windows as visitors departed, it cast them all in silhouette. Their heads and shoulders were black against the light. Lined up as they were, they looked as though they belonged in a gallery of the dead, each one tacked up against a wall of stone.

"Second floor," my father said, "there she is. Third from the left," and he pointed up to the darkened faceless form of my mother. But I didn't need to be shown. My eyes found her instinctively, immediately, as easily as if she were a picture I had hung there myself.

CHAPTER EIGHT

It was clear to Merle that I was hell-bent on driving her crazy too. Crystal clear. I knew the sound of crystal. My mother had one piece of it, a tiny Christmas tree that my father had bought for her the first year they were married. Sometimes we took it out and sang at the top of our lungs to see if it would crack. Joan had tapped it with a fork once to test if it was crystal and not cut glass. Ping. That was the sound it made, ping, the exact sound Merle's wedding band made when she swatted me in the back of the head. My skull bone sang. She hit me for three reasons. I knew what the first was didn't I, Miss Tattle Tale Tit? I thought of her tit, how it seemed to rise toward Mr. Birdseye's hand. The reason for the second slap was that I was a born liar; nothing had transpired between her and Eddie Birdseye. I was seeing things. It was true. I kept seeing her tit no matter how hard I tried not to. The third reason for hitting me was that I was digging a grave for her right here in Four Corners. And if I didn't knock it off, she was taking me with her right into the frigging grave. I'd be buried with her for all eternity. How would I like that? Merle didn't like the idea very much because the next day she wasn't taking me into the grave with her. Instead she was giving me fair warning, if I didn't learn to keep my big mouth shut she was packing her bags and leaving the lot of us. One of these days we were going to wake up and she'd be gone. Then who would be here to take care of our sad asses? We'd be wards of the state, the five of us. Our heads would be crawling with lice. And where would she be? California. California, where the oranges were as big as our goddamned skulls.

For days afterward, she *sang Tattle Tale Tit, get your lip split, all the doggies in the town will have a little bit.* And when she finished, she'd run her hand over her lips and call Clover over to lick her fingers.

My father was never home. When he wasn't working, he was over at his friend Carl's studying to be a machinist. Carl took courses from *International Correspondence School.* ICS was the monogram on the cover. Once my father brought two of the books home, small blue books the size of the catechism book I was studying. But evidently the questions in his books were more complicated than *Who made you? Who is God?* and *Why did God make you?* because my father couldn't concentrate with all of us standing around the table staring at him. The sort of questions he was asked had a lot to do with precision. Did we understand what he meant by precision? We did not. At least I didn't. I stayed at the table with him.

"The measuring capacity of a micrometer is so precise it can measure the width of a strand of hair," my father read to me. He pulled one of his own black hairs from his head and laid it between the anvil and spindle. "Three thousandths of an inch," he said. "Take a look." I did. And there it was.

"Your hair," he said, laying a strand of my hair across his finger, "might be thicker." But he wouldn't pull it out, that was how precious every hair on my head was to him. That's how much he loved me. He wouldn't hurt a hair on my head. Ever. He measured my hair where we sat. Four thousandths of an inch.

"If a job is off by just that much, it's ruined," he said. It took a lot of concentration to learn about these instruments. It wasn't just micrometers. There were calipers, bevels, and bits to contend with as well.

"A machinist cherishes his tools," my father said. His children too.

We should know that by now. We knew how much we were loved, didn't we?

"Four thousandths of an inch," I said. My father laughed. He was glad that someone in the family had a sense of humor.

I was a barrel of laughs, Merle said. But she wanted to give me some advice. I wouldn't have much to laugh about if she left. And the way things were going with Uncle, she just might. And she would cut my tongue off if there was another word on the subject of Eddie Birdseye. I knew what would happen if Uncle got wind of this, didn't I? Jesus Christ Almighty. He was the last person in the world I wanted on my side. Merle hoped I knew this much at least. I did know it. I heard the ugly things he said to Merle when they fought. *Whore. Bitch. Cunt. Cunt. Cunt.* That's what his punches sounded like when he hit the soft parts of her body. The day after, she graded the fights, assessing her arms in the mirror. *That wasn't a bad one.* Or, *he damned near killed me, the son of a bitch.*

Don't let him fool you, Merle said to me. Don't let him weasel any information out of you. Did I know what would happen if he did? Here she started humming, *California here I come, right back where I started from.*

In the weeks to come that tune had the same effect on me as the raised iron had on Uncle.

My father thought that my good behavior had everything to do with my increasing religious instruction. My First Holy Communion instruction had begun in earnest because of my age. I should have received the sacrament at seven but that was when Toby was born and my mother's legs welted with bulging, deep purple veins. It looked as though worms crawled under her skin, and just as they seemed to crawl away, Kevin was born and they came back. Now, I was two years behind in my lessons. But to compensate, instructions were held for several hours on Saturday as well as Sunday after Mass. Father Leary was to hear our first confessions but this would only be a trial run. We needed to practice going into and out of the confessional booth. Some children were afraid to go into it by themselves.

They were the ones with brains, Merle said. You wouldn't get her inside a booth with a grown man in a dress smelling like a fifth of whiskey.

It was wine, Emily said. The blood of Christ had changed into wine. She practiced singing *Eat His Body and Drink His Blood* for choir practice. Sister Francis Jerome thought that Em had a vocation, a calling to be a nun. She'd talked to my father about it after Mass. My father smiled and nodded. He said Em was a little young to make that decision. Sister nodded and smiled too, not everyone is called, she said. We didn't have a phone. I was glad for that.

The blood of Christ smelled just like Uncle's breath. We didn't have to drink this but we did have to practice eating the body of Christ Made Whole Again. That came in wafers the size and hardness of the chips Merle and Uncle used in poker. The ones we used to practice with were not blessed, and so if our teeth accidentally bit down on them we were not biting the body of Christ. I thought of Toby. He had nearly stopped biting Kevin.

On the third Saturday in December, ten of us queued up along the wall under the stations of the cross waiting for our turn to tell our sins. Seven girls and three boys, the smallest group of communicants St. Paul's had had in twenty-five years.

Even though this was only practice we weren't to use made-up sins. We had to tell the real sins. Venial and Mortal. Those were the categories open to us. We were to take this time in line to reflect upon our souls, according to Sister Francis Jerome. She was in charge of us and our souls until after Communion when we would take over. I was fourth in line for confession and couldn't reflect for very long. Because it was Saturday there wasn't anyone else in church aside from us and Roger Smith, the altar boy who would serve Mass with Father. Roger Smith had swallowed a night crawler in our front yard the summer before. I reflected on that for a while.

Empty, the church was as cavernous as the turkey Merle had earlier gutted for dinner. And as mysterious. I had reason to study that bird. After Merle had gutted it she pointed to the tailpiece. "Hey Miss-Tattle Tale," she said, "do you know what this piece is called?" I only knew that you weren't supposed to eat it. Joan had said it was filled with shit. I shook my head no.

"The Pope's nose," Merle laughed and brought her hand down hard on the yellow breast. After she left the room I pulled a chair up to the bird to take a better look. The tailpiece was pocked with holes from where Joan had plucked the pinfeathers out with tweezers. It was shaped more like a heart than a nose. I looked inside the turkey. It was dark and deeply red and the ribs crisscrossed with the same delicate precision as the arches in St. Michael's Cathedral in the Bronx, where we used to light candles for the souls of the departed. I put my hand inside the bird's cavity. It felt cool. I pulled my hand out and peered inside remembering the crack I'd heard when Merle first opened the turkey. Nothing was broken as far as I could tell. I could see clear through to the end of the bird where the breastbone curved. I saw the marbleized membranes that covered the gizzards, the transparent silvery webs, the blood pooled along the backbone. A backbone was what I lacked, according to Merle. If I had a backbone I wouldn't be afraid of Harold Birdseye. I wouldn't be afraid of anyone. Unfortunately, I was born without one. The whole damn bunch of us were.

I was thinking of this when the girl behind me nudged me to move up. It was nearly my turn to go in. Emily told me that the confessional booth had two sides. Father Leary sat in a special box between the two sides, hearing one, then the other confession. The box had sliding wooden windows and if you strained your ears, you could hear the soft shuffle of sins dealt to Father from the person on the other side. Underneath the wooden windows were dark screens so that Father could hear but not see the confessor and so that the confessor didn't have to see the priest, though we all knew Father Leary and he knew us. He sometimes played baseball with the boys after Mass, running around the bases, cassock and beads flying. He never lasted more than an inning, but this was because of his weight, not because of his calling, my father said. He was a natural athlete.

When I knelt on the kneeler, I could hear Father slide open the side opposite me. With the sliding window shut on my side the booth was completely black. I couldn't see my folded hands before me, but I had them pressed tightly together, and leaned into them, smelled the coppery odor of my damp palms. I was bent toward the screen when the wooden window on my slide opened. I was so startled I couldn't remember what to say. I wasn't afraid of Father Leary, but I was afraid of the situation I found myself in. I'd forgotten my sins.

"Yes," Father said. He sat with his face turned to the side, leaning his ear toward me. Some of the light that came through the latticework in the door to his box filtered through, and I could see his head in silhouette.

"Bless me Father for I have sinned," I began. "This is my first confession."

"What are your sins?" he asked. I had to admit I didn't know.

Father asked me very gently if I could think of one. It was hard to think of anything in the dark. Even at night, when all was black around me and everyone else slept tightly, I needed some light, some sense of shadow, to think of anything. I needed something to scare me into thinking, the way slashes of lightning made me think of my mother. My mother. Suddenly, there it was slipping into the darkness between us. I couldn't have held it back, though my tongue ached in anticipation of being cut out by the roots.

"I drove our mother crazy," I said. Father sighed.

"Who told you that?"

"Merle," I whispered. I thought that everyone had heard of her.

"Merle?" Father asked. "Is she a parishioner?" No, I said, she's my aunt. She's taking care of us. Our mother's in the nuthouse. I said this very quietly in case Merle was standing outside.

Father coughed then. The confessional filled with the smell of Christ's blood. Father asked if Merle ever came to church. Emily had warned me that it was a mortal sin to tell a lie to Father. Mortal. That meant I could drop dead if I did, so I told Father that Merle said she wouldn't be caught dead in church.

"You must be a very good girl and listen to your aunt while your mother's away. I'll pray for her. And for your aunt," Father promised. He would like me to do a special favor for him. Would I do it? I nodded yes. He would like me to offer up a special prayer for Merle every night because she was a Good Samaritan, the same name as the hospital that had taken my mother from us. You didn't have to be a saint to be a Good Samaritan, Father said, and then he gave me a special blessing. Not everyone got this blessing. Father said, he was singling me out for it. He told me to bow my head and close my eyes and I did. Though I couldn't see, I felt the movements he made as I knelt beside him, I heard his urgent whisper, the rise and fall of it, like the secret sounds I sometimes heard coming from my parents' room where Merle and Uncle now slept. I felt my body fill with heat and something else that I couldn't name right then. Some vast longing. And even though my eyes were closed and it was very dark, inside of me all was light. My body started to tremble. The bony knob at the back of my neck felt electrified. Current ran along the length of my spine. I felt completely alert, excited. I felt amazed. Then the screen slid shut and I was released. I believed myself to be blessed. I believed this with all my heart.

I knelt at the altar rail for several minutes reciting prayers, mostly Hail Mary's because they were shortest. And then I sat in a pew near the back of the church because if there was one thing that infuriated Merle it was not being able to find one of us when she needed us. It was a mystery to her that whenever she didn't want to find us we were right under her goddamned nose. But when she wanted one of us to go get her cigarettes, or help with the dinner, there wasn't a one of us around.

When she dropped us off someplace we were to stay put in the exact spot until she came for us. We were not to move. Not even a muscle. Because she wouldn't be caught dead in church, she sent Joan in for me. Bareheaded. Without even a tissue pinned to her hair. Joan said she didn't care if she went straight to hell for it. She wasn't wearing a snot rag on her head. As we left, I dipped my hand into the holy water and Joan dipped hers into the open poor box.

Em had told me a story about a boy who'd done the same thing, that the poor box had been left unlocked as a temptation. When the boy came outside of the church he was struck dead by the hand of God. The pennies for the poor burned into his palms.

But no such thing happened to Joan. Instead we were given a reward. Merle said that we could go to the movies. She had some things to do in town. She was in high spirits. She drove us into Keansburg checking her lipstick in the rearview mirror, her mascara, her rouge. Her eyes shifted from green to blue as easily as she shifted from second to third. She checked over her shoulder so often that we began to look out the back window until she screamed at us to stop. We were making her a nervous wreck. We were to stay inside the movie theater at all costs. We weren't to come out and start looking around for her. When the movie was over we were to stay in the lobby until she came for us. Joan was to keep a close eye on me. And no, we couldn't have any money for candy. Joan and Emily had just had a sandwich and hadn't I just swallowed the body of Christ. For Chrissakes. She didn't understand about confession. At confession you got nothing to eat. But Joan had money for candy from the poor box. She'd put a dime in each sock. Separately, so Merle wouldn't hear them jingle. When she rolled down her socks as we sat in the lighted theater before the movie began, I could see the silver circles they left in her flesh. I knew this was a bad sign, that God knew about the money. I also knew that I wasn't going to share any of the candy she bought with this money even if by some remote chance Joan offered us a piece. Let her bear the full force of God's anger because she was not only a thief but she was a selfish one.

The lights dimmed. The curtains parted, swaying back and forth momentarily, gracefully, over the stage floor the way that the new chenille bathrobe Merle wore swayed as she crossed our own floors on her way to the coffee pot every morning.

I knew Joan wouldn't go for the candy right away. She'd wait to make certain Merle wasn't lurking in the lobby checking up on us.

Merle knew Joan like the back of her hand.

The movie was *The Miracle of Our Lady of Fatima*. We'd heard about her and the three peasant children she appeared to in Portugal. She gave them the secret of world peace. They had just been walking along through the woods the way Joan, Em and I often did, when out of the blue the Blessed Mother appeared in the sky. The children fell to their knees.

"Oh brother," was all Joan could say to this, then, "come with me to get some candy." But I wasn't going anywhere near that candy. I shook my head. Joan raised a fist but didn't punch me. Instead she tried Emily, but Emily couldn't be lured away. Just wait until we asked her for something, Joan said. Then we'd be sorry. We were seated in the front of the theater, bathed in the light from the screen, close enough for Emily to see. As I turned and watched Joan disappear into the dark, I was sorry I hadn't gone with her. Though she was older than me, I knew that she needed me as much as I needed her. She wore her blond hair in the same single braid that she'd worn all week. Strands of her hair had come loose and wavered like cobwebs in the light from the projector. Those strands were the same golden color as the braids of silk on the Blessed Mother's veil. I watched as she vanished as completely, as easily as the Blessed Mother through the clouds. My skin rose up in goose bumps, as though it too wanted to rise and follow her. I forced myself to turn back toward the movie screen. If I got out of my seat, walked up the six dusty steps to the stage, I could have walked right into the movie, been one of the three children who had been chosen to receive the secret of world peace. I thought about going into the woods near our house, the three of us. Em, Joan and me. We could fall down on our knees and pray for the Blessed Mother to appear to us too. I would have to stop telling secrets, and Joan would have to give the money back to the poor box. Em would just have to stay the same. It might have worked, except that Joan emerged from the gloom with a bar of Turkish Taffy. I knew taffy could pull our teeth from our heads. Two of my baby teeth were loose, one hanging in place by a thread, and though I was mortally afraid of pulling it out and knew, according to Joan, that I could choke to death if I swallowed it in my sleep, I still hoped with all my heart that Joan would give me a piece of her candy. She opened the wrapping carefully. I could smell the sweet, sticky smell of it as she bit and pulled and chewed. I tried to find the place in me that was blessed. That place had made me feel such release. I closed my eyes and tried to concentrate. When I opened them I looked at Joan. I couldn't help it.

Don't ask, was all she said to me when she saw me eyeing her. So I knew not to ask if she would come with me to the bathroom. My mother had told us never to go into a public bathroom alone. Children were often snatched from them. But I had my own secret fear that somehow I'd get locked in and never get out, so I leaned across Joan and asked Em if she would come with me. *Shh*, was all she said. All everybody around us said. The Blessed Mother had just appeared again. I would have to miss it.

I got up from the seat and made my way up the aisle. I was relieved to see that there were little lights on the aisle seats near the floor. I could see where my feet were headed if nothing else. I kept my eyes on the floor, one foot in front of the other up the aisle. I walked slowly into the dark and toward a line of startling light that bordered the lobby doors. I had just put my arm up to push those doors open when someone pulled me from the aisle and into the last row of seats. The hand on my arm was firm, tight, and tightening. My eyes were not yet used to the dark. All I could see was the shape of a man. At first I thought it was Father Leary, but it wasn't.

"Stay with me," he whispered. It was not a command, not like something Uncle might say, though I thought it could be Uncle. He smelled the same. He was fat too. "Stay," he said and pulled me down on his lap. I stayed. He rubbed my arm, he pulled me back against him. "Stay with me, stay with me," he whispered this into the back of my neck. I knew this was bad, that this was something that Merle had warned about, but it felt so much like goodness that I didn't want to leave. I closed my eyes. He kissed the place where I was blessed. That same feeling overwhelmed me. And I stayed. I stayed while he rubbed his hands along my arms and kissed my neck. I could feel his whiskers as he rocked me back and forth. "Stay on my lap," he whispered. He rocked me very gently, the way my mother sometimes rocked me. And then he rubbed my legs and my hind end. *Shh,* he whispered though I hadn't made a sound. I was alive to every sense, but I felt asleep. I felt as though I couldn't move. He wasn't hurting me. I sat absolutely still while the Blessed Mother revealed the secret of world peace to the three children. I would have sat there all day long if the usher hadn't come up the aisle. The man slid me off his lap. I stared straight ahead even when the usher flashed a light on us. He asked me if I was supposed to be with the man and I nodded yes. He flicked the flashlight off. The man and I sat side by side for the entire movie. He didn't touch me again. He had his hand on the armrest and several times I wished with all my power that he would touch me again. I even prayed he would. But he didn't move and neither did I though my bladder ached. As the first transparent curtain closed over the screen, the man stood up and brushed past me into the aisle, then he was gone. I stayed until the lights came on and Joan and Em came up the aisle. Em walked right by me but not Joan. She was looking for me because she hadn't kept an eye on me.

"Why are you waiting here," she demanded. "Why did you stay here?" I wouldn't look at her. I was thinking of the Blessed Mother behind the curtains. I wanted to reach out to her and feel the softness of her hand, feel her take me up into the clouds with her, the clouds that had the silver linings that my mother told me about. Every cloud had one. I wanted to feel exactly as I had when I was blessed. But Joan wouldn't let me go. She took hold of my shoulders and shook.

"You can't stay here all day," she yelled. Why was I staying there? Answer her that.

"Because," I said, the word suddenly hanging as loose as my tooth. Dangling by a goddamned thread. Merle had reached for that tooth to yank it out. But I was too quick for her.

"Why because?" Joan insisted, looking at me closely. The sweet smell of taffy stuck to her words. I was afraid to breathe, afraid that her sticky question might pull the words from my own mouth. Regardless, I really couldn't have said why I'd stayed with the man, but at the same time I knew that Joan was probably the only person who would understand why I didn't want to share the pleasure I took in being touched. David had been chosen for pictures, and Eddie wanted pictures of Joan, too. And Em had been called. But this was mine alone. For the first time in a long time I felt truly blessed. Finally I got up from my seat and went straight to the bathroom. Everything I did had import. I folded the toilet paper in neat packets the way my mother had taught me. I wiped from front to back careful not to let my bottom touch the toilet seat. I flushed, retied my sash, then washed my hands. After I was finished I went outside. When I did, the day dazzled me.

CHAPTER NINE

We waited over an hour for Merle. Normally she'd say that was too damn bad, but this time she said she was sorry for being late. Then she took us out for sundaes, the three of us, hot fudge sundaes with whip cream, the cherries bleeding softly into the cream the way Merle's lipstick bled into the milky skin around her lips. I felt doubly blessed. The sweet tooth that my mother said I had throbbed with each spoonful of ice cream. Merle watched us eat. Her full upper lip formed the initial of her name, *M*, and she traced it over and over again with her finger. Because of all the candy Joan had eaten, she couldn't finish her sundae. After a while Merle pulled Joan's sundae to her and took a few spoonfuls. The ice cream raised goose bumps on her arms and she rubbed herself warm. She pulled her red sweater up over her shoulders and sat staring out the window. The sun was setting in the western sky, bright orange falling away to red at the horizon. Everything lay bare and lonely in the December light. Merle watched the sun slip from the fingers of the bare trees that stood at the horizon, then roused herself. She pulled her lipstick from her purse and in the reflection of the glass freshened her lips. She rummaged around in her purse for something to blot them with and finding nothing reached across to where I sat and took my unused napkin, slid it between her lips and pressed down. Once, twice, three times, moving the napkin from the right to the left. Instead of crumpling the napkin and throwing it in her purse, she left it there on the table. I looked back at it as Merle slipped a quarter under the napkin for the waitress. The imprints were smoother M's than the true line of her lip, more like the soft arch in the heavy wings of the first Canada goose I could just then see against the sky. When we opened the diner door to leave, the wind lifted the napkin up and it floated momentarily, as though it was borne aloft by the red birds imprinted there.

We drove along slowly, leaving everything behind. Merle, when she wasn't taking long drags on her cigarette, rubbed her legs softly, exactly the way the man in the theater had rubbed mine. What was left of the daylight was parceled out in meager splashes of light that occasionally illuminated Merle. She smiled to herself, and whenever she did, she'd trace the skin on her lips with her finger. I'd watch as the glow of ash made a red revolution around her mouth. She was so pre-occupied that she missed the turnoff to Four Corners. We didn't say anything, not wanting to break the spell, hoping for a moment that she might take us to California, where she appeared headed.

"Jesus Christ," she swore softly. The way she said it wasn't a curse. Were we all asleep? Reminded of us once more, her anger sparked.

The next morning Eddie Birdseye came to our house. He'd come over to ask if he might use one of our stables for Shadow. His barn was ready to fall in on itself. The weight of another snowfall might bring the roof down. Merle pressed herself into his fender as if she might fall in on him. She said she'd have to ask our father. It'd be nice to have a horse here, Merle said. Joan scowled. Her mother hated horses. Eddie said it'd be even nicer to have an excuse to see more of her.

"Since when do you need an excuse?" Merle said. She was rubbing her hand down her own backside.

"When I don't get an invitation," Eddie laughed.

"Since when do you need an invitation?"

"Right about now," Eddie laughed. It seemed to me that he was eyeing up the barn.

"I'll give you a rain check," she promised, then pushed back quickly from the truck and looked over her shoulder.

"I bet she will," Joan muttered. "I bet she'd like my father to break her neck too."

Em and I wondered if having Shadow in our barn meant we'd have to see more of Harold though normally Merle wouldn't let him on our property.

"Probably not," Joan said. She didn't sound convinced. "But Bess will, your mother will," she said, almost savagely, shifting immediately all the blame to her.

I couldn't believe that our mother was coming home again. Another trial run. This time I'd be very careful to keep my big mouth shut. I didn't know where to start so I didn't defend my mother to Joan. Instead I walked out of the barn with my lips pressed shut so tightly that when my father came home from work early to get cleaned up before leaving to get my mother he couldn't force a smile from me.

Merle waited until he'd taken a bath to ask about Eddie boarding Harold's horse in our barn.

My father didn't want any trouble, he said. He didn't want anything to upset my mother. In the long run he didn't think it would be a good idea. It wasn't the horse he was worried about. Merle knew what he meant, didn't she? She was leaning against the kitchen sink, with her one arm wrapped around her waist blowing smoke straight from her nose. Toby was running from one end of the room to another. Sometimes, if he got it into his head, he'd run like that for hours. Kevin was sleeping face up in the playpen, his undershirt stuck to his neck where the pabulum had dried there. Wayne was polishing his shoes with liquid polish. He'd put newspaper down on the table to protect the fresh cloth and put both shoes on it. New shoes on the

table were bad luck. That's what our mother had always told us. I
didn't know if old shoes were. I watched to see what would happen as
Wayne put the balled wand into the bottle and brushed the brown liquid across the leather, holding a shoe in his one hand gracefully, exam-
ining the arch in it much the same way I'd seen Merle slip her hand
into her nylons and check for runs.

Merle didn't say one word to my father, and neither did we. Our
bad luck was changing into good luck. We wouldn't have to deal with
Harold after all. Emily was reading *The Lives of the Saints*, in anticipation of becoming one. Joan was in the barn sweeping out a stall. My
father looked around at us, then back at Merle.

We were a mess, he said. We needed to get cleaned up, take baths
and put on fresh clothes before our mother came home. Our heads
needed shampooing. No one moved. Wayne had finished polishing
his shoes. They gleamed like Merle's eyes. Both heels were worn into
his same down-turned smile. Merle stared out the door. A flock of
Canada geese were making their way south. They honked wildly above
our heads. We could hear their excitement. If things didn't change
around here, that's where she was headed, Merle said. I could see that.
So could my father. He threw up his hands and turned to her. He
guessed it would be all right. About the horse. Then he patted his
pocket for his glasses, slipped them on. When he did, he could see us
more clearly.

"For Chrissakes, do something with their hair," he said. I thought
of how my mother used to cut paper strips and rags and wind our hair
up in them, how in the morning we'd have curls that she'd wrap
around her finger and pull slowly as though the dark ringlets bounc-
ing down our backs were Chinese puzzles, meant to hold her fingers
there.

I wanted to ask Merle to do this as she reached above the tin medicine cabinet over the sink for the comb and tried to pull it through my hair. My father watched her for a minute then shook his head sadly at the sight of me, red-eyed and begging to be let go each time Merle lifted the comb.

"Do whatever you can," he said to Merle and left the house. Our father seemed to think Merle had nothing to do all day but stand around and comb our hair. He must think the goddamn leprechauns came in at night and cleaned the house. The Irish bastard.

He wasn't even out of the driveway when she took the scissors out. We believed her when she said that we needed bobs, that they'd be easier to manage come summer. We'd thank her for that. We'd thank her because there'd be no more tears in the morning. We'd thank her too because we'd be cooler in the summer. There was an endless list of what we'd be thankful for it seemed. She elaborated on them as she cut my hair up around my ears, locking me between her knees, warning me not to move or she might slip, cut off my ears. Which wouldn't be such a bad idea. It might just cure me of the sneaky habit I had of listening to other people's business.

"I'm no beautician," Merle said at last and with some satisfaction. She pulled back to assess her work and to take a drag on her cigarette before sending me upstairs to look at myself in the mirror. For some reason I imagined myself with a fluff of curls around my head like the baby picture my mother kept of me. It was the only one that showed what a head of curls I had. My mother loved that picture. Her only baby with naturally curly hair.

I carried this image upstairs to the bathroom mirror. I felt better than I had in months. I dragged the footstool out from under the sink. When I stepped up on it I felt ten pounds lighter. Then I saw myself.

I was stunned to see that my hair had not sprung into curls, that instead it lay flat against my head and that my face looked like a melon with ears. Wayne walked by just at that instant and called me Dumbo. It was more than I could bear. From where I stood I could hear the clip, clip of the scissors rising up through the grate. I thought I heard Em's hair hit the floor. I stepped off the stool.

It seemed to me that when I started down the stairs my knees wouldn't bend. I began to jump, leaping from step to step waiting for Merle to yell, take it easy on those steps, and it seemed that she was about to say just that when I reached the kitchen and raced at her. It was as if my arms were propellers, pounding into her soft belly, her hard chest. I wanted to kill her and she knew it. She raised her hand up as though she wanted to kill me too.

Go ahead, I said. I was sticking my chin out toward her the way I'd seen her do a hundred times. My lips were trembling uncontrollably. "Go ahead and hit me," I yelled.

"Jesus Good Christ Almighty," is all Merle said. Jesus Christ, get her the hell out of here before I take the scissors to that damn tongue of hers. The ungrateful brat.

Joan dragged me upstairs and threw me on the bed. I began to cry. Joan still had her pale white braids. She twirled them around, studying them while I cried. She crossed them under her nose but I didn't laugh. She tied them in a knot under her chin and pretended to throttle herself. She took the end of one and tickled my face. Nothing worked. She gave up finally, sat on my bed, sucked her two middle fingers for a long minute, then stood up and walked out the door. I turned to the wall and vowed not to leave my room until my hair grew back. I wouldn't even go downstairs when my mother came home. But as soon as I thought this I started to cry. And I didn't stop, not until the door opened and Joan came back with the scissors, sat down beside me and cut her braids right off too.

It was my father who was more shocked by our hair than my mother. Or so it seemed. The day was endless. We'd long since stopped looking up the road for the car. We'd tried every trick we knew to get the car to appear. By nightfall we'd given up completely and given ourselves over to boredom when finally we saw the car heave over the hill and coast down to our house. It had taken much too long for my father to bring my mother home, as far as I was concerned. Instead of feeling happy I was miserable. Merle took one last look at me, and let that be all she had to do in the future, take one look at me to make me keep my mouth shut, then she went outside to her sister.

Normally, Merle told me to wipe that grin off my face, but when she helped our mother up the stairs and set her suitcase inside the door, she turned to me and pushed at the corners of her mouth. Smile. I did. I had made my mother a gift, a doll's cradle out of a Quaker Oats container. She had made them for us, once, for Em and me. Toby had made her a drum. When she walked in the door he began banging it. He started walking too, marching from room to room until my father scooped him up in his arms and put him over his shoulders like a sack of potatoes. That's what my father called him. It was my father who did the walking. He kept going with Toby, up the stairs and into the bedroom the sack of potatoes shared with David, until David could calm him down. Emily had bought my mother a gift, a crucifix that looked pale green in the daylight but that glowed in the dark. Kevin was chewing on it and staring at my mother. He looked shocked to see her. And my mother to see him. He had hair now and that astounded my mother. It didn't astound her that Em and I had none. She said we looked like pixies. She rubbed all our heads. Kissed

Kevin's but didn't reach out to take him. I gave her the cradle I made. She brought it up to her face and smiled.

"Rainey," she said. That was all. It wasn't enough but at the same time it was everything. Em handed her the crucifix. Her hands were full then so she couldn't touch us, pull us to her, instead she held the crucifix and the cradle against her chest. When David came downstairs with Toby, he grinned at her. It was the same grin that he wore in the proofs that Eddie Birdseye had brought to our house months before. David had had to stick his head into a barrel of water for these shots. It wasn't easy he told us. The water was ice cold. But that was what Eddie was after, he said, a startled smile. And that's just the picture my mother got.

We weren't allowed to monopolize our mother, and for my part I resisted getting too close to her in case she started to shake her foot again. But this time she was different. This time she made herself coffee, and we sat at the table watching her drink it. Joan and Wayne had come into the kitchen to sit with us. She couldn't believe how tall Wayne had gotten. She put her hand on his shoulder. I couldn't understand how she could bear to touch him. I wanted to tell her that he called her a screwball. But I knew what would happen if I did. She pulled Joan to her. Joan, it seemed, was getting more beautiful everyday. She went red in the face, red right up to her scalp when my mother said this. It was true. Her short hair had changed her. Without her braids she looked older. Where the weight of her hair had previously pulled at her, kept her closer to our age, freed from the rubber bands, from the confinement of braids, it released her into adolescence. Her hair sailed along the curve of her jaw line. Under the glare of the kitchen light I could see the silver and the gold strands that brought out the flecks of yellow in her gray eyes. We were in winter but suddenly Joan seemed to belong to spring.

Joan was going to be a knockout my mother said standing back from her. Uncle and Merle were going to have to beat back the boys from the porch. Merle looked like she was ready to do just that, ready to start swinging right that very minute, but then my mother looked from Joan to Merle. She has your beauty, my mother said. Merle raised her eyebrows and held them arched for a minute. We waited for her to say something mean. But she shrugged, turned away, caught a glimpse of herself in the glass above the sink, and smiled. Uncle came in a few minutes later, swatted Merle on the backside and went for his ukulele. We needed to celebrate, he said. My mother's homecoming demanded a song. But before he would begin to play, before he could sing, he needed some liquid libation. I thought that was something new and waited to see what he'd pull from his pocket but it was the same old flask. And the same old song. *Danny boy, the pipes, the pipes are calling, from glen to glen and down the mountainside.* Even so, even as we steeled ourselves against it, within minutes he had us all in tears.

CHAPTER TEN

Joan's fourteenth birthday arrived the day before Christmas along with the deep freeze that normally held off until late January. It was too cold to go outside. It was too cold to snow. There had been a small attempt at it but it seemed the sky thought twice about it. All around us, the land lay flat and still under a thin film of white the same thickness as Merle's slip. She still wore her slip through most of the day but added layers of sweaters and flannel shirts over it. For Joan's birthday she made an effort to dress early. My mother had baked a cake. My father had brought something home in a bag and hurried into the living room to wrap it. It better not be a damned cat, was all Merle said. We weren't poor my father had said the night before my mother came home. No, he wouldn't go so far as to say that. What we were was *strapped*. This was something totally different. It meant we had to be careful. Things were a little tight. We had to make sacrifices, my father said, so I was totally unprepared for Joan's gift. My father bought Joan a pair of ice skates. They were so white, they hurt my eyes. I sat in stunned silence. Joan seemed afraid to touch them. She sat under the light of the kitchen bulb like a thief being interrogated. For a moment I was afraid that Joan had stolen them, and she seemed afraid she had too. The blades glinted guiltily under the light. Women's. Size five. Figure skates.

"Well, lass, all you need is the figure to go with them," Uncle said. "She has a beautiful figure," my mother said. *All her geese were swan.* I remembered that, remembered that she loved Joan and Wayne as though they were her own. "She's a young lady now," my mother said.

I looked at Joan very carefully. She was. Merle handed her one of the gifts she bought her. It was an unmentionable, Merle said. My father left the room in the face of this. Merle had bought Joan a white bra with a pink flower in the center of it, though Joan had said she wouldn't wear one. Ever.

"You're an optimist," Uncle said, eyeing the cup size and Joan's chest. By that time Joan had unwrapped the wine-colored sweater that I immediately coveted. Merle had bought it from Mrs. Zook. It was made from the wool of her own sheep. Hand-dyed, hand-made. It was both a birthday present and Christmas present, so she might want to leave it under the Christmas tree, Merle said to Joan. This took some of the pleasure from it, I could tell.

"Well, what do you say?" Merle urged. But it wasn't in Joan to say thank you. We all knew that. "Her face says it," my mother said, beaming for Joan. I smiled for Joan, too, trying to make her smile back. My father had come back into the room and my mother squeezed his hand. Joan held the skates to her chest, then, to everyone's amazement, she bent down and tried them on. We watched as she wobbled across the old linoleum. It seemed the blades would slice it in two. For once Merle had nothing to say.

At first it seemed to me the ice skates were too grown up for Joan. Too adult. They reminded me of Merle's high heels, the way they changed the shape of Joan's legs. Where just the day before she was all muscle and bone, now her calf swelled round and womanly above the graceful rim of the skate. More than the bra, the skates seemed to lift Joan out of childhood, hers and ours. I couldn't take my eyes off her. She'd need to practice, my father said, but she had perfect balance. Joan was breathtakingly poised for a moment, But then, compliments being new to her, both ankles gave way.

By the first week in January the Sucker Hole was frozen to three feet. Because of the leeches we seldom swam there. But in the winter it was a perfect place to skate. It was large for a pond and small for a lake though just the right size for skating. The Zooks owned it, and their son kept it cleared of snow. He pushed a broom over it again and again, until someone told him to stop. He would have swept through to water if we let him. He was adopted. This made his being retarded acceptable. We called him Jay though he was older than our parents. He tested the ice as well. "All right, all right," he said as he inched his way out. He was scared, we could see it. I thought his father made him go first because he didn't care about him, didn't care if he fell through the ice. Merle called him the village idiot. She was mad that she had to check the ice before our mother would let us skate. Freezing her goddamn ass off, she said. She ought to put on some drawers, in that case, Joan said.

"Six inches," Jay crowed, as we approached. He must have been waiting hours for us. The ice was swept clean. It was at least twenty-four inches. It would have to be or there'd be no skating allowed.

"Sixty's more like it," Merle said, whacking the surface with the baseball bat she'd brought along to test it.

"Sixty inches, six inches, what's the difference," Jay said, sounding just like one of the old men at Moe's store.

"Fifty-four," Merle said. We all laughed.

Fifty-four, fifty-four, Jay said, marching across the ice. He reminded me of Toby right then.

We knew what to do in case we fell in. We knew about the air pocket between the layer of ice and the water. We were to stick our noses in it. Merle said I'd be a natural for that. She didn't care if we became human ice cubes, if we fell in, she wouldn't pull us out, so we better make damn sure that we didn't go through the ice. We stayed close to the edge just in case. After her first few falls, Joan made progress quickly, mainly because Jay announced each new fall sadly. He was only concerned with mistakes. Finally he got bored and left us alone. We could see him wander back toward the farm and the dirty sheep huddled alongside the barn. He stood staring at them, arms akimbo, for a long while.

Joan wouldn't let Em or me skate beside her, so we held on to to each other. I still skated on double runners. These attached to my shoes like roller skates. Em was wearing an old pair of David's ice hockey skates. Her ankles were weak. Every time she fell, I fell. Because the freeze had come on so fast, cattails and the wild grasses that grew along the shallow banks were frozen in place. When I looked down I could see clumps of weeds caught in the ice under my feet. I liked this clarity. I liked the way things stayed put. There were deep cracks in the ice where it had split and rejoined and this left the surface ragged. But out toward the center where Joan practiced, the ice was smooth. She didn't try for style. She was far more interested in speed. She kept trying to go faster and faster and instinctively kept her body low. The wind was spiteful. Our faces ached, our lips split with the same suddenness as the ice did. Joan's face blazed the same color as her sweater. Her blood had changed. Instead of turning blue when she was cold, she now turned deep red. This happened inside the house as well as outside. Sometimes she seemed to burst open from the force of it and bleed from between her legs. This mortified us all. We lived in fear of Merle finding out, of spots on the sheets giving this away. But so far this had not happened. Merle was too busy with our mother.

Sometimes Mr. Zook or some other adult would start a fire near the ice and roll logs close for us to sit on, though Jay was as afraid of fire as Harold Birdseye ought to be. He'd light a match, toss it on the dried leaves and twigs, then run for it. As often happened, after we'd been skating, other people would join us, an occasional parent and some of our classmates, people we knew quite well, but who treated us like strangers since our mother's hospitalization. We were suddenly shy until we grew so cold that we gradually came to the fire. The heat was as intense as the cold. It didn't matter whether we sat or stood, whether we were cold or hot, we couldn't get comfortable. Still, we stayed as long as we could. We weren't far from our house. Because the land was so level it was easy to pick it out, solitary, and built of limestone the same gray as the sky. That house wasn't going anywhere. Besides, the red barn seemed a huge stop sign in its path.

Normally our mother would have sent David to call us home, but it was hard to know what was normal now. So it didn't surprise me that Eddie Birdseye was the one who came to round us up. He was able to drive right up to the pond off the Zooks' dirt access road. We were small enough to squeeze into the front with him, he said. But we weren't really. I had to sit on Em's lap. She didn't care, neither did I, so grateful were we for the sudden warmth of the truck. Eddie did smell like smoke, Joan was right. She usually loved being right, but this time she didn't brag about it. She didn't say anything. None of us did, though whenever Eddie Birdseye said anything I wanted us all to smile. Em and I were the ones pressed up against him. I stared at his hands on the steering wheel, rubbed smooth from years of his touch. I stared at his fingers and wondered what they'd feel like on my own flesh.

He'd heard Joan had a birthday. Joan just nodded.

"Your mom and dad buy you those skates?" Joan shook her head. The skates and any information about them belonged to her alone.

"My father did," I blurted out. Joan stared straight ahead. It was impossible to know if I would pay for this later.

"I guess it's hard to find places to skate in the Bronx." Joan shrugged. We all did. We weren't sure.

"About as hard as finding places to ride a horse, I'd say." We had nothing to say to this either. Then Eddie said he'd brought Shadow over. Something changed in Joan when she heard this, the red of her cheeks seeped to her neck. Her tongue flicked over her ripped lips. We'd pulled into our driveway by then. The door on Joan's side had no doorknob and so we couldn't get out. We had to wait until Eddie opened the door for us. He'd taken his pipe out from his jacket and tapped the rim on his palm. Then he took a pouch of tobacco from his shirt pocket and filled the pipe. The tobacco smelled like cherries, something he should eat instead of burn. When he was satisfied his pipe was filled, he stepped outside the truck and lit the match, took a long draw, and blew the match out with the smoke he inhaled. When he opened the door for us, he pointed the stem toward the direction of the barn, said we could take a look at Shadow if we wanted. He could use the company of some pretty girls. What male couldn't? I was happy to hear this, happy to think there might be a chance for my picture to be taken. I smiled with all my might. Then Eddie smiled down at Joan. And to my amazement she smiled back. She did this so quickly I barely caught it. It was so rare an act, it shocked me. I wasn't sure if Eddie realized this. But he did. He put the pipe back in his mouth and winked. For the effect he'd had on Joan, he might have been smoking a goddamned peace pipe for all I knew. Of course this wouldn't have any effect on Merle. We still weren't allowed in the barn. She didn't trust that damn horse. I didn't either. I had no intention of going near him.

Joan tried to appeal to our mother, but she still wasn't back to her old self. She slept most of the time, though not in her bedroom. She couldn't bring herself to go back in there because that was where she heard the ghost of her baby brother crying. Edmund. The one who died from lack of TLC, which I thought was an abbreviation for talcum powder, not Tender Loving Care. Edmund cried incessantly, it seemed. That crying drove my mother crazy. I heard her tell this to my father the first night she was home. We'd all gone up to bed but I couldn't sleep. I stared out the window. The sky opened up, spilled blue. The stars sailed by. My brothers and sister, even Joan, were deep in sleep, more soundly than they'd been in a long time. I got out of bed and stood in the hall for a few minutes, torn between going downstairs and staying where I was. Finally, I went into David's room and stood over the open grate trying to get one last look at my mother, trying to recover the mother she'd once been in the figure she now was. Uncle had asked about the sleeping arrangements. He could sleep anywhere. He was just a guest in our house, after all. Family, my mother said. Uncle was family. The sleeping arrangements weren't going to change. He and Merle should stay right where they were. In my parents' bedroom. In that case he was going to bed, he said. Merle too. I could see her clearly enough, leaned back against the stove, her arms crossed against this news.

They'd have plenty of time to talk in the morning. My father agreed. My mother needed a good night's sleep. It had been a long day. My father was going to have my mother all to himself. I knew that was what Merle was thinking. She crumpled up her package of Pall Malls into a wad and aimed for the trash. I couldn't see if she missed or not. Her parting shot, is what Uncle called it and pulled her off to bed. My father and mother sat for a few minutes in silence. When it was clear that Merle wasn't going to come back into the kitchen, my father got up and came over to the stove. I could see the top of his head, the soft moon of white that was starting to appear there. He reached for the coffee pot. Empty, he said, and he shook it back and forth. Did my mother want him to make another pot. No, she said, she'd never sleep.

About the crying that kept her awake. If that was the only problem, if that's what my mother was worried about, my father was going to make sure she never had to worry again. After she was completely better, back to her old self, he was moving their bedroom upstairs, to our room. Em's and mine. He'd move us downstairs. We'd be the ones who'd have to listen to Edmund after that.

I would have done this gladly if it meant my mother would be able to stay home for good. But there was no way of telling when this would occur. It was anybody's guess, our father said. God knows he was as anxious for the answer as we were. We'd have to take it day by day. Don't rock the boat, keeps things on an even keel. In my father's estimation our mother was getting stronger. This explained why she was so heavy, at least to me. She no longer shook her foot but her fingers trembled. She held them against both sides of her head, rubbing her temples, pressing flat the veins that throbbed there. She held them there even when she laughed, as though that much happiness might make her head explode. If we ran or made any sudden movement, she was startled. When this happened Merle would make her hand into the shape of a gun and point it at us. It had the same effect Harold's rifle had on us. But he was nowhere around. It was so bitterly cold, it wasn't safe to take Shadow out. He could get cooled down too fast and get pneumonia.

Eddie drove up with feed and hay for the horse a few days after he stabled Shadow with us. For once Merle wasn't home, so it was Joan who answered the door. For all her talk about how she hated Eddie, how he gave her the creeps, she went right up to him, followed him right into the barn. It could have been her wearing a bridle and lead instead of Shadow. I followed right behind Joan.

There was a bad storm brewing, and Eddie wanted to make sure if he couldn't get out to feed the horse one of us would. Did Joan think she could manage it or should he ask David? Joan could do it. She ran her hand along Shadow's flank, across the place she'd once bitten him. Shadow seemed to have no memory of this.

The year before we'd had a lot of snow. Eighteen feet. Not all at once, of course, but if it happened again, if we had another bad winter, there might be times when Eddie and Harold wouldn't be able to get out to the horse. Could they depend on her? Shadow meant the world to Harold.

"You like horses, don't you, sweetheart." Sweetheart nodded. She was running her fingers through Shadow's mane. She put her hand right on the horse's muzzle and held it there.

"Girls always like the feel of that," Eddie said, shaking his head as though he couldn't quite believe this himself. I was shaking my head, no. I didn't like the feel of that.

There was something about a girl and a horse, Eddie Birdseye said. That combination was irresistible. He sure wished he could talk her mother into letting him take some pictures of her on Shadow.

"Have you ever ridden?" Joan didn't answer. She didn't want to lose this chance though I saw my chance of being photographed fading. I'd never be able to ride Shadow.

Joan was an artful liar, according to her mother. She understood immediately that Eddie could check with Merle if she said she had. Still, I could see she was going to risk this. She nodded her head. Later, she'd tell me she didn't *say* yes. There was a difference.

Eddie studied her carefully. I could hear the catch in his voice. *I-rene*, I thought. Shadow's hide twitched, rose up in ridges. Joan rubbed his side, settled him.

She was a natural. For a city kid she sure had a way with horses. Did she want to mount the horse? Eddie wondered. Then it was Joan who twitched, grew anxious. Eddie bent into the horse's flank and made his hands into a stirrup. Joan pulled back.

"You've sure got the legs for it," Eddie said. "You could ride bareback if you wanted. Never even use a saddle."

The air outside the barn suddenly soured, the clouds curdled. Shadow could feel the storm move in on us. His skin prickled again, his eyes rolled back. I heard our names. Rainey, Joan. My mother, calling us in from the storm. "We're not allowed in the barn," I said.

"She's not," Joan lied.

Eddie put his finger to his lips and winked at me. This will be our secret then, he said, his voice sounding smoky and private, the voice he used with Merle sometimes. I was so seldom let in on secrets that I readily agreed.

But the storm held off. We had to stay inside anyway. We had to entertain Toby after Merle came home. I played stone school with him on the stairway between the kitchen and living room so I could listen to my mother and Merle in the kitchen She was trying to talk some sense into our mother, though my father had told her not to do this. God knows what she might trigger. Merle didn't give a damn what anyone said. Our mother was being coddled in the nuthouse. That was the problem. It had been her problem her entire life. She never learned to stand on her own two feet. Never had a backbone. It was because she was the younger sister. She always had Merle looking out

for her. She could count on her sister. But Merle? Well, she'd had to
fend for herself. Nothing brought her to her knees. Nothing.

Kevin was set between them in an old wooden highchair. Merle
had taken Uncle's belt, the only one big enough, and wrapped it
around the baby's belly, through the spindles, around the back and
secured him in place. If my mother wasn't there, she would have said,
that ought to hold the little bastard. But my mother was there. I think
she would have liked to hold Kevin on her lap, but he was still afraid
of her. He had that look he used to get when I was mean to him, when
I spun him around by his feet.

My mother said that she remembered sitting in a highchair just
like that one when she was a baby. Merle just nodded. She didn't like
my mother to talk about her past. In this she was like my father. Don't
encourage her, he told Merle before he left for work.

"I remember Belle was kneeling down on the floor in front of me
scrubbing it. It was wooden. I remember that smell, the smell of the
wet wood as if it was only yesterday." Merle said, tell me about it, she'd
broken her own back on our floor the day before. She'd been down on
all fours though she'd just said that nothing brought her to her knees.

"The house looks beautiful Merle," my mother said, her eyes taking in the floor, the clean windows, her sister's sharp face. Clean windows were the final touch, she said. Merle was drinking a beer and
using the cap for an ashtray. Behind her, a tail of smoke curled up
from the kitchen counter where my mother had forgotten a cigarette.
The burned tobacco left a greasy smear on the porcelain sink the exact
color and consistency as the wax in Kevin's ears.

"The children look beautiful too, Merle. I don't know what we
would have done without you. I don't know how Andy would have
managed." At the mention of my father's name, Merle threw back her

head and snorted. My mother took a handful of raisins and put them on the highchair tray for Kevin. He stared at them as though they might come alive any minute and begin crawling around. My mother had loved the raisins Belle had given her when she was small.

"I thought Belle was my mother. For years I thought that. But she was old enough to be my grandmother. Her hair was the color of Crisco. She had deep finger waves. I remember looking down at her from where I sat."

"Our mother had fiery hair," Merle said. "Close to mine."

"Belle went white early. Redheads do."

"Not this one," Merle shot back. "Belle was an old maid by the time she was thirty," Merle said. "She was in love with the greengrocer but Grandma D. wouldn't hear of it. Belle was the oldest daughter. She had to take care of her mother. That's the way it was done in those days."

"It left her bitter," my mother said. "She should have married and had children. Children sweeten a woman."

"Belle had a child. Our mother. Belle raised her. Spoiled her rotten, just like you do these kids. Grandma D. didn't leave the bed after our mother was born."

"She had a heart of gold," my mother said.

"Belle?"

"No. Our mother."

"Hah," Merle laughed. "She was selfish. If she'd stayed home with us she wouldn't have died."

"She wasn't selfish," my mother said, stricken. "She was out helping a neighbor woman who was sick with scarlet fever. That isn't being selfish. It's what killed her. Scarlet fever."

"Who told you that? Belle? Bullshit. She died of scarlet fever all right. That's Belle's name for shame."

"That's not true, Merle," my mother said quietly. "She loved us. She loved her children."

"She was in bed with another man, that's what killed her. Scarlet fever, my ass. She put her head in the oven when she was caught."

My mother sat smoking in silence. Head bent. She was scraping the ashes that had fallen to the table into little mounds, little gray graves.

"I've thought about that, too," my mother said.

"You have not. You're nothing like her, Bess," Merle said, standing up her collar, pulling her hair free from where it caught on the chair. "I take after her. Except I wouldn't stick my head in the oven for any man."

Our mother would give up her life for my father, for any of us. We knew that. Hadn't she always told us that? But she didn't say this to Merle. Instead she turned to her and said she'd always missed her mother. There wasn't a day that went by when she didn't think of her. It wasn't just her loss either that she worried about. It was ours. We didn't have grandparents. I had never thought about this, though I realized it was true. Our father was an orphan, too. He was just a boy when his mother died, but he'd kept his dad until he was twenty-two.

"Well, we had grandparents," Merle said, "and they weren't any bargain."

"All the children have is you," my mother said and then repeated that she didn't know what she'd do without her sister.

"Get inside," Merle said to me when I came into the room, drawn there by my mother's sadness.

"She can sit with me a while," my mother said. "It's all right, Merle. The children miss me. They miss their mother." I could not believe my victory over Merle. Neither could Merle. She narrowed her eyes. The ash from her cigarette dropped onto the floor she'd broken her back over. She stood up. I tightened my shoulders when she walked behind my chair, but she didn't hit me on the back of my head.

"Are you afraid of the storm?" my mother asked when she saw me shiver. I said I was. She put her arm around me and pulled me close. Don't be afraid, she said. She smelled of Johnson's Baby Powder and Ivory Soap, exactly the same as she had before she went crazy. The smell of sulfur from the match she struck made me want to crawl onto her lap. Time to light the lamps in case we lose power, she said. But no one moved.

I could feel the wind, the places it found to get into the room. It didn't feel like a winter wind.

"The temperature is rising," my mother said. "There must be two systems coming together. We're in for some snow." She switched on the radio but there was nothing but static. Storms made my mother anxious. "We're in for some snow," my mother said again.

It better not, Merle said. She went to all the windows, pulled the curtains back and looked at the sky menacingly. It wouldn't dare snow and upset her sister. It didn't. The temperatures rose ominously. It reached 60 degrees within an hour. There was the low growl of thunder from the storm and the steady pressure of the wind. It set the cradle I'd made for my mother rocking. My mother looked at it in alarm. Merle followed my mother's eyes.

"Get this thing out of here," she said to me, shoving the cardboard cradle into my hands. This time my mother didn't try to keep me. Her hand went to the side of her head. Her foot began its wild swing. It was the empty cradle that made her think of Edmund again, made her turn the conversation back to him instead of her mother. I knew that

Merle would blame me for this sooner or later. I put the cradle under the china closet. The wind gusted. The parlor door blew open and set the dishes chattering. Toby was sound asleep on the sofa. Joan was upstairs. I could hear her feet padding from our room to David's room. David and Wayne were gone with Uncle to pick up pinecones. Emily was somewhere practicing to be a martyr. St. Stephen or St. Jerome who'd had his skin peeled off his body and put on inside out. Joan had read this to me from stories of the martyrs a few days ago. Skinned alive, she said and lay the book down on her belly. We were side by side in bed. I was hoping Joan made this part up as she often did when she didn't understand words, but she shook her head. It was on my mind to go find Joan when I heard my mother's chair scrape back against the floor.

Edmund had been dead for a day and a night before they found him, my mother told Merle. By that time his eyeballs were sunken in his head.

"That's horse shit," Merle said. From where I stood I could see the picture of Edmund on the mantelpiece. His eyes did look caved in, his whole head did.

"Where do you get these ideas?" Merle said, looking around the kitchen for them and seeing nothing, looking straight at where I stood in the hallway.

I stepped outside then and closed the door. The wind dropped so suddenly I nearly fell off the porch. There was no place to go but the barn. Despite my fear of Shadow, it was safer than staying in the house with Merle. When I was certain no one was watching me, I slipped through the barn doors. Shadow was in his stall. I didn't like to be in the barn alone with him. I was sure Shadow was just as mean as Harold, just as willing to trample me to death without any prodding from him.

I stood watching Shadow. He stood watching me too. It was that that made me nervous, made me climb up the ladder to the hayloft. Splinters of wind slid through the siding, and pieces of hay sailed and settled in the weak light. The siding creaked, the upper story trembled in the wind. From where I sat I could see some worn-out tires, David's maroon Schwinn bicycle, and my sled leaned up against the wall below. Shadow had gone back to staring at the barn door, waiting for Harold or Eddie, I thought. But it wasn't either of them who pushed open the door. It was Joan. For a moment Shadow looked startled, as though he was afraid to be alone with her the way I was with him. I could see the barn mice scatter, then slide along the edges of the barn. They were the color of the sky behind Joan's head. She moved to where the horse stood. She murmured something to him but it was lost in the gloom and space of the barn. There was a roll of thunder. I counted seconds between the thunder and lightning. Seven. A second a mile, David said. That's how far away the storm was from where I sat in the barn. Still, I knew I was in the worst place I could be in a storm.

I knew there were three lightning rods on the roof, but that hadn't spared other barns from being struck. Lightning came into our own kitchen. It leapt out of all the outlets. When that happened our mother would take us all into the living room, make us sit on the sofa and warn us to keep our feet off the floor. She'd tell us the story of the girl who got up for an instant to close a window and was struck right in the face. When they found her body, it bore the imprint of a lightning bolt on her chin.

I was thinking about this, feeling the wind press against the siding, and looking out the loft doors considering what to do. I didn't want Joan to see me. She hated to be spied on. It wouldn't matter that I had been in the barn first.

I decided to sneak down the ladder behind her back. This seemed possible only because she was so fixed on Shadow and I was so fixed on the lightning. What stopped me was Harold Birdseye's face in the barn window. At first I thought it was an apparition, something horrid the wind had whipped up. Joan had her back to him. It was impossible to tell if the look on Harold's face meant harm or good, but at that point nothing could have compelled me to come down from the loft, not even the lightning I was so deathly afraid of. It seemed to me Harold was frozen to the spot, just as I was. He may have wished that Shadow would trample Joan to death. I couldn't imagine him wanting to share his horse, the only thing that meant the world to him. Shadow, like the air around us, seemed electrified. His tail switched. Joan held her hand steadily against his flank. We couldn't have known that she wanted to mount him. When she stepped up onto the side of the stall, it only looked as though she wanted to get a closer look at him. Her pale head against his chestnut flank held me there. Held Harold too. In another instant she straddled the horse. Shadow accepted her easily. She sat transfixed, like Joan of Arc bathed in the light of Christ's holy vision just before she rode off to do battle.

I felt Joan had stolen the horse right out from under Harold's nose. Or what was left of his nose. Beyond my fear of what she'd done, even beyond my fear of the storm, of Harold, I wanted her to keep the horse. I wanted her to have the horse because of how she looked as she sat astride him. The horse meant the world to her too. I could see that.

I was foolish enough to think that she could take possession of Shadow just by claiming him. I believed that she could start by coming out in the evenings to sit on the horse. She could grow daring and take the horse out of the stall. I could see her walking the horse around the barn at first, and see the horse following her obediently. I could see her eventually opening the barn doors and taking Shadow to the barnyard. I could even see her galloping around the pasture. She'd learn to canter, to gallop, to post.

I could see all this, was seeing it, when the lightning struck. It sounded like a rifle shot. For one moment I thought Harold had fired on Joan, that he'd brought his rifle with him and shot her straight through the heart. In the next instant I saw her fly through the air — coming straight at me — her eyes coolly blue and blank as she hit the ladder. I remember only that I'd reached out to her, felt her dress graze my fingers as she dropped to the floor. But I couldn't have hid. She'd taken the ladder down with her. It clattered to the floor just missing her body. She looked folded in two. Shadow was still rearing and bucking in his stall. The thunder took me by the shoulders and shook, and the rain, having held off so long, let loose above my head. The moment held so much noise, so much terror that I nearly leapt from the hayloft in my fear. Had I done this, I would have landed on Harold's back. As it was, I teetered, swayed there above his head as he bent to Joan, took her against his chest and said, *My darling, my darling*, over and over again. I was glad for an instant that someone held her, even if it was Harold. But Joan couldn't feel anything. Her eyes were still open, still coolly blue and blank, and they would remain so long after I summoned up the courage to scream for help, to scream for Merle who was going to bury me in the goddamn silo under two tons of corn if I set foot in that barn again.

CHAPTER ELEVEN

After Merle carried Joan in and lay her on the sofa she slapped us all because Joan was unconscious. Uncle came home, swaggered into the kitchen and Merle whacked him for being the useless drunk that he was and then chased him out to go call the doctor from the road-house, and to get my father home, too.

Dr. Maybee came as soon as he could. He shooed us all out of the room. We stayed with our mother who sat staring out the window. She was doing the church trick with her hands. *This is the church, this is the steeple, open the door and see all the people.* She wasn't saying the words though. I said them for her, over and over again. Uncle kept screwing and unscrewing his pint until Merle grabbed it from him. Give me that damn thing, she hissed, then tilted her head back and drank. Dr. Maybee came in with gauze that was covered with plaster. He soaked it in a pan in the kitchen sink, his head glowing absolutely pink under the bulb.

Joan's leg was broken. A clean break, not a compound, not a greenstick. We could count ourselves lucky on that score. And she had quite a knock on her head, Dr. Maybee said. A concussion. We'd have to watch her closely for twenty-four hours. If she started vomiting, or if she fell asleep and we couldn't rouse her, we'd have to bring her straight in to the emergency room. He could be there in five minutes. He was sorry that we didn't have a phone. It was a nasty night to be out, and he hoped that he was the only one who'd have to go out in it. His hands were dusted white. Plaster of Paris was stubborn, he said. Resilient too. Like children. They bounced back. He'd seen that a mil-

lion times. Then he turned to my mother. She was staring at his white
hands, then at him as if he were a stranger.

"Bess," he said, "you look like you just saw a ghost." That made
her stand up and start brushing at her skirt as though all the little people that spilled from her hands were running around there.

My father had come home as soon as he could, but he hadn't come
into the house. He stood smoking on the porch, watching the barn
until the doctor was finished. When the doctor stepped outside, my
father shook his hand, threw up his hands in mock despair and came
inside. His hair was dripping wet, his teeth a gash of white.

"Christ, Merle," he said. "This is what I was afraid would happen."
He sounded as though he was half-laughing.

"She'll be all right," Merle said. "She'll be fine. We just have to
keep an eye on her."

"She's my wife," my father said. "I'll keep my own damn eye on
her if you don't mind."

"Joan," Merle shot back. "It's Joan I'm talking about."

"Andy," Uncle warned. "No trouble lad. No trouble now. Blood is
thicker than water."

My father turned his back. He said he needed a twankquilizer.
When he was upset he couldn't say his *r*'s. Emily, who was as confused
as my father, put her hand to her mouth. Wail-woad, she whispered.
My mother, coming suddenly back to her old self momentarily, said,
someone get your father a beer.

David offered to stay up all night and watch Joan. But as it turned
out none of us could sleep. Every time one of us heard a noise, we all
crept downstairs. Joan slept deeply. A bruise the shape of an elephant's
ear covered the left side of her face. A black star marked the place a
nail had punctured her cheek. The cast on her leg was bright as noon

though the room was still in shadow. Merle sat across from Joan. She'd been drinking all night. She'd been able to wake Joan only once and if Joan didn't wake up soon and stay awake, then they'd have to take her in.

"Turn off the light," she said, rubbing her temples when I came downstairs. "I have a splitting headache." My mother, her hand pressed against her own head, was in the kitchen boiling water for tea. She had set the table for us, six bowls, a quart of milk, the cream choking the neck, a box of raisins, the flaps like hands held over the head of the Sun-Maid Raisins girl, the box of puffed rice shot from a cannon, the waiting teapot, the pattern Briar Rose, the roses twisted through with thorns, the can of evaporated milk, the carnation in the center, like a red heart waiting to explode. I couldn't speak to the strangeness of the scene except to say I was afraid to go into that room. The room with my mother. Instead, I shut the light off for Merle and pulled a chair close to Joan. It had been thirteen hours since she'd been thrown from the horse.

My mother called to Merle. She'd made her tea, some hot tea would help her nerves. She came into the room and placed it on the arm of the chair. That chair was made of horsehair. So was the sofa Joan lay on. The thought filled me with dread. Merle brought the cup to her mouth. The cup shook so badly that it took both her hands to steady it. She held it to her mouth and stared into the tea, as though it were a crystal ball that held Joan's future. Or hers. Joan's brother hadn't come out of his room all night, though he had left his light on. Uncle sat on a wooden chair in my parents' bedroom leaning forward as though listening to a voice on the other side of the room. We were all straining for some sign that Joan would wake up. Even my father, who couldn't bear the sight of any one of us hurt and had once thrown the newspaper at David when he came home from work and saw

David's foot soaking in Epsom's salts. Jesus Christ, he'd hollered, what have you done to yourself? Even my father couldn't tear himself away from Joan and tend to my mother.

Our house was on a small ridge. The alcove that held the bay windows, the crumpled morning sheets and blankets of my parents' bed, faced south over the winter hill that we'd sledded down just the month before. One of Toby's mittens was held fast in the mud and lay like a hand reaching up from the grave. I was staring at that, the blue ribbed mitten, as the sun came over the hill in the way it did. Immediately, as though on rebound from where it dropped from the sky the night before. The rising sun was too bright to look at and we were not to try it. My mother had told us the story of a boy she knew who stared at the sun in eclipse though he'd been warned by his mother not to do it. Now his world was black. Black as if a knitted cap had been pulled over his eyes. Black as it was when we tied a scarf around our own eyes and played blind man's bluff. The boy could not see even a pin of light when the doctor brought the flashlight to his eyes. Because of this I watched the field, watched it as it suddenly flooded with light and so missed the moment we'd all been waiting for. The moment Joan opened her eyes.

Merle sprang from the chair. Jesus Almighty Christ in Heaven, she said to Joan. Her voice was shaking like the cup in her hand. "You'll be the death of me."

Joan looked around at all of us. Her broken leg lay across the blanket white as a Yule log. She could see that she'd been hurt. But she couldn't feel it. I knew because when Merle went into the kitchen to get her some ginger ale, the ginger ale we'd left out all night so that she could drink it flat if she woke up, I leaned over her and asked if hitting her head on the post under the hayloft had hurt very much and she looked at me in disgust and said, no it didn't hurt. It tickled.

Dr. Maybee drove up in late afternoon. By that time Joan was sitting up. That's what he wanted to see, he said. His bald head beamed. He sat on a chair beside her, the same one I had sat on, but that didn't mean I could stay in the room when he examined Joan. That was private, he said, reaching into his bag and pulling out the light that David said lit up the inside of your skull the way a candle in a pumpkin did. We waited in the kitchen taking turns holding the flashlight against our fingers, believing that the insides of our bodies were experiencing light for the very first time. I personally believed that we glowed, like the crucifix that Em had given our mother.

We could move Joan up into her own bed, the doctor said when he was done. He stood up and let us all back into the room. Kevin had pulled himself upright in the playpen for the first time in his life and stood wavering. His knees were dimpled. He held a black crust of toast in his hand. His face was smeared with apple butter.

"They'll eat a pound of dirt before they die, mother," Dr. Maybee said to my mother. Her hand flew to the side of her head. She smiled but the laugh didn't come. Dr. Maybee leaned down to steal Toby's nose. He had it between his pointer and middle finger and was about to give it back when Toby spit at him. My mother was sorry for that. It was something he'd just started. Normally, Merle would have whacked his ass good, but she wasn't yet back to her old self either.

In the meantime we'd have to figure out where to put Joan. She needed to lie still for a few days to give the bone in her leg a chance to set and her brains time to settle down. She couldn't sleep between Em and me because I was a restless sleeper. David and Wayne were the only ones who had their own beds. Toby did too, but it was the big crib, the one with all our teeth marks in the rails from trying to

chew our way through the wood. Just like rats, Merle had said more
than once.

Joan couldn't sleep where Wayne did because there was no heat in
the summer kitchen and the cot was too narrow. Besides, the bathroom was upstairs and Joan couldn't manage the steps. David would
have to give up his bed and sleep on the sofa so Joan could have his
bed. This turned out to be a good arrangement for two reasons. One
was that David stopped peeing the bed the first night he slept on the
sofa. The other reason was that the chair I sat in next to Joan's bed was
right next to the grate in David's room.

This was where I was sitting when I heard my mother say to Merle
the next day that they were lucky that they weren't loved as children.
That they were free.

"Free from what?" Merle wanted to know.

"No one noticed us," my mother said. "No one cared if we lived
or died."

"They cared plenty if we did something wrong. Remember
Gladdie?" I knew the story of Gladdie. Part of it. Gladdie was one of
the seven sisters and five brothers who couldn't find it in her black
heart to care for my mother and Merle after their mother had died.
Twelve frigging brothers and sisters and not one of them could take
their sister's children. Merle had told us this the summer before. Her
mother, according to Merle, was rolling over in her grave because of
this.

Gladdie was the poor sport who was married to Ira. Ira had the
webbed fingers. He was marked. Merle had told us that much. It had
happened when his mother, Grandma D. had gone to the well for
water. She had just drawn a bucket to the top and was unhooking it
from the crank when it slipped. The handle spun free, whacked her

good on her hand. She dropped the bucket and grabbed her right hand. In that same moment Ira moved in her womb, and she knew she'd marked him. It was his right hand that was webbed. I remember when Merle had told us this we'd studied our own hands carefully. Merle had just stared out at the clothesline, at the diapers, at the sheet-draped clothesline pole, the way the wind shifted it back and forth as though it were some creature struggling to free itself from the tangled linens. It was early evening. Merle was quiet for some time. It seemed her stillness silenced us all in the softness of that summer's night. I could hear the peepers and the terrible ripping sound the crickets made. But that was all. Then Merle turned back to us, made aware and suddenly uneasy by our presence. She said, then, looking back to the clothesline, that if a woman hung clothes on a line when she was pregnant she stood a good chance of strangling her baby. The cord just wrapped around its neck. Choked it dead. She said she'd lost count of how many times she'd wished Grandma D. had gone to the line instead of the well the day she marked Ira.

"I think it was Ira behind that," my mother was saying to Merle. Her voice came to us from far off. I knew she was sitting by the window. My father had had to drag the parlor chair back into the kitchen for her. She was hearing the ghost of her baby brother crying in all the other rooms. "He didn't want us there after their baby came," my mother went on. Gladdie had taken Merle at first because she was ten years old and could help around the house. Then my mother had come to stay after her father sent her back to the Bronx from Chicago. She was six years old at the time.

"Ira may not have wanted you," Merle shot back. "But he sure wanted me. I was afraid to be in the same room with that old fart."

"Shh," my mother said.

"Shh, what?" Merle said. "Let them get an earful." I heard the clatter of dishes.

"He got his just desserts in the end. He's dying of cancer you know."

"Cancer," my mother said, her voice snagged on the word. "Cancer of what?"

"Cancer-of-what-do-you-think?" Merle laughed.

"His pecker," Joan said.

"That's right," Merle yelled up between my legs. She'd made her way over to the stove and heard us. We sat in silence then, staring out the window. We could see the barn. See Harold Birdseye bring Shadow out into the light, lead him to the field. Merle must have heard the barn door open.

"Is that Eddie?" she asked, her voice rising light, coming right up to us.

"Harold," my mother said. "Joan gave him a terrible scare. Poor soul." *My darling, my darling*, I thought.

"Imagine the scare he would've given her if she opened her eyes and saw him staring back at her. It probably would have killed her."

"What does she mean by that?" Joan scowled. She didn't remember that Harold had been there at all. She didn't know that Harold had run to her instead of the horse.

I shrugged. Joan pinched me so hard I had to tell her. She didn't say anything at all. Instead she watched as Harold led Shadow from the barn into the pasture. After he closed the gate, he looked over at our house, then hung something on the barbed wire. It looked like a piece of tinsel. We both stared hard at it.

"I can't stand sitting in this goddamn bed," Joan said at last. She started plucking at her eyelashes. One by one. She said she was going to pull them all out if she had to stay in bed one more day. I told her that she was supposed to make a wish whenever an eyelash fell out, that my mother had told me that. She pulled an eyelash out and balanced it on her finger.

"Now make a wish," I said, "and blow the eyelash away." Her eyelashes were the same golden white as her hair. Curled and long as her brother's but not as thick. She had the one eye stripped bare within a few minutes. I didn't know what I could do to save the other eye, I only knew that I had to do something.

"I wish to hell I could get out of this damn cast," Joan said.

"I'm going out and see what's hanging on that barbed wire," I said. Even as I said this, I was wishing I hadn't. Harold was still out in the field somewhere with Shadow.

"You wouldn't dare," Joan said. I said I would. Joan looked at me. Her one eye, without its lashes, could either make you laugh or make you cry, it looked so odd. I wouldn't chance either and headed downstairs. My mother and Merle were still in the kitchen. It was on my mind to tell Merle, your daughter's up there pulling her goddamn eyelashes out, when my own mother said to put on some boots if I was going outside. Just like that. As though every day I had a mother who reminded me about coats and boots. I was amazed by this and pulled the door shut too hard. I mouthed the words, "The Door," even before Merle had a chance to. I was feeling that kind of power, the kind of power I needed to go across the road through standing water on frozen ground and grab whatever it was that was sparkling in the sun before I was trampled to death by Shadow.

Once in that very same field a bee had landed on Em's finger. It sat like a bright yellow flower on her ring finger and stung her. Stung her good. But instead of brushing it off and running, she continued to walk through the field and toward our house with that bee stinging away. I remember trying to figure out if what Em had done was because she was very brave or very scared. We knew better than to bring a bee into the house with Merle there, but that was what Em seemed ready to do. That pain drove her to it. Which was what was happening to me. I walked directly to the silver glinting on the wire. I saw only that, saw only a tiny silver heart hanging from a chain that was hanging from the wire. I had it in my hand, nearly to my pocket, when Harold galloped up behind me.

I stood staring down at my galoshes. Their clasps looked like miniature ladders, eight small ladders lying on their sides, the way the ladder in the barn had looked when Joan had hit it and sent it flying. I had put on my boots but not my shoes. My feet were numb from the cold and that numbness climbed very quickly, up my legs, my stomach, my chest, until I couldn't feel my body. At that moment I was not a bit afraid of Harold Birdseye.

"That belong to you?" Harold said. I didn't even look back at him. I just reached over and put the necklace back on the fence. Shadow lowered his head and starting chewing on some long grass, startlingly green, near my feet. His head was inches from my right side. I could see his dark horse eyes, his rich black eyelashes.

"She's laying up there pulling her goddamn eyelashes out," I said. He knew who I meant.

"Give her that," was all he said and rode off.

"What did he want," Merle asked when I came back inside. I said he wanted to know how Joan was doing. "Tell him it's none of his goddamn business."

"Merle," my mother said softly, "she can't do that." But in truth I could have.

I went upstairs and put the necklace into Joan's waiting hand.

Some sort of lightness spilled into the kitchen in late afternoon. My father was working a double shift, and so Merle had our mother to herself. Uncle was at the stand trying to come up with an idea of what to sell in the dead of winter. He still had bushels of pinecones left from Christmas and some dead wreaths. Wayne was with his father, helping him come up with an idea that better be good or we'd be eating pinecone soup for the whole next week. Both Merle and my mother had freshened up, combed their hair, and put on starched blouses.

Merle had taken Kevin out of the playpen and was walking him around the kitchen holding onto his hands. Toby was in my mother's lap. She had her face buried in his hair. Emily was making crosses from cardboard, one for each of our rooms. David was out at a shoot with Eddie Birdseye. I had spent most of the day upstairs with Joan, but despite that, despite the silver necklace, she had pulled all of her eyelashes out anyway. Because of this, I was drawn downstairs, to the sound of Merle's laughter, the warm smoke-filled kitchen, the ham baking, sweet potatoes boiling on the stove, Clover barking as she followed Merle around and around the room.

"He's ready to walk," Merle said. My mother nodded. She remembered when Toby first learned how to walk. She'd walked him around first by his hands for a few days, just like Merle was doing, and then by the straps of his overalls for another few days. At some point she let go and there he went. He was overjoyed that he figured this out, my mother said. But he hadn't gotten it quite right.

"The first few days he walked by himself he kept his own hands on those straps," my mother said. "He thought that was part of it. Holding himself up by his straps."

Merle threw back her head and laughed. Her neck was as white as the spout on the pitcher my mother kept on the washstand. It was the only spot on Merle's body that wasn't freckled. Kevin, in imitation of that laugh, threw his own head back and crowed. We all stopped what we were doing and laughed. Kevin was amazed by his sudden power over us and repeated himself. We laughed so hard, even Merle, even my mother, that tears were running down our faces. We couldn't stop laughing. Toby slid off my mother's lap and began prancing around the room with his hands to his shoulders. We only laughed harder.

"Stop that laughing," Joan yelled down through the grate, but that just made it worse. Clover was chasing her tail, the coffee perked and pulsed against the glass eye of the pot, the potatoes tumbled on the stove, the ham sizzled in the oven, the very air sweetened by the brown sugar glaze and the sound of our dry and harsh laughs.

Merle was the first to run to the bathroom, hands cupped between her legs. We all settled then, wiped our eyes. Toby had the hiccups. My mother stood to get him some water, to check on the ham, put a fork into the potatoes. David came up the driveway, but Eddie Birdseye, who usually stopped in, put his car in reverse and left. When David opened the door to the kitchen we tried to tell him what had happened, tried to pull him into our mood. He stood ready to smile, wanting to smile, but of course it was too late. Above our heads we heard Merle. She'd stuck her head into Joan's room to see if she needed anything.

"What did you do to yourself?" we heard her ask. There was still some laughter in her voice. It was a strange thing about Joan's eyelashes. If you hadn't seen her pull them out you wouldn't notice they were gone, but at the same time you knew that something was missing. We couldn't hear Joan's answer.

Merle was still perplexed when she came back into the kitchen. "Take a look at Joan when you go up," she said to my mother who was heading to the bathroom herself. "There's something odd about that girl. I can't put my finger on it."

It was not her missing eyelashes that my mother noticed. It was the rash. It covered most of her body. What Joan had was the measles. Not German measles either. She had the kind that could make your temperature soar, make your gums bleed, make you go blind, and possibly kill you. She also had the kind that made our house quarantined. Dr. Maybee himself brought the notice and tacked it up outside our front door. It looked the same as a *No Trespassing* sign, and it meant that we all had to stay inside and everybody else had to stay out. Joan had to wear dark glasses and the shades had to be pulled. Even so, any light at all made her eyes sore. I thought this was made worse because of her missing eyelashes.

After Dr. Maybee left, Merle said she'd come and go as she damn well pleased. And she did, so did all the adults. My father had to work, and so did Uncle. Our mother worried about exposing our neighbors to measles, but Merle didn't. It would serve them right, she said. Not one of them had offered to give her a hand. In fact, they bent over backwards to avoid her. Our mother said that she cared. She lived here. This was her home. The last thing she wanted to do was be responsible for causing someone to get sick.

"What about me?" Merle said. "If I have to stay locked up with this bunch of maniacs I'm going to get sick. It'll be me who's in the nuthouse next."

My mother was stricken by this remark. And confused. She wandered into her old bedroom where the ghost of her baby brother was and sat on her bed.

Merle said we better make damn sure that we didn't get sick. But we wouldn't because except for Kevin, we'd all had the measles. We'd had the mumps and whooping cough as well. We'd even had chicken pox.

Merle was holding out for smallpox then. Had we had smallpox? We weren't sure.

"There's always hope," Merle said and went to find my mother. She had to bring her back to the alcove and lie beside her until she stopped crying.

Diphtheria was really what had killed Edmund, our mother's baby brother. But it's what saved our mother. She'd gotten it too, but Belle heard about this and had come to the foundling home and brought my mother home. She nursed her back to life. She was at death's door. I pictured death's door as the same rotted door that led to our cellar.

Diphtheria slowly choked you to death. It closed your throat until you couldn't breath. So it couldn't be Edmund's ghost that my mother heard, Merle told our mother. It was all in her head. There was no ghost. Merle would bet her life on this. So my mother just better knock it off. She was giving Merle the creeps with all this ghost shit.

But my mother still heard the ghost of her baby brother. She didn't want to hear it, but she couldn't help herself. Merle told her to stay out of the damn bedroom then.

We all listened for it, even Toby. Once he thought that he heard it. "Oh Christ," he said. But it was only Kevin. Kevin caught the measles a week after Joan. Her case had been mild but not Kevin's. His fever was so high that we couldn't keep our hands on him. Or off him. He didn't have red spots at first. What he had were white spots in his mouth and some difficulty breathing. We'd have to watch him carefully because he could go into convulsions if his temperature spiked. If this happened Merle or my mother would have to wrap him in a towel and put him in tepid water. Tepid. I had no idea what that meant, but if it wasn't tepid, it could send him into shock. My mother hovered over Kevin all day long. He couldn't bear to be held and she couldn't bear not to hold him. She'd made a bed for him in the kitchen by pulling two armchairs together, hers and the other one from the parlor.

Merle let my mother tend to him. She had enough to do, she said, but actually she was afraid of coming down with the measles herself. She'd read an article about the effects of childhood diseases on adults. Chicken pox could kill a grown man. Mumps, well, she didn't want to say what mumps could do to a man, but he'd need a wheelbarrow to carry his privates around in.

Kevin lay splayed open in his makeshift bed. He reminded me of the frog Joan had dissected in late fall. We'd thought it was dead, it lay so still. If it had a heart we couldn't feel it, and maybe that's what Joan was looking for. The frog had puffed itself up to appear bigger to its enemies, but we didn't know that. We thought it was a fat, dead frog. Joan lay the frog on its back and took a double-edge razor and sliced it down the front. I don't think the frog made any movement, but it immediately deflated and when it did we saw that it had a belly full of eggs. Emily turned and ran into the house. Joan leaned back on her haunches, turned her head to the side, and tried to cover her mouth. But still she vomited. I saw her do it, but neither of us said anything about it. Emily came back with a box to bury the frog. She lifted it up and buried it, eggs and all, near the ditch.

Joan had not really turned green when she threw up, but she had turned gray. Kevin, lying on the cushions between the chairs, was just that same color. Shadow gray. My mother took a fold of his skin between her thumb and index finger and gently pinched. What Kevin was was dehydrated. I looked at his eyes. They were dark like mine.

They'd started out as bluish brown when he was born. When I'd pried his eyes open to check the color, he seemed mad about this. For months after this some of that blue hung onto the outer rim of his irises stubbornly. But by the time he was six months old, they were as black as mine, and I liked this about him, because we were the only ones with dark eyes. But as Kevin deflated, the brown seeped out and pooled in the quarter circles below each eye. I went into the parlor to check on the picture of Edmund with his sunken eyes. Kevin's looked exactly the same. David saw me looking at the picture and went to it and laid Edmund flat down on his face, then went running up the road to Birdseye's.

Merle wanted to go to the hospital with Eddie, but that meant measles for sure. I tried to imagine her with measles *and* freckles, but it didn't seem possible. My mother really had to bundle Kevin up and while she did this, Eddie kept the truck running so it would be warm for the baby. Then he carried Kevin out the door. After they left, Merle stood at the door and watched them drive up the road, then she went into the dining room, to the alcove below the bay windows, and watched as the truck made its way up over the hill to the bridge, where often it seemed our hopes rose then fell.

As it turned out, Eddie had saved the day. Merle took this news as a compliment to her. My father was sitting at the table smoking one of Merle's Pall Malls. She didn't care. She'd shoved the entire pack over to him. Kevin had had a seizure on the way to the hospital and Eddie had saved his life. My father owed the man an enormous debt. He'd kept the baby from swallowing his tongue. Intravenous was what Kevin needed. His body chemistry was out of whack. This was nothing new to Merle. She didn't say so. She didn't have to. He'd be fine in a few days. Home in a few days, we heard our father say. Our mother would be too. Though this was a setback, it wasn't as bad as it appeared because our mother *asked* to be taken back to the hospital. She knew when one of those spells was coming upon her. That marked some progress no matter how you looked at it. How I looked at it was the empty chair by the kitchen window.

"Ah, Jesus," my father said, when I began to cry. He threw his hands up above his head. We knew not to ask him any more questions. It wasn't just because he looked worn out, he looked out of whack too. He'd put on his work shirt inside out, though he'd buttoned it perfectly. When he was about to leave for work, Merle said softly, "Andy." She almost sounded like my mother. He stopped dead still. "Your shirt," she said. He looked down at his shirt. "Jesus Christ," he said, and tucked it in.

What a piece of work, Merle said shaking her head. But there was no meanness in her that afternoon, nor in the weeks to come. The change in her behavior, her mildness, was reflected in the weather. The days softened. The clouds at sunset were the color of peach petals, and as though in honor of this transient mildness, Merle changed the color of her nails from red to pink. Beyond the lip of the sill, the wild geese landed, then lifted. Merle stopped whatever she was doing to watch them, circled her mouth with her finger, then dropped her hand to her throat and rubbed it, as though easing a sudden ache that throbbed there. The late afternoon sky was an inkwell of pastels that the geese dipped into over and over again, each time rising against the sky in formation, finding their bearings, and heading farther south. I knew how badly Merle wanted to leave, to follow their flight, how each of my mother's setbacks tethered her once more to us, the house, the life that was hers, and ours, as we marked the seasonal migration of our mother's love.

CHAPTER TWELVE

We saw no more of the geese until spring, but I would always think of them, search for them, whenever Merle stood at the window and looked out over the fields, as one mild day after another fell under the advance of a cold front coming in from Canada.

We all knew what Merle was looking for, had heard her tell Uncle a dozen times, whenever he'd asked. A way out. That's what she was looking for. She should have thought about that before she made the grand gesture, he'd say, smelling of whiskey, his hair smelling like the cradle cap that cupped Kevin's head. She was brittle as the icy windowpanes. A loud noise could shatter her nerves. At the same time, my teeth began to crumble, laid waste to the gum. For weeks my teeth wouldn't ache, but then one night a tooth would shatter my face with a pain that was ear splitting. On Valentine's Day, in anticipation of the miniature candy hearts our father always gave us, two started. The pain shifted from one hollowed, rotten molar to the next. I lay awake listening to the sound of Em's breathing. The noise seemed unbearable, seemed to echo in my throbbing gums. I placed my pillow on the cold floor for as long as I could, then balled it up under my chin. The cool fabric was a comfort against my cheek but didn't penetrate the dark recesses of my mouth. The pain pounded my head so hard, I felt as though it lifted me off the bed. But it hadn't. Every time I shifted my position, Emily moaned. Across the hall Joan sucked harder and harder on her fingers. I looked out the window at the stars. Their icy brightness sent shocks through my body the way cold water on my teeth did. I closed my eyes against them. As the night continued and grew quieter, the pain became stronger. It was as though its source was the comic character Mr. Pain, who was featured in an advertisement for Ben Gay in the *Daily News*. Mr. Pain was green with a stubbled chin and wore a black bowler hat. In the ad he had a double-sided ax that he used to torment backs and shoulders. But in my case he was in my tooth. The ax hit rhythmically on the exposed nerves of one, then another molar, like ascending notes on a musical scale. I couldn't stay in my bed. I thought if I went downstairs Mr. Pain wouldn't be able to find me. I crept down the steps and sat in the upholstered chair my father had brought into the kitchen for my mother. My mother always woke suddenly when we were sick. She knew, like Miss Clavell in the story of Madeline, that something was not right. But for my father, it was our sadness that woke him. Or our fear. I heard his bare feet on the floor. The nightlight on the stove blinked on, then off and when it did, my father switched on a light above my head.

"There you are," he said. "I knew I'd find you." I felt blinded by pain. My teeth howled. Light, heat, was excruciating. The sound, the weight of my father's feet, echoed in my teeth. There was nothing to be done until morning. He sat on the floor beside me then and rubbed my face. He told me stories about the Norsemen. Story after story about how they carved their boats and sailed the seas, about their gods, Odin and his eight-legged horse Sleipnir, Thor who smashed monsters with his mighty hammer. This made my teeth hurt more, and so my father switched to the goddess Freyja whose chariot was drawn across the sky by cats. Cats? Can you imagine, Rainey? My father often tried to teach me lessons through stories. These stories were like stubborn knots that had to be worked and worked before the lesson came loose. So it was when he told of Loki the trickster that I listened carefully because Loki had a mean streak. Merle said I was

developing one and it was going to rot me to the core. Loki was the
father of a wolf who could stretch his jaw from the earth to the sky.
He was often bad and set his wolf on others. In my deliberations I
thought this wolf was the one that ate the little boy who cried wolf all
the time and that this story was meant to instruct me on the conse-
quences of meanness, but my father went on. It seemed that the gods
finally seized Loki and tied him to a rock beneath a poisonous snake.
His wife caught the poison in a bowl but when it was full and she left
to empty it, the poison fell on his face and the earth shook while Loki
struggled. I understood this to be connected to the poison in my jaw.
I felt the poison splash against me until I couldn't bear the weight of
an eyelash on my cheek. I couldn't bear my father's story, and so I
begged him to get the pliers and pull my teeth out. To my relief, he
said he would and for the briefest moment the pain lessened. As soon
as my father left the room, however, the pain returned with a
vengeance. I could hear him in the dining room looking through all
the drawers, then I heard him make his way down the cellar steps.
He'd yell up from time to time that he was still looking.

I took great comfort in this, that he, too, was as determined as I
was to yank the teeth out. Every once in a while I'd hear him mutter:
"Where are those damn things." By the time he went out to the car it
was nearly dawn. When he finally found them I was sound asleep. The
gods and goddesses had entered my dreams, floated me through the
sky on cats, carefully outwitting the poisonous snake. When I awoke,
I was in my own bed, and my molars sound asleep. I didn't dare open
my mouth to do anything to disturb them, not even when Merle
brought me the whiskey-soaked cotton my father told her to lay on
my gums. I wouldn't open my mouth though Merle said I'd be sorry.
My father's story was a distraction that was all. I didn't believe for a

minute, did I, that he would pull the molars from my head with a pair of pliers? For Chrissakes, hadn't he'd told me how he wouldn't hurt a hair on my head. I was going to go to the dentist, like it or not, and if I gave her one bit of trouble, she'd be more than happy to pull the damn teeth from my jaw. She didn't know about my father, but one thing I could be sure of, she was not going to lose one more night's sleep over me.

The problem with me was that I had an overactive imagination. Just like my mother. And I was gullible, just like her, too. Anyone would be able to take advantage of me. That's what *gullible* meant. She was feeding the guppies we kept in a bowl on the mantel because if it was left up to us, those suckers would have been belly up weeks ago. I didn't like the guppies because when they had babies, they swallowed them whole. I swallowed everyone's story whole, Merle said. Hook, line, and sinker. A sucker, that's what I was, that's what my mother was, a sucker for any sob story she heard. Not Merle. No one got a foot in the door with her. No one pulled the wool over her eyes.

I didn't care what Merle said, I believed everything my father said. And everything my mother said, too, especially the piano story, which I told to Joan the next day when her leg itched so much that instead of sucking her two fingers, she bit them so hard that it looked like she was wearing red rings on each finger.

"This is the piano story," I said as I moved around David's room, straightening the bed, making hospital corners the way my mother had taught me. It was sort of like diapering Kevin. I filled the pitcher that was as white as Merle's throat with cold water and brought Joan our pillows, mine and Em's that we'd cooled off for her in the basement all during the day.

What had made me think of the story was seeing Merle lying

down on the sofa with the wet dishtowel on her head while our mother continued getting the good, long rest she needed in the nuthouse. The dishtowel was white with six red stripes each the width of a finger.

"Our mothers," I told Joan, "hadn't seen one another for one whole year." This was when my mother had been sent to live with her father and his new wife in Chicago.

"And the new wife hated your mother's guts, right?" Joan said. She was mad about her eyelashes. She was missing them, but I'd grown used to how she looked, and she looked very strange and beautiful to me. The puncture wound had closed but left the black star on her cheek.

"No," I said, settling in beside her. "Her father hated her guts."

"Big deal," said Joan. She was picking at her cast. She had already gotten my wooden ruler stuck inside it when she was using it to reach an itch near her knee.

"My mother was sent to live with your mother at their Aunt Gladdie's house. The Protestant side of the family. Gladdie was the one who was married to Ira. Joan made her hand into the shape of a claw and inched it toward me.

"They had to sleep in an attic. On a cot in the attic. That attic was freezing in the winter and suffocating in the summer."

"When was your mother there?" Joan wanted to know. "Summer or winter?"

I didn't know. My mother said she would have gladly slept in hell if it meant she could be with Merle.

"Summer," I guessed. It was Merle's job to do the dishes. It was my mother's job to dust the furniture, but never the piano. It was Ira's pride and joy.

"He couldn't play the piano the way his hand was," Joan said. She had started sucking her fingers again.

"He could play the piano very well," I said, using the exact words my mother had when she told us the story.

My mother was warned not to touch the piano. She could touch anything else but not the piano. And she didn't remember touching it. But there were fingerprints on the wooden lid that covered the keys. Eight fingerprints, each the size and width of my mother's fingers. Gladdie measured them after she'd brought both girls into the room. She slapped my mother across the face, not because of the prints on the piano, but because she had lied.

"And your mother went berserk," I told Joan. She went at Gladdie as if she meant to kill her. Ira had to pull your mother off Gladdie, but by then her milk had dried in her breasts and she couldn't nurse their baby. So your mother and my mother had to leave. It was the red stripes on my mother's face that made Merle turn so ugly. She would have killed anyone who touched my mother, I reminded Joan. Then I waited for my favorite part.

"It was because they meant the world to each other."

"Where did they go?" Joan wanted to know.

"Your mother went to the Catholic relatives and my mother went to the Protestants. We could have been Protestant," I said, thinking of how this would have doomed us, how we would not be able to ascend to heaven. But our mother went to a Protestant service once and the minister was making fun of Catholics because we worshiped false idols. He didn't understand about the saints, so she changed her mind. That's why we were Catholic. If we passed the Protestant Church when services were letting out, my mother would shake her head at the parishioners and whisper, *There but for the grace of God go you or*

I. When she said this, I truly felt sorry for them.

"What other stories did your mother tell you?" Joan wanted to know. They were all there, suddenly, right inside my head.

Once a stranger had come to the door and she made us all get up and out of bed and stand, sleeping on our feet, in the kitchen until the man left. Even though not one of us remembered that this had happened, my mother would never be able to forgive herself for it.

My mother's aunt Emma's hair turned white and fell out overnight the day she learned her son had been killed in the war, I told Joan. Belle's hair turned white because she couldn't marry the man she loved. She'd gone off raving into the night once and her brothers were sent to find her, and thank God they had because when they did, she was lying next to the railroad track with her head on the rail, her hair white as snow.

Joan yawned. I knew she was getting bored. My mother knew a man who sat on a bedspring and died just at the moment when he had everything to live for, I went on.

"Like what?" Joan asked. A new job, a beautiful wife, a new home. It was on my mind to throw in a horse for Joan's sake, but I didn't want to remind her of her own sadness. She was fingering the silver heart that Harold Birdseye had given her. She kept it under the mattress most of the time so Merle wouldn't see it and think she'd stolen it. Or that I had. Show me a liar and I'll show you a thief, Merle said to me whenever she caught me making something up. Joan had let me hold the necklace. The heat from her entire body seemed gathered in that heart.

"He was on his honeymoon," I told Joan.

"Who?"

"The man who died just when he had everything to live for."

"How did he die?"

"The bedspring snapped and burst his rectum." We couldn't help it, we had to laugh. Both of us.

"You're making that up," Joan said. I was.

"My mother had a silver ring from her mother," I told Joan handing her back her necklace. Belle gave it to her when she graduated eighth grade. It was the only keepsake she had of her mother's. Belle warned her to take good care of it and my mother had. She even took it off when she washed her hands so she wouldn't get soap on the stone. The stone was a sapphire, my mother said.

"What's a sapphire?" Joan wanted to know. I said it was a precious gem that was orangish red, the wild color of our grandmother's hair.

The sapphire ring disappeared. My mother remembered with a sinking heart that she'd left it on the sink back. That was the last place she saw it. She went to Belle and asked her if she'd taken it. Belle said no. But my mother never believed her.

Joan scowled. "If Merle lays a hand on this I'll break her neck." Then she slid the necklace back under the mattress.

Joan had a story of her own to tell. She had touched a man's pecker once. She hadn't wanted to do it but the man twisted her arm and made her. I assumed that this had happened in the Bronx. But it had not. It had happened when she was walking home from school right here in Four Corners. The man had dragged her into his car and made her touch it. She'd never tell me who it was, never tell anyone, actually. I thought about all the men we knew, the old men at Moe's store. Mr. Moe himself. That one of them would drag Joan into his car was unimaginable to me. I could hardly believe that they had privates they wanted touched and that they'd twist an arm to get this done.

"Mr. Moe?" I guessed him, but Joan said I wasn't even close. I was glad for this news. Mr. Yetter? Mr. Zook? Joan couldn't tell me because we both know that I couldn't keep secrets. I had kept a secret, I said in my own defense.

"Which one?" Joan asked. I almost told her about the man at the movies, but I realized the trick in time. If I told her it would be further proof that I couldn't keep a secret. I told her I couldn't tell. She said too bad, she'd just then made up her mind to tell me who it was. I hated Joan right then.

In the afternoon Eddie Birdseye stopped by to see the patient, he said. Joan did not want to see him and pretended to be asleep, but Merle sent him up anyway. Eddie had brought Joan a box of chocolates, a Whitman Sampler, in a yellow box, stitched round the edges in the same cross stitch my mother used on our dresses.

Joan's face reddened when Eddie stuck his head in the room. She'd pulled the covers up around her neck. Eddie sat down by her and said he wanted to sign her cast. He wanted me to go downstairs and get him a pen. Joan shook her head. She wouldn't let Eddie write on it even if he had saved the day with Kevin's measles. I knew I would have, he could have signed his name on me anywhere.

"Aren't you going to offer anyone a candy," Merle teased. She'd come up behind us and stood leaning against the door. For some reason Eddie jumped up from the chair as though he was afraid he'd done something wrong. With Merle you could never tell.

Joan didn't look like she wanted to share the candy. I knew that much for sure, but she took the cellophane off, lifted the top off. It came away reluctantly, as reluctantly as the act of sharing came to her. She was about to remove the quilted white lining from the chocolates themselves when Eddie said no. No, the candies were hers alone. She was the one who deserved them. And he was making her a promise. As soon as she got the cast off her leg, Eddie was going to teach her how to ride Shadow. Merle smiled for Joan. She offered Eddie a beer. A beer sounded good, he said. Where's the old man? Over to Syracuse. Syracuse? What's in Syracuse?

"Ukuleles," Merle said heading down the steps. "He's taking his in to be re-strung."

"What's with her eyes?" Eddie asked. He sounded worried.

"Whose? Rainey's? Watch her, she doesn't miss a trick."

"Your daughter's. Her eyelashes. They're gone." His words trailed down the stairs, one step at a time behind Merle, but her answer was lost to us. We heard her once more quite clearly as she came around the corner into the kitchen and grabbed two beers.

"What does a woman have to do to get a box of chocolates out of you?"

"Plenty," Eddie said. I don't know why but at that moment I got the chills.

"She's asking for it," said Joan, sliding the box of candy under the bed, but even so the smell of candy lingered in that room all day.

Toward evening, Dr. Maybee came to check on the swelling in Joan's leg and to give her something for pain. Merle said Dr. Maybee ought to write her a prescription too. We were such a pain in her ass. That's what she told us. She told Dr. Maybee that we were a pain in her neck and that that was moving it way up. A smile was the only thing he gave her. It seemed that was enough for Merle. She smiled back. Rubbed her arms. She wanted to know when Joan could go back to school. Dr. Maybee thought in another week, though the leg would have to be elevated. Kevin was coming along fine. All they were waiting for was for him to be able to hold down solids for twenty-four hours. If no one else got the measles, we'd be off quarantine in three days.

No one else dared. Within a week we were all back to school including Joan, who tried everything to avoid this. But Merle didn't care. Not only were we going to school, but Joan was as well even with her leg. She was going to school if Merle had to put her on her back and carry her there herself.

Uncle couldn't drive her. He was up early to scour the country looking for abandoned houses and barns and whatever furniture was left behind and salvageable. Sometimes he was gone for days. He'd transformed the vegetable stand into a used furniture stand for the winter. My father couldn't drive anybody anywhere because he was on call. If the opportunity arose, he'd go to work. He worked days and nights whenever he could because of the money situation. We weren't poor, no, far from it. My father wouldn't want anyone to think that, least of all his children. Things were tight. We were in a bit of a financial bind. Whenever my father said this, I looked at Joan's white figure skates, their sharp blades that ended in serrated tips, and imagined slicing the bind we were in wide open. We weren't too poor to go to school as Merle had often been. She'd had to leave school after eighth grade and get a job. Joan was in eighth grade herself. She said she'd be happy to leave right then but Merle was determined to find a way to get her there.

We didn't know what Merle did during the day. We didn't think that Toby and Kevin could be that much work. Usually she just propped Kevin's bottle. And if Toby was hungry, she'd scrape some of her breakfast or lunch onto his plate. By the time we came home from school, she handed Kevin over to me and Toby to Emily. Uncle said Merle lolled around all day long. Dolled herself up. Oh, she was a great one to complain about how hard she worked, but he never had clean clothes to wear. And try and get a decent meal out of her. I'm no cook,

Merle would admit. Somehow she managed to turn this around to a plus. She had her hands full, but she still liked to have her days free, which meant we couldn't stay home. Not even if we came down with typhoid, cholera, or polio. And that included Joan. She was going to school whether she liked it or not. She was going to school if Merle had to put her in Kevin's carriage and push her there.

I thought that maybe Harold Birdseye could ride Joan to school on Shadow. I offered this idea to Joan. Instead of punching me, she sat staring out the window at the barn. I knew she longed for another ride on his horse. But the snow was too deep, and it was bitterly cold and besides it would be weeks before she'd be able to use her leg.

It was Eddie Birdseye who saved the day again. The man was a saint, my father said. He didn't know what we'd do without him. He offered to drive Joan because he felt responsible for what had happened to her. Uncle had thought about suing him. His daughter might turn out to be a cripple. They might be stuck with her the rest of their lives. He'd like to get his hands on some of Birdseye's money. He was sure he'd cleaned up after the fire. But since Joan's accident happened on our property, we'd be liable, my father said, and we didn't have insurance. Still, Uncle said, he'd like to have Birdseye's luck. Then you'd have to take his loss, my father said. Uncle seemed to think this over for a minute, a dead wife, a scarred son. Merle shot him a look, her cigarette butts lying like spent bullets in the saucer under her cup. He'd do anything to avoid a hard day's work. We all knew that.

"Two can play that game as well as one," Merle said. He'd better think twice about it and sleep with his eyes open, Merle said. Uncle laughed, tried to nuzzle Merle's neck before he left, but she shrugged him away. Once she was mad she'd take her damn sweet time getting over it.

"Is this any kind of send-off for a loving husband?" he appealed to us. But we knew better than to side with him. He should consider himself lucky she wasn't sending him off in a casket, Merle said.

We were all up early the next morning waiting for our ride. When my father saw us, dressed and ready to go, he wondered why we were so anxious to get to school. We reminded him of the ride we were getting. But he shook his head. We weren't getting the ride. Joan was. Eddie only had the pickup truck, and our father wouldn't hear of us riding in the back of it. Good Lord, that's all he'd need, one of us to go flying if Eddie hit a bump. That's all he needed, another broken leg in the house. We could all squeeze in the front, Em said, we'd done it before. But with Joan's leg in a cast there wasn't room. No, we'd have to walk. We'd have to walk past Harold Birdseye's house without Joan to protect us and risk more than broken bones.

But danger didn't come from that quarter anymore. Danger came from Wayne. He'd always been mean to Joan, but she'd learned how to stay away from him. She never walked into the barn or the shed or his room without checking in case he was lurking inside, ready to pull her in. When they lived in the Bronx he had made her play strip poker, she told me. He'd held a saw to her neck out in the woods and made her take her clothes off and dance. And he would have let her drown in the river. I remembered that, didn't I? I did. She doubted that he'd ever hurt me or Em because we weren't his sisters. If he did, I was to tell her right away. She'd pay him back, she'd get even with him if it was the last thing she did. I didn't see how since she was so much smaller than him, but I reminded myself of how she had brought Harold Birdseye down.

After Joan broke her leg what I hoped for was that somehow Wayne would die. This was a sin I'd have to put on the list I was keeping as a record before I received Communion. Em said she didn't know if I'd be able to receive absolution because I wasn't sorry for it. I wasn't. I intended to tell Father Leary the whole story. How Joan had broken her leg and was sleeping in David's bed the next night and Wayne had come up the stairs and into the room with a glass of water. I thought it was in case she got thirsty in the middle of the night, but instead Wayne threw it in her face. Joan was so startled awake that she almost leapt from the bed, broken bones and all. I was as startled as Joan and just as helpless to do anything about it. It would only make it worse if we told. Despite Merle's weekly recitation of "A Justice Story," we'd seen very little of it in our own lives.

But the next night the sheriff came to our house, and I believed for a moment that justice would finally be served, that Wayne would be locked up for good. The sheriff had come to speak with Merle and Uncle about him. There had been a complaint about Wayne peeking in windows. One of Harry Hess's daughters had seen him in the field outside her bedroom a few nights before, and now Mrs. Zook had caught him looking in hers just about an hour ago. Could the sheriff speak to Wayne? He could. But Wayne was nowhere to be found. This was the country, the sheriff said. At night men came to their doors with guns. They'd better speak to their son. It may be all in innocence, a lonely kid, wandering around at night, but he could get hurt.

He could get his goddamned head blown off, was more like it, Merle said, when Wayne came home. She wanted us all there to hear what he'd done. Maybe it would put some shame in him. What did he think he was doing slinking around at night like some frigging night crawler? Jesus Christ Almighty. His father needed to have a talk with that boy. "Treat all girls like your sister, lad, and don't smoke until you're eighteen," Uncle advised. Merle was so mad she blew a stream of smoke straight at Uncle. Then she turned on Wayne.

"Well, let me tell you, Buster, if I catch you sneaking out again, I'll put you in reform school. You can bet your ass I will," Merle warned. To make sure he didn't sneak out at night, Merle put a padlock on the summer kitchen door. Now if he wanted to go out, he'd have to come through the main kitchen and use the back door, and that door was right next to Merle's bedroom. She bragged that she was a light sleeper, but in truth I was. I'd roamed the house at night, both asleep and awake, and she had never once heard me. Nor did she hear Wayne a week later when he climbed out of his bedroom window. I watched him walk across the silvered fields in my father's navy pea coat and skullcap. The moon was crisp and quartered and as distinct as Wayne was indistinct. Within seconds he'd become a shadow, then less than a shadow. He seemed to vanish completely. This was exactly what I was praying for. I stayed by the window waiting for the shot I was sure I would hear. Across the hall Joan slept soundly. She was sucking her middle fingers. I knew that sound got on her family's nerves, but because doing it made her feel better, it didn't bother me at all. She sucked her fingers steadily until she fell deeper into sleep. When she did, her mouth stopped moving and her fingers slowly slid from her mouth. Every time this happened, she would suddenly startle awake and bring her fingers to her mouth and start sucking all over again. Each time she did, I'd think about the night Wayne threw the glass of water in her face.

The shot I was waiting for never came. Or it had come and I missed it. I'd fallen asleep waiting for it. When I awoke I didn't know what time it was, or even if Wayne had come back. I slid out of bed and crept down the stairwell. Above our kitchen door Jesus glowed in the dark. The lamp we left on for my father illuminated the clock. It was nearly one in the morning. The bar would close, and my father would be home soon. I went to the door to look for him. Just knowing my father was home helped me sleep. Across the field I heard some dogs start up, Zook's hunting dogs, tied to their houses, mad at something. Wayne for all I knew. I pictured him lying dead in the field outside the Zooks' bedroom. Or he could be sound asleep behind the closed door. The road was empty. My fervent wish was that Wayne's bedroom would be too. I put my hand on the doorknob. It was made of porcelain, the same dark brown color of my eyes. I wished it was a huge eye that could see if Wayne was in there or not. The knob was loose in its fitting and jiggled. Wayne could be on the other side of the door just waiting for me to push it open. Then what? He'd wring my neck. He'd cut my throat with a saw. It wasn't worth the risk. I slowly released my grip on the knob and on my breathing. Simultaneously, it was as though all the night sounds released theirs as well. I heard again the distant outrage of the dogs as something eluded them, I heard the wind slip through the frozen branches of the trees, and the muffled *whomp* as the snow shifted, then slid from the roof to the wooden doors that led to the cellar way. That sound reminded me of my father's footsteps on the porch, and so I went once more to the window, saw that there was some light at the top of the rise that might mean his car. That's when I saw Wayne. Wayne who'd been warned what would happen if Merle caught him. Reform school, where the teachers were former drill sergeants and the inmates were forced to stand at attention for twelve hours at a time without relieving themselves, and if they fainted or peed, or threw up, well, it was solitary confinement in a dirt hole with rats for friends. Some of those boys were never seen again.

It was as though I'd spent my whole life rehearsing for just this one moment. Without hesitation or thought, I slipped into Wayne's room and latched the window. Let him freeze to death, I thought, the idea of it, the warmth of it, filled my entire body.

I stepped back into the stairwell, slammed the door so hard the plaster sifted down on me. By the time it settled, Merle was out of bed, cursing that everyone better be in theirs or there'd be hell to pay. And there was. Merle took her shoe and whacked the hell out of Wayne. She hit him so hard and so long that her shoe collapsed. Then she threw the shoe at him and anything else she got her hands around. She beat him right into his room. He tried to cover his face with his hands but she got him good. She'd have slapped the eyes from his face if she could have.

My father didn't understand why Wayne did what he did but he knew it had to stop. Good God, he had to live in this town, and he wanted to be able to hold his head up in it. What Wayne did was a reflection on all of us. I didn't see how it could be a reflection on me, but I kept quiet. My father's form of punishment was different from Merle's. We all made mistakes. These were opportunities to learn a lesson. Worse than the crime itself was not owning up to it. Owning up to it cured it, as far as my father was concerned. The next morning he took Wayne to the Hesses and the Zooks and made him apologize for what he'd done. And let that be the end of it. But of course it wasn't.

There was no way that Wayne could have known I locked the window, yet he did. He knew it just by looking at me. And he watched me all the time. This made me sick to my stomach. I knew that it was only a matter of time before he sought me out. In the first days I'd thought about owning up to what I'd done as he had been forced to do. It had worked for Wayne. He hadn't had to go to reform school, after all. But I remembered how he'd snapped the twig in two. I knew that he didn't have to do very much to cause pain. I'd seen him bend

Joan's finger backward until she went down on her knees. He could break my fingers, the two that turned the window latch. But after the first week he seemed to forget about it. He went back to his old ways. He stayed in his room working on a model airplane. The wings were made of paper as thin as moth wings. He had several models hanging from the ceiling. The one that he was working on was a Stuka, a two-seated dive-bomber. He leaned over it with infinite care, the strips of balsam as delicate as bird bones. He worked with a razor, a small knife, and a pot of glue. If we touched his workspace, if we even came into his room, he'd cut us to ribbons. He had it booby-trapped so he'd be able to tell. I had no intentions of going into his room ever again. I trembled like the planes tacked to the ceiling every time Wayne opened the door.

Before Joan had come to stay with us, I really had no friends. David and Emily had each other and often they excluded me. I hadn't known about this until my mother told me. She said they shut me out. They'd done this since the day I was born. And she didn't like this. It actually broke her heart. Sometimes she forced my brother and sister to include me, but more often than not they left me alone. I didn't mind. I liked to be alone. Toby and Kevin seemed one continuous baby to me and weren't much company. But since Joan had come to stay with us, she sometimes sought me out. Emily was too much of a goody-goody, she said. I was not. In order to live up to this, I'd picked up some of Joan's traits. In fact, I'd begun to steal candy for myself. Sometimes I showed off and said Jesus Christ Almighty. Joan loved this, loved anything I did that was forbidden. So I didn't think that she would mind if I took her figure skates and tried them out without asking. I knew quite well that had I asked she'd have said no. I took the skates one day right after I'd gotten home from school. It was a day that Eddie was going to be late bringing Joan home as he had to do a shoot in Keansburg. Joan would have to stay after school and wait for him. She could use the time to make up work she'd missed when she was sick. God only knew how long that would take, Merle said.

But I knew I wouldn't have much time. The days were short and mostly overcast. What little light came into the mornings gave up without a fight right after lunch. An hour after I got home from school dusk had settled in, and deer dotted the fields just as the first stars did the sky. So I'd have to act quickly. Any hesitation and Merle would have wondered what the hell I needed in the cellar that was so important. For Chrissakes the rats were just waiting for any opportunity to come inside and warm their frozen asses, and here I was opening the door and extending them a goddamn invitation.

I bunched newspaper in my pockets, lifted the skates from the nail in the cellar way and left through the rotted cellar doors. I headed out across the field to the Sucker Hole. I stayed along the edge of the woods in case Merle looked out the window. I had the feeling she was watching me anyway and wanted to turn around to check, but turning around might have revealed the skates. In anticipation of this I went farther into the woods. The snow was undisturbed and quite deep. Each time my foot broke through the crust of snow I sank to my knees. Long before I reached the pond I was already cold. I could see people on the ice, see that someone had a fire going. I could see Jay standing with his arms on his hips watching the skaters. He was too afraid to try it, but he seemed compelled to watch. He reminded me of our old hound dog, Buster, and the way he paced along the edge of the lake and worried furiously all the while we swam, then tried to lick us dry when we came out. Buster was not a swimmer, not like Clover, but he was a very good watchdog. My mother said that up until the day he died, he wouldn't leave our sides for a minute. She always felt better when he was outside with us.

I sat on one of the logs and pulled off my boots and slipped on the skates. Even with the newspaper stuffed in the toes they were much too big for me. The sheer size of them convinced me that they'd hold me up. But they didn't. My ankles flopped almost immediately. I thought of Joan, how once she put the skates on, she'd seemed in command of them, but this was not the case with me. I wobbled upright again but didn't chance a step. Below me, under the ice, bubbles staggered toward the surface. As they'd risen, they froze in place. There were deep splits in the ice. The ice was as hard as our dinner plates, and what lay below its surface seemed as indistinct as the faded pattern on each dish. A blue hair ribbon frozen in place could have been six inches below my feet or sixty. What's the difference? I remembered Jay saying. I understood, then, what he had meant. I watched the older girls, the ones with Norwegian sweaters and flared skating skirts, float across the ice. The older boys didn't skate, instead they socked each other in the shoulders, smoked cigarettes, threw snowballs at each other or at the girls. Jay beamed at them.

All the while I tried my best to stay up. I saw another girl, my age, learning to skate. She leaned forward and waved her arms as though they were the heavy wings of the great blue herons I sometimes surprised near the streambed across from our house. I half expected her to fly away, she seemed that determined. My ankles burned. I wondered how the older girls did it, how they managed to perfect what seemed to be the miracle of balancing. Even Joan had been able to do it after only an hour. I risked a step and fell. Suddenly the ice popped, the girls screamed. They were like a flock of noisy birds, as easily disturbed as they were settled. Before long they skated back over to the log, warmed themselves by the fire. I was reluctant to leave but I knew from long habit I was to be home before dark.

Instead of going straight across the field, I retraced my steps through the woods, thinking that I'd made it to the pond without detection and this might guarantee I'd make it home the same way. I'd tied the skates together and slung them around my neck the way the older girls had. As I walked, the blades sounded like the noise my father made when he sharpened our knives. I was afraid of knives and the sound made me edgy. I was also afraid that Merle would know what I'd done. I was never allowed to skate without my sister or brother. And the cold made me afraid too. My skin rose up in goose bumps. I tensed my body, trying to gather my own skin around me for warmth. I could see my house in the distance, the smoke curling from the chimney like a cat's tail. The Meekles, whose farm was across from the Yetters, had lost a cat because of the freeze. She climbed up under the hood of the car to stay warm, and when Mr. Meekles started the car in the morning she was caught in the fan. I wondered why she hadn't heard Mr. Meekles open the car door. Or maybe she had, but it was too late. She was cut in two by the fan. In my mind, when I thought about this, there was no blood. She was simply cut in half like the woman in "A Justice Story" that Merle had read to us two days before. The husband claimed it was an accident. He said he was an amateur magician and he was just trying to imitate Houdini. Merle said if that was the case he shouldn't have any problem getting out of the tight squeeze he now found himself in. It was a two-part story, and we'd have to wait until Sunday to see if he did.

The woods, as the evening light bore down on them, seemed a field of black bones. The trees that had fallen haphazardly, one bringing another down, scissored the snow. Everything I looked at seemed a sharp angle. Shards of ice stabbed from branches. The ice crust broke like glass under my feet. I had such a sense of dread, and such a sense of anticipation of harm, that when Wayne finally grabbed me I wasn't really surprised. Whether he followed me there or was taking a short-cut, or was peeking at the girls as they skated by, I didn't know. "You little bitch," he said. "Now you're going to get it." All I could think of was that he was going to take one of the skates and cut me in two. There was a pile of deadfall that looked like a puzzle of trees, like the random spill of pick-up sticks that we sometimes played at night. Wayne dragged me over behind them. I wanted to scream. I could hear the older girls screaming in the distance as though screaming in my stead, but Wayne had his hand over my mouth. I don't think my heart was beating all this while because it shocked me when I did feel it jump in·my chest. With one hand Wayne unlaced the figure skates and took the laces and tied my hands together behind my back, then tied me to a tree. Somehow this seemed just to me. I had wished that he would freeze to death that night I locked him out, and now my pun-ishment was what I hoped for him.

"I'm rubber, you're glue, whatever you wish for me bounces off me and sticks to you," was what Joan said if anyone wished she was dead.

When Wayne was finished tying me up he stared at me for a minute. Then he started fumbling with his fly. I thought he was going to pee on me. He might have except that he heard something behind him. The noise surprised him. He turned and picked up the skates, threw them as far as he could and headed away from our house, which I could just then see beyond the woods. I watched as the sun fell behind it and as the sun's ray ignited each window. I knew that no one was going to come look for me. Merle wouldn't miss me for hours. Joan couldn't try to find me. Em would have her face buried in a book.

David wasn't home and neither was my father. Freezing to death was just like going to sleep, that's what David said. One minute you felt cold, and then the next minute you felt sleepy, you felt like lying down and just going to sleep. The snow became a pillow and then a blanket, and then a grave. I was wide-awake and was glad for it. Later, as the sun set, and one of the older boys walked by not more than fifty feet away, I didn't call out for help. Instead I looked away, hoping he wouldn't see me standing there, the sockets of my arms burning, my wrists rubbed raw.

I stood and watched the night come straight for me. I didn't cry. I didn't blink. I stared straight ahead. All around me the fields were silent. My back was to the pond but I knew it was empty. The skaters had all gone home. The Zooks' flock of sheep was in the barn for the night. Even the deer didn't come to feed. The snow on the ground seemed as devoid of life as the silence surrounding me. Not a single star shone in the sky. I stood. I stood until my legs felt as though they'd already walked away from my body and left my arms frozen to the tree. I stood still and waited. Finally, in the sky above my head, the moon came out, a quarter moon, the same shape it had been the night I'd locked Wayne out two weeks before. Then it had been the first quarter. Now it was the final quarter and enclosed what I had done to Wayne in a pair of perfect parentheses. Bursts of cloud shot across the sky. Though the sun had disappeared and no trace of it remained in the sky, its distant glow illuminated the moon, cupped it, like my mother's palm often did my cheek. I felt her presence in me for the first time in weeks. I wondered if I was ever going to see her again. I tried to turn my head toward the pond. From the corner of my eye I saw fire and ice but nothing else. I no longer had any sensation of pain in my fingers and toes, though my face still burned. My lips split as suddenly as the ice on the pond had. I could taste the blood as it leaked into my mouth. A car pulled off the hard road and made its way past the Birdseyes' and rose above the ridge before our house, then was lost from sight. It came into view again, but was far, far from where I stood. I closed my eyes, felt the wind pick up, heard something rustle near me. When I opened my eyes I saw two pins of light. I thought they were the eyes of something fierce. A bobcat, or a wolf. But then I could hear footsteps.

At first I was frightened that it was Wayne coming back to kill me, but then I saw another pin of light, and another. It was as though the sky had tipped and all the stars were falling to the ground as the men rushed to me. I heard someone call my name. *Rainey*. A chorus of *Raineys*, my brother's voice. Eddie Birdseye's, Mr. Zook, some of the Yetters' sons. The noise that came from me wasn't my voice. I sounded like one of the Zooks' dogs. I was afraid that the men wouldn't know it was me. But they did, the men came running through the snow, the lights zigzagging wildly. The one who found me first was Eddie Birdseye. He tried to lift me up, tried to wrap me in his jacket, until he saw that I was tied there. Then he took his penknife from his pocket and cut the laces. My father had thrown his flashlight down and his glasses. He stood pounding the tree. He said he would find and kill the bastard who had done this to me. Just give him the name, and he'd rip the arms from his body. My father was trembling too, as I was, my arms going into spasm. Then he was lifting me and holding me against his chest. Jesus Christ Almighty, what was the world coming to? What kind of person would do such a horrible thing as this? Who did this, my father demanded, the men then standing all around, shaking their heads. But the only name that came from my mouth was my own. *Rainey,* I said, repeating my name over and over again.

CHAPTER THIRTEEN

I couldn't get warm despite the bath that Merle had drawn for me. The tips of my fingers and toes had some mild frostbite but Dr. Maybee thought there'd be no permanent damage to them. But he wasn't sure about the damage to my psyche. He'd seen some awful things in his career, but this was one of the cruelest acts he could remember. He didn't want anyone asking me questions just yet. I was in shock. Besides, I might have my mother's temperament. When I was ready to talk about it, I would. Isn't that right? I nodded though I knew I would never be able to talk about it again. What I needed was rest. Dr. Maybee would leave a sedative with my father if I couldn't fall asleep. But Joan had no intention of letting me sleep until I told her who did it. She sat beside me on the bed. She promised that she wouldn't be mad about the skates if I told her who it was. But I couldn't bring myself to say his name. I couldn't bring his name into the room because I thought he might follow. I shook my head.

Merle said the goddamn country was more dangerous than the city. Her voice rose on the waves of heat that wafted through the grate. It can be, the sheriff admitted. I heard the *skutch* of his chair each time he shifted his weight. He was just glad that Mr. Zook had finally taken his son seriously. Jay was like a little kid. He sometimes told tall tales. But what convinced Zook was that Jay wouldn't stop jabbering about it. He said he saw a fellow grab her and drag her into the woods. That's when he ran for his Dad. He could have told any of the boys at the pond what happened, some of those boys were as strong as their dads and they'd have chased the fellow off. Or scared him off. But Jay only knew to tell his Dad when there was trouble, and that's what he did. Not that Jay would do anything to help, he was afraid of his own shadow.

He didn't know who the fellow was, but he recognized Rainey. Jay might be simple but he wasn't dumb, the sheriff said to Merle. That saved some time. Another hour and he might be coming to our house with different news.

"If anyone can get some answers out of Rainey, it will be me," Merle said. And then she'd take matters into her own hands. She'd kill the son of a bitch with her own two hands. She had a feeling she knew who it was. Harold Birdseye. He gave her the creeps.

"I don't think he has it in him to hurt a kid," the sheriff said.

"He had it in him to throw his puppy against the barn and kill it," Merle shot back. Joan looked at me. I shook my head.

"Well," the sheriff said, "I hope it is someone she knows. I'd hate to think we had a stranger going around snatching little girls."

"Most victims know their attackers," Merle said. She'd learned this from the Justice Stories.

"Isn't that the truth," the sheriff said. After a while Merle came upstairs. She'd made me chamomile tea with honey and milk and tried to spoon it into my mouth. Each time she put the spoon to my mouth she opened hers. But I wouldn't open mine. As much as I wanted to keep Wayne's name a secret, I wanted to blurt it out. My teeth chattered uncontrollably, as though they were as shaky as my resolve. Jesus Christ, Merle swore softly, though more in wonder than anger. She put socks on my hands and feet and stood over me. When I still didn't stop shivering she went and got her chenille robe and wrapped it around me, then she stared down at me, tried to stare the shivers down, as well, but still I trembled. It wasn't the cold anymore that made me. Merle knew this. Though she didn't know of anyone who'd ever died from a case of the shivers, she wasn't going to take any chances. She didn't want me sleeping alone. Joan was going to have to sleep on one side of me, cast and all, and Em on the other. Joan thought she was pretty hot stuff lately so it couldn't hurt.

"Jesus Christ," I heard her say again when she rejoined the sheriff and my father at the kitchen table, "she's scared to death." And I was. My father came in to me then with a small blue pill and a glass of warm milk. He sat down on my bed and told me that if it made me feel better, he'd sleep in David's room across the hall.

I didn't know what Wayne would do when he came home and found me. I didn't think he'd come upstairs and try to kill me. But I knew that he'd want to. Despite this, despite my fear, I fell sound asleep. When I awoke in the morning Merle and the sheriff were still at the table. I thought that the sheriff had stayed all night to protect me, but he hadn't. He'd come back because he wanted to see if I could remember anything about what had happened. What had happened seemed impossible in the light of this day. The kitchen was sunny-side up. That's what my mother used to say when the sun rose and shone directly into the kitchen. Outside, prisms of color glinted off the snow. Inside, sunrays shimmied on the ceiling. Even though it was bitterly cold, the sun on the roof melted the ice. All around water dripped from the icicles hanging from the eaves. A steady drone played on the floorboards of the porch.

Wayne's door was cracked open. To every question the sheriff put to me, I shook my head, no, and I meant it. No, I wouldn't tell, I'd never tell. I could see Wayne's boots slouched in the corner of his room. That's all I needed to see.

Joan was toweling off her skates. The sheriff had retrieved them earlier. He teased Joan about them, about her broken leg. Every time he looked at her the blood rose to her face. And his too. She didn't even need to wear the skates anymore to look grown up, all she had to do was hold them.

But it wasn't just Joan who was hot stuff. I was too. I was a celebrity, Merle said. She hoped I didn't let it go to my head. Two of the Yetters' boys had stopped by with gifts, a kaleidoscope and a magic slate. The Yetters had the farm south of us, next to the Meekles. Merle said it wasn't so much a farm as a parking lot. She'd counted seven vehicles in the yard, and if they were anything like barn cats there'd be dozens more by fall. That's what came of having a house full of males. Mrs. Yetter had had five boys. They all had biblical names: Gideon, Ezekiel, Jonah, Jacob, and Seth. Delivering her sixth son killed her. Merle called him Cain.

Eddie Birdseye had stopped by to see me too. He reached right down for me and picked me up, sat me on his lap, rubbed my chafed wrists with his thumb. I'd had some scare. He knew that. He wanted me to know the scare I'd given him, everybody really. My father was out of his mind with worry. If I didn't want to tell the sheriff who tied me up, I could tell him. Whisper it right in his ear. He'd keep it a secret. I wanted to with all my heart. I looked over at Wayne's door. He was in there all right. I leaned back into Mr. Birdseye and shook my head. What I really wanted was to keep Mr. Birdseye there rubbing my arms. More than that, I wanted to take his long strong arms and knot them right over me, as tightly as Wayne had tied my hands. What would I like him to bring me, he asked, eyeing my gifts. I looked over at Joan. I thought about her Whitman's Sampler, but I knew better than to ask for that. Joan was already mad at me as it was. She didn't like sharing the limelight, according to Merle. She didn't like sharing, period.

The kaleidoscope made me dizzy but it was better than watching Wayne's door. The sheriff said that if I could think of anything to let him know. I thought he meant about what I wanted from Moe's store. But he meant about the man who grabbed me.

Though my lies were often good, I was not a good liar. Something in my face gave me away. I'd tried on several occasions to see what it was. I stood in the mirror and lied. I looked the same as always. But Merle said she could see it in my eyes, the way I rounded them. Wide-eyed and not so innocent. So I tried to squint when I told about the man. He was an old man, I said, and he had a sack with him. I was thinking of the man I'd seen on the road when we'd taken my mother to the nuthouse three months before. He had something in that sack. Something that was struggling about as much as I was with the truth. It wasn't just that I was afraid to tell on Wayne, somehow I knew that I wouldn't be a celebrity if people found out that it was just Wayne.

The sheriff was interested in the sack. But I couldn't think what to say about it. What was inside the sack? Kittens, I thought. I shrugged. I had some power over the sheriff, I could see that. Wayne came out of his room and stood by the sink. The sheriff watched him carefully, the same way that Wayne had watched me. Wayne stared down at the floor.

"I don't want to talk about it anymore."

"Of course you don't, honey. I don't blame you one bit." But he didn't want to see what had happened to me happen to someone else. He'd come back tomorrow to check on me. In the meantime it would-n't hurt if I stayed in the house a few days.

Merle knew I was lying about something. After the sheriff left, she took me into her bedroom and asked me if the man had touched my privates. I could tell her if he had. I said he hadn't. "Did he make you touch his privates?" I knew I had to tell her something so that she'd let me go. I nodded my head.

"I thought so," Merle said, slamming down her pack of Pall Malls, satisfied she'd gotten the truth out of me.

As soon as I could do it without detection, I went upstairs and pulled out the sheet of yellow paper where I listed my sins and added three lies. Another two and I could put a slash through the set.

Wayne didn't try to kill me again, but he did try peeking in windows once more and was caught by Mr. Hess. This time Mr. Hess came to our house with Wayne. Merle refused to let either one of them in the house. She stood outside on the porch smoking her cigarette. Don't bring him here, she said. Take him to jail. I stared at Wayne through the window. He was crying, his face collapsing like soft clay. I was glad that my mother wasn't home because she would have never let anyone take him away. Not one of hers. She would have put her arm around him and brought him into the house. She would have sat with him on her bed and talked to him quietly. She would have said there's good and bad in everybody. She would have said that people who are the hardest to love need love the most. Not Merle. She'd had it with him. She flicked her cigarette into the snow. For a moment it held there, turned the snow orange, then it hissed and went out. When she came back into the kitchen, she tore a beer from the refrigerator, shut off the light, and stood by the sink in the dark. Her silence scared us more than her temper and so we made our way up to our beds. She spent her whole frigging life trying to stay away from perverts and here she'd gone and raised one, that's what she shouted up to us as we gathered in our rooms. She'd murder him if he came in the house.

But Wayne didn't go to jail. Instead, Uncle took him back to their apartment in the Bronx. There was more opportunity for him there my father said. He needed a job, he needed to keep busy. Merle said he'd be busy all right. There were a hell of a lot more windows to peek into there. Uncle would have to stay in the Bronx with Wayne. He needed more opportunity as well. A better market. He'd loaded up his panel truck with broken chairs and scarred tables, and Wayne, of course, who sat hunched over in the front seat, the acne that would gouge his face just beginning to spread. Uncle would be back in a month. Maybe by then we'd have our mother back and he'd get his wife back.

Being a celebrity didn't extend beyond a few days. It didn't extend far enough into the future to secure a ride to school in Eddie Birdseye's truck. The answer was no. I was still to walk to school with my brother and sister. There was safety in numbers. Still, when Eddie came for Joan, I liked to sit next to him while he waited for her. So did Merle. From that first morning on, Merle was up and completely dressed, make-up and all, before he arrived. She made him a fresh pot of coffee and arranged her chair so that her knee touched his when she sat down. She touched his hands lightly, said no matter how cold it was they were always warm. Sometimes she put her hand on his thigh as though she couldn't find anywhere else to rest it. When Joan came down the steps, Eddie stood up, helped her on with her coat. I half-expected Merle to grab hers and walk out the door with him. She seemed that ready to leave. As soon as Joan saw Eddie, her face flushed. She'd make a beautiful model, Eddie said. A model for what? A thermometer, Merle snorted, when she saw the red rise in Joan's pale face. Joan never looked directly at Eddie, even when she spoke, either she looked at the ground or to a spot above his shoulder, unlike Merle who couldn't take her eyes from him. Yet, it was clear that Joan was pleased with the effect she had on Eddie Birdseye.

He always carried Joan's books and her lunch bag and ran around to open the door for her, helped her into the cab, slid the crutches out from under her arms and put them in the bed. I knew the truck was heated, and that always made me feel colder walking to school. By the time we got to school, Joan was settled in near the wood stove, her foot propped up on the firewood box, while Mrs. English helped her with the work she missed. When Eddie drove her home, Merle said Joan looked like Cleopatra on the barge. He lifted Joan's crutches from the bed of the truck, set them up for her, and slipped them under her arms.

She was a sweetheart, Eddie told Merle, though of course, Joan never said thank you for the ride or have a nice day. She just hobbled upstairs and lay down on the bed, closed both eyes and sucked her fingers raw. She wouldn't talk to me until late afternoon, when she and the sharp edges of winter softened in the failing light.

I missed my mother most at this time of day. It used to be the time she wanted us near her. She didn't know why it was but every year when Daylight Savings Time ended she was relieved because it meant that nightfall came in earlier. And so did we. By late afternoon we all gathered around her in the kitchen. She knew where we were. Safe at home with her. In the long evenings she read books to us, *David Copperfield, Oliver Twist, Jane Eyre*, all orphans like herself.

They weren't half as interesting as the ones Merle read to us on Sundays. The last one she'd read was called, "The Fatal Secret." It was about a woman whose husband murdered their daughter. The woman kept it a secret all these years. She told her husband she wouldn't tell even if she was put on a rack, even if she was drawn and quartered. And that's exactly what her husband did to her. He put her to the test.

We all had secrets in our house. Secrets thick as the wallpaper that layered our walls. I sometimes confused them with sins and wrote them down. Once they were on paper, it seemed they were out, and so I had to scribble over them and hold the paper up to the light to make sure they couldn't be read. But mostly I guarded mine carefully.

I helped Joan guard hers. Harold Birdseye left notes for her, which I was forced to fetch but forbidden to read. He'd given her a bracelet that matched the necklace. Sometimes he left money for her as well. Whenever I brought these gifts to her, she bent forward, her silver hair parted, opened, then whisked closed over each offering like the transparent lining of the velvet drapes at the movie theater. Then I would feel the hair on my neck rise, remembering the man in the back row.

Even though I wasn't allowed to touch her gifts except when I brought them to her, Joan said I should be grateful for them. If it wasn't for her, Harold would have probably shot us by now. Or turned Shadow on us. She was doing this for our sake. Emily's and mine, so when she left Four Corners he'd never bother us again. I hadn't thought about Joan leaving because I couldn't imagine my life without her. I could picture Merle walking out the door, but not Joan. I looked at her carefully. She was looking out the window toward the Zooks' pond, the Sucker Hole, which she now called the Shit Hole because just the week before she broke her leg, she'd gone through the ice there. Joan saw me looking at the silver necklace and the bracelet and slid them under the mattress. She knew I wouldn't dare take her things, but she was afraid she might relent and give me something as a bribe. If she did, then she wouldn't be able to take it back. Once something was taken from her, she'd never take it back. Even advice. So, even though she advised me never to take presents from Harold for myself, she wouldn't listen when I told her not to take anything else Harold offered.

Despite their generosity, Joan never seemed pleased with what Harold or his father gave her until the morning Eddie came and said that his son was going into the hospital for a skin graft, and he wanted to know if Joan would take care of Shadow's leg for him. He'd sliced his right leg on some barbed wire and needed to have salve put on it twice a day. It would have been easy enough for Eddie to do it, but Harold had asked specifically for Joan. This was a real privilege, Eddie said, smiling down at Joan. He was staring at the top of her head, as though he could read her thoughts.

Harold didn't trust Shadow's care to anyone. But he was going to be laid up for a few weeks. The doctors were going to try and rebuild his upper lip. Eddie was too much of a gentleman to say where they were going to take that skin from, but it was a sensitive spot. Probably the arch of his foot, I thought, the place I couldn't stand to be touched.

So, if it was all right with her mother, Eddie was wondering if Joan could tend to Shadow's leg. He was surprised how good she was with the horse. Shadow didn't let too many people close to him. Merle shrugged, it was fine with her. There wasn't anything that he asked for that she wouldn't give him. He ought to know that by now. Eddie smiled, tipped his hat, and went outside.

Joan followed him out to the barn so that she could see what she had to do. Did Joan think she could manage what with the crutches and all? Yes, she did, she said, and rubbed her hand against the horse's neck. "Don't try and ride him," Eddie said, reaching over and giving Joan a squeeze. "Promise me that?" Joan nodded. Then she smiled. I smiled too. Eddie looked over at me and winked.

Joan wouldn't let anyone near Shadow. She wouldn't even let me in the barn with her. I had to stand outside the door and look in. She said I might spook the horse, that Shadow could smell my fear and that might cause him to rear again. I couldn't argue with this. We both knew I was afraid of the horse.

Joan didn't just take care of Shadow's leg. She currycombed him, sliding her hands into the handles on the brushes as though they were mittens. She brought him oats and treats from the kitchen, and he took them in that same thankless way Joan took the things Harold had given her. Sometimes when Joan held an apple to Shadow's mouth, his lips would curl up, close around her hand and I would think of Harold, lying in some hospital bed, with a worm of skin inching its way across his lip. But if Joan ever thought of him she never mentioned it.

February, the shortest month, seemed to have the shortest days. They were hauled off before we used them up. For a week we were up to our necks in snow, then after everything that could had fallen from the sky, the night came on. Sitting in our beds we'd be up to our necks in stars. David said that the days were getting longer, but they felt as short as Merle's temper. She was edgy, restless again. She hated February with a passion. News came that our mother was getting better. It was about time, Merle said. She had her craw filled to here with us. We were choking the living life out of her. We never went to the nuthouse to see our mother. Our father didn't like us to see her there. Still, I remembered the nuthouse quite clearly, the long steps, the dark windows. Whenever my father said our mother was making progress, I saw her white feet take one step closer to us.

When it became certain that our mother was set for a visit in March, Merle decided to clean house. Spring cleaning she called it. She was full of energy. The way my mother cleaned house was stripping beds, turning mattresses, starching curtains, washing windows and polishing them with old newspaper. It meant beating the rugs, washing and waxing the wooden floors then tying rags to our feet and letting us buff them. It meant changing furniture around, rearranging cabinets, putting fresh newspaper on the shelves.

What spring cleaning meant to Merle was getting rid of any article of clothing that she hadn't worn in the last year. It meant throwing out her cotton brassiere and buying a satin one, getting two slips, and a pair of nylons. Taupe, that was the color. I could no sooner hope to learn how to pronounce that word as I could to slip my hand inside one of the legs of the stockings. They came in a box with tissue paper, and Merle put them away at the top of the closet where my own white nylon socks lay wrapped unworn.

Spring meant buying a hat, a cloche, and a pair of slings, open toed. Bright red. All of these articles of clothing cost one dollar if we were ever asked by Uncle, and all of them disappeared into the closet after she modeled them for us. Spring was in Merle's closet just waiting for a chance to make an appearance. Sometimes it was all that I could do to keep from standing in that closet with the door shut surrounded by all that luxury.

Merle was definitely happier. She would generally start smiling at seven o'clock in the morning and keep it up until Eddie arrived an hour later.

When I was in school, I sometimes looked at the clock and when it reached noon I imagined Merle beginning to smile in anticipation of Eddie bringing Joan home three hours later. She would be standing by the door when we got home. She'd open the screen and let us in and although she didn't say anything, it was still amazing to see her open the door to us at all.

One afternoon Eddie was late. By the time he pulled in the driveway she'd had a few beers. He'd had to stop and pick up some enlargements in Keansburg and he couldn't call. We had no phone. He didn't think that Merle would be angry but she was. She told Joan to get the hell inside, upstairs, and never mind about the goddamned horse. We all knew to get inside, outside, or upstairs with Joan. We could hear the exchange of words from our various hideouts.

"Whoa, whoa," Eddie said to Merle. "Slow down." He didn't have to answer to anybody. What about Uncle, Merle wanted to know, Joan's father?

Uncle was the last person in the world Eddie would answer to. Since when did he need Uncle's permission to do anything? If it was going to come to that, that Eddie had to answer to either of them, well, he'd rethink a lot of things.

Merle's voice softened, gave way to that husky laugh. No, Eddie wouldn't stay for a beer. Another time. Ask him another time. Then he left.

We thought we might be in for it, but Merle seemed to have forgotten her anger at Joan. She'd always wanted to be a Rockette. Did we know that? Had she ever told us that? Someone get her a beer, and she'd tell us about her audition at Radio City Music Hall. Merle had come close. Oh, she'd come very close, she had a good voice, but her legs were too short. She'd given them an eyeful, anyway. Something they'd always remember. She could still do a kick. Come here and she'd show us. She had to put her beer down. We went to her. We stood just at the threshold flanking Merle. She put her arms across our shoulders, Em, Joan and I, and then, to our amazement, Merle kicked her leg, the right one, over and over again above her head, as we held her up, or she us. We began to laugh. Intoxicated with this, we all started kicking our legs. Can-can, we said. But Merle wasn't having any of that. It was her show. She alternated her legs, first the right and then the left. But it wasn't the same. She couldn't get the height. She needed the heels. She wobbled into the bedroom and wobbled back out with the red slings, slipped those on and motioned to us again. We came to her. This time she had it. One and two and three, her leg flashing, Kevin mesmerized in the playpen, all of us really astounded, watching as the red sling came free and flew with sure aim over our heads and straight through the windowpane, right into spring for all we knew.

Later, we had to put Merle to bed. We hoped that she wouldn't forget she broke the window. If she did she'd break our goddamn necks. Joan sat in the living room looking at the broken pane. Six over six, that's what my mother called the window design. Six panes over six, all hand blown. Those panes were irreplaceable. We'd retrieved the shoe, wiped it off, and put it back in the closet. David slid the glass from Edmund's picture out of the frame and set it in the window. It was all we could do.

We decided on cocoa, Em and I, remembering our mother's claim that it had amazing properties. David said he'd make it. We let him. He got the powdered chocolate down, added the water and then some sugar, and put it on the stove. When it started to warm, he added some canned milk. Before long we were sitting at the table as we'd seen our parents do, playing cards. War, Memory. Go Fish, for Toby, and later when we got our baby brothers to bed, Poker, Five Card Stud, David near the door, Joan in my father's place, Em and I between the two of them drinking cocoa. Joan polished off her mother's beer. We all looked at her, then shrugged. After what we'd been through, nothing surprised us anymore.

CHAPTER FOURTEEN

Our mother was on the right track, the track that would lead her back to her old self. Back to us. The doctors were trying something new, some medicine that calmed her nerves. She was high-strung it seemed. She was making progress but she could still be derailed. We had to remember that. No loud noises. Nothing sudden. No stories. She didn't need to know about what had happened to me. It would make her feel helpless. She was too protective of us, of anybody she loved. That was part of her problem. Jesus Christ, that's all my father needed was for our mother to lose the ground she had gained. Of course, she needed rest, plenty of rest, plenty of help, too. We couldn't slack off. We'd done a pretty good job so far, and our father was proud of us. If it was up to him, he'd put all our pictures in the newspaper.

If it was up to Merle she'd give us the medicine instead of giving it to our mother. All it was was glorified sleeping pills. They turned her sister into a zombie. My mother's progress consisted of moving from the bed to the chair by the window, according to Merle. My father said that we couldn't measure her progress by that. I thought about his micrometer, how that was the way we'd have to measure it. But my father whispered, *no*. He had brought her home to us while we were at school. She lay asleep on the day bed when we got home. Each one of us sat someplace near her hoping we'd be the first she'd see when she opened her eyes. Merle said the sight of us, our long faces, would send her sister back to the hospital. It would her. She'd rather see an ax murderer standing over her than one of us.

"Oh for Chrissakes Merle, leave the kids alone for once," my father said. She'd like to leave us alone for good. She had plans of her own, a life. She was going somewhere, making tracks of her own. Then she started humming *California, here I come.*

Later, when our mother woke up, she smiled. She said she hoped she wasn't dreaming. Was it her imagination or had we all grown a foot? Right then, we felt as though we should, David, Em, and me. Even Joan. We straightened up, straightened to the five feet she needed us to be, made a fence of ourselves around her, she seemed so fragile to us all.

In the days that followed the circles darkened under her eyes; she looked as gray and limp as her nightgowns hanging on the clothesline.

Week followed week. The pussy willows budded, broke open, their furry backs like the winter coats we discarded. The weeping-willow branches in first green hung like the crocheted chains our mother sat and worked into loops around her feet. All the pear trees in the old orchard bloomed white, startlingly white, like the new cast Joan wore. Her bones just wouldn't heal. Our mother's mind wouldn't either. I could see how we got on her nerves, how our roughhousing made her edgy, how Kevin, now that he could climb, worried her sick. I could see that Merle was right, that we drove her crazy. But what I couldn't see was how to change this.

Merle wasn't going around walking on eggshells. Not anymore. She was sick of it. She wasn't the one who'd gone and had five kids, she told us. She was angry at any sign of weakness in our mother. In fact, she said one morning in exasperation, our mother was driving *her* crazy.

It was April Fool's Day but none of us would risk a joke, not with Merle in the kind of mood she was in. Joan sat at the table with a pair of scissors in her hand. She wasn't paying attention to what she was doing even though she was holding the scissors against the curtains, staring right at her hand. As Merle moved from the stove to the table, to my horror, Joan cut right through the fabric. For a moment I thought this might be part of an April Fool's prank, that she would pull back the scissors and the curtain would be whole again. But it wasn't. Because of this, we fled the house before Eddie came for Joan.

The day was overcast. The grasses were still brown, the fields stubbled. The rosebushes near the end of the yard were brittle, the thorns, sharp brown tongues that lashed at us as we passed by. Em and I and David. It was not a day that I could take much comfort in.

We had to walk a mile to school. It was a two-room schoolhouse. The first four grades occupied four separate rows in one room, and in the second room, grades five through eight. That was Joan's room. She sat in the third row from the door. Once when Mrs. English asked her where she was born, Joan had said the hospital, and not the Bronx. All four grades had laughed at her. But Mrs. English didn't laugh, and after Joan broke her leg, she shared lunch with her because Joan couldn't go out to the playground. She let Joan sit by the woodstove, which was in the center of the building between the two rooms. It was a place of such dizzying warmth, that if I sat near it I could barely finish my sandwich before the bread had hardened.

It was to that woodstove that I headed on April Fool's Day. We arrived just as the bell rang and the brown shellacked doors swung shut. We went to the cloakroom, settled our coats and lunch bags, and slipped into our seats. David and Em in Mrs. English's class and me next door in Mrs. Washburn's. Mrs. Washburn was wearing a cameo brooch that had been her mother's. She took it off and passed it around the classroom. It was carved alabaster, the face of the woman chiseled stone. That brooch had been in Mrs. Washburn's family for over a hundred years. It was an antique. Roger Smith's sister raised her hand then and said there was a spider on Mrs. Washburn's shoulder. She jumped up and brushed at her blouse. *April Fools*, everybody screamed. Even our teacher. She admitted she'd been fooled but warned us we had work to do and let that be an end to the nonsense. We were to put such silliness out of our minds. Even so, Mrs. Washburn's face stayed red until the bell rang for lunch.

We could stay inside while we ate our lunches, but even though the day was raw, both teachers thought some fresh air would be good for us and ushered us out to the playground. I hadn't expected to see Joan on the playground and didn't look for her. When we were filing back to class, Mrs. English asked Emily about Joan. She hadn't come to school. Was she ill? Em shrugged. Mrs. English looked at me, but I didn't know either. Maybe Joan had gotten into trouble for cutting the curtains.

In the afternoon we had to make cards for Harold Birdseye, who was still in the hospital. Mrs. Washburn was his aunt by marriage. Imagine what it was like to lie in a bed for weeks at a time with no company? Mrs. Washburn knew that our cards would bring a smile to his face. It was hard for me to imagine this because of his lips, but I made him a card anyway, one of Shadow galloping across the pasture, his bad leg all healed. I made one for my mother as well, a bouquet of lilacs, with their green heartleaves.

I was somehow cheered by this card, remembering the spring before when my mother had gone out to the yard and cut armfuls of lilacs and put them in milk bottles in all the rooms. That had been in late May, the month of our birthdays, my mother's and mine. I was born in her month, she said. I took great pride in this, and so when I left school the day had taken on some color. We passed Moe's store, the green wooden benches on the front porch glistening in the light rain. We stopped for a minute at Willy's Garage. He had the only television in town. We stood in a cluster and tried to make out the figures on the eight-inch screen, but it was more interesting to watch Willy bent under the hood of a car, his legs barely touching the ground as though he were Jonah being swallowed by the whale.

I'd forgotten about Joan, didn't think about her until I passed the Birdseyes' house and saw Eddie's truck in the driveway. Then I felt sorry for her. She'd had to stay home all day long with Merle. I imagined Joan upstairs in our room, punished. Merle would be furious on two counts, the curtains were ruined and so was her day. Joan would be happy that she got to stay home from school, but mad because she'd had to stay in our room. Even if we weren't sick, the living room was off limits because of our mother. I thought of my mother again, how my drawing would make her smile. She might even tell Merle to tape it to the refrigerator door though Merle insisted that this was inviting a fire because of the nearness of the stove. We'd all be roaming around the goddamn countryside with blistered faces. And if she caught anyone of us putting paper or cloth near the stove, we'd have blistered behinds as well. Joan probably had one because of what she did to the curtains. As I neared our house, I pictured Joan upstairs on the bed, scowling, peeling the wallpaper off in strips. When I reached the ditch alongside our property, I stayed to the middle of the road, even though it had been months since Harold threatened us with Shadow, and even though I knew he was in the hospital. That's where I was walking when a horn beeped behind me. I was so startled, I nearly jumped into the damn ditch. But it was only Eddie Birdseye. I thought briefly about riding the rest of the way home with him. Then I looked again. Alongside him Joan was huddled against the window.

For a minute I thought that this was another April Fool's joke, that Joan had tricked us all, that she had been in school all day, maybe in the cloakroom ready to jump out and laugh at everyone who'd ever made fun of her. But then I looked at Em. She put her fingers to her lips. *Shh.* But who would we tell? Not Merle. Merle, who at that minute was tucking her hair behind her ear, pulling up the collar of her blouse, getting her smile ready, when Mr. Birdseye brought Joan to the door. I stood stock still, watching as he turned his truck into our driveway. No, I would never tell Merle. I'd handed secrets over so effortlessly in the past, but this one, like the man in the movies, like Wayne, wouldn't be one of them. At least I hoped it wouldn't. Then, for one brief moment, I thought that maybe Eddie had simply taken Joan to Dr. Maybee's for a check-up. That there was a simple explanation. Perhaps he'd taken her in to see Harold, who needed something more than our cards to bring a smile to his face. But I knew the lie this was when we walked into the house a few minutes later. Joan's books were slumped on the table, Merle was wondering why Eddie was always in such a hurry anymore, that surely there had to be some way to repay his kindness.

A beer would do for now, he said, raising it up when Merle handed it to him, toasting her, then seeing us coming in the door, turning and toasting us as well.

Joan was not on the bed when we went upstairs. She'd shut herself in the bathroom. We heard the water running. We didn't know what had happened to her except that since she hadn't been in school and hadn't been home, she must have been with Eddie. For my part I saw this as a plus. It was far better than spending the day with Merle. I tried to imagine both Joan and Eddie Birdseye sitting around, talking about Shadow, but all I could see was me, sitting there talking to him about my secrets, about who really tied me up to the tree.

I sat on the edge of the bed and waited. Finally the toilet flushed. I remembered then when Joan had first come to us, how she'd tried to shock us by swearing or doing something wild, taking dares, leaping once from one of the old pear trees into some horse turds below. Barefoot. Her toes thick with shit, she'd come upstairs, walking on her heels. We followed. We thought she'd climb in the tub and rinse her feet off but instead she stuck them in the toilet and flushed. For one sudden moment I thought the water would suck her down the drain along with the manure. But it didn't. Still and all, I was shocked that she had put her feet in the toilet in the first place but not as shocked as I was when I saw my cousin's face the moment she came out of the bathroom. It was completely white, hard and white, carved just as cleanly as the woman in the cameo that Mrs. Washburn wore.

She knew that we knew she wasn't in school and she didn't give a damn. From now on in, she was going to do whatever she wanted. She lay down on her bed then. We could hear Eddie talking to Merle. Joan smiled to herself. I knew how much she hated school. As unlikely as it seemed, it looked like she had talked Eddie Birdseye into letting her stay home. At his house. She had that effect on him, I could see that.

I didn't think it was possible for Joan to be more secretive, but she was. Some days she came to school, some days she didn't. But always she was home by the time we came in. For personal reasons she wanted to sleep in her own bed. This was because of the bleeding spells she had. So much had happened to her body since she came to us, that nothing surprised her, or me. Merle said that she could take her brother's room, the summer kitchen. Aside from being a sneak, she didn't have any of her brother's traits, so the door didn't need to be padlocked. But Joan often locked it against me. I could see her sometimes, lying on the cot, naked. Em saw her too and complained to our mother.

My mother said to leave her be. She was growing up. And she was. Now she stole cigarettes instead of candy. Except for the cast on her leg, she looked pretty glamorous as far as I was concerned. When she came through the rooms, my mother tried to grab her, make her sit next to her. We all wanted to, even Merle who sometimes looked at Joan greedily. But she moved beyond us, broken leg and all. Corn silk, that's what my mother said the color of Joan's hair was. It had darkened some, taking on the soft luster of spring. Like Joan herself, her hair refused to be held, barrettes slipped out of it, rubber bands, hair combs did as well. Her eyelashes had grown back lush and blond. Where once Joan's skin seemed lightly blue, it was now the color and texture of cream. She was flawless, every bit of her as beautiful as the satin my mother had bought for my communion dress. That fabric was gone. I'd seen it once on the sideboard and again in my parents' room on my mother's sewing table, slippery and white, and after that it disappeared for good.

Sometimes Joan let me sleep with her if she heard me wandering around at night. She often couldn't sleep herself. Then we would lie together and watch the stars. They seemed in bloom like so much of the world around us, like Joan herself. Because she'd lived in the Bronx all of her life, Joan wasn't used to stars. She didn't know about the Big and Little Dippers or the Milky Way. She'd never seen a shooting star, though I'd seen many. She didn't have the patience to wait. I might lie beside her and see two or three in a matter of minutes, but she always missed them.

One night, when we were lying side by side in the dark, she began to tell me about sex. She'd found out some more about it, what it was a man and woman did. I was ten years old, old enough to know, Joan said. She had been younger than me when she first learned about sex. I knew better than to ask any questions or to question what Joan said, so I kept quiet.

What sex actually was, she said, was taking off your clothes and lying side by side like we were doing. Then the man's pecker grew hard. This was called a hard-on. I stared out the window, stared hard at the stars. The man rolled over on top of the woman and began kissing her. Above my head, the stars thickened. There was a place in a woman's body that opened. Between her legs. The man knew exactly where to find it. I could see the Little Dipper quite clearly. It looked like a window opened to another world. When a man found this opening — it wasn't the pee hole either in case I was wondering — he put his pecker in it. It hurt at first. Like popping a blister. *In and out, in and out.* Then the man actually peed inside of the woman, only it wasn't pee. It was more like milk. I looked up at the Milky Way, saw its swirl and spill of stars. One star suddenly flared, rainbowed across the dome of the sky. I lay there in silence. One word and the spell would be broken. Still, I wanted to point out the star. It was astonishing really, that star. It was the longest and brightest shooting star I'd ever seen. That was it. That was sex. Any questions? I shook my head. I heard Joan sigh. Pretty soon she'd be asleep. Into the shimmering darkness around us, I whispered that she had just missed the most amazing star I'd ever seen. After her news, it must have seemed of small account because she said she didn't care if she ever saw a shooting star.

"I don't believe you, anyway, Rainey. I don't believe a word you say anymore," Joan said, mad that I wasn't interested in what she told me. Then she rolled over on her side to make some room for me. I curled against her. I looked up at the sky. It was still, sure as secrets. I laced my arms around her waist. "Stars don't move," she said. I nodded, shut my eyes, moved closer to her. When finally her breath evened, I looked out against the night. If I wanted to, I could have waded out into stars as thick as water, I could have ridden their dark, invisible currents through the night and into morning. But I didn't want to leave Joan. Couldn't have left her. I wasn't even mad that she hadn't believed me about the stars. I knew the stars. I knew they moved. As for what she said about sex, I thought we were even. She hadn't believed one word I'd said about the stars, and I hadn't believed a word she said about sex either.

In the days that followed, Joan would be kind, sharing what she had with me, but just as often she could be mean, terribly mean. Once she made me take off all my clothes. She tied a scarf over my eyes, tied my wrists to the bed and tickled me with a feather, rubbed the feather against the arch of my foot until I wet the bed. Another time she pulled me into the barn, held my hand under Shadow's mouth until his teeth came down hard on my flesh. There was something in this meanness, something in the way she held a match to my fingertips, both of us watching in horror and fascination that seemed to burn us clean. For days Joan would leave me alone, and I would stay far from her, but then a night would come, she'd offer some kindness, hold up her silver necklace, let me touch it. She'd close the door, take off her blouse, make me take off mine, then she'd unsnap her white bra, the pink flower the same color as her nipples, and she'd press her titties to me, and I would let her hold me, all the while knowing the match would come again, the needles stuck in my fingers, Shadow's teeth on my flesh.

Joan still wore the cast, but she could finally put weight on her foot. Harold got out of the hospital and soon started leaving things for her on the fence. When he did, she'd go out and get them herself, throwing that one leg out in front of her as if it was a net she was casting for all the gifts he left her. After the necklace and bracelet, he'd brought her earrings. Silver hoops. She'd have to pierce her ears. But Uncle said no, that she had enough holes in her head as it was. He'd come back for more furniture because he'd sold the pieces he took to the Bronx. He was happy about that, but mad about the changes he saw in Joan and Merle. Neither one was happy to see him. I was happy to see he hadn't brought Wayne. Wayne, it seemed, had taken off.

Joan said she'd pierce her ears anyway, and she took a threaded needle and pushed it right through her lobe and into a piece of potato she held behind it. I threw up, but Joan went ahead and did the other ear. We didn't know it was his mother's jewelry that Harold was taking. Not until he left the ring, a single diamond caught in fisted prongs. I told Joan that she'd have to give that back. But it was hard for her to part with it. She hoarded things, pushed everything under her mattress. I warned her that Merle was going to find out one of these days. Maybe one day while we were at school, Merle was going to clean the room and find all the jewelry under the mattress. She would think Joan stole it. Then what would happen?

Merle was too damn lazy to clean her room, Joan said. Besides, she didn't care. The jewelry was hers. But just in case, she was putting it where no one would ever find it. Not even me. Then she walked out to the pasture and vanished behind the barn. Harold was near the row of poplars that bordered our land. He was exercising Shadow, but he never tried to approach Joan. And she never left any clue that she'd gotten his gifts. But he must have known. He was always around, always out in the field with his horse, his face blazing red as a bandanna through the tender green of the trees.

David's face was going to appear on a billboard for Wonder Bread. Well, there was a good chance it was, Eddie Birdseye said. He'd finally gotten the name of a contact in Manhattan. That's all it took, knowing the right person. Merle smiled at this news, but not the smile that meant in a pig's ass. On our way to Mass on Sunday, I saw an empty billboard by the side of the road. I'd never noticed it before. I imagined David, in the middle of a field of wheat, far above me, looking as surprised to find himself there as I was.

Joan was going to be next. Eddie had started taking pictures of her already. Just her head and shoulders because of the cast. She practiced poses in her room using her sheet for a robe. It was hard to know what she was going to pose for exactly, but as far as I was concerned she could have posed for anything, she was that beautiful. Em and I felt as ragged as weeds next to Joan. We ran outside without our coats every chance we got. Put something on, Merle yelled to us, but she didn't make us. If we got croup, whooping cough, or walking pneumonia, keep on walking. We were enough trouble as it was. She didn't need anything else to worry about. She had enough problems of her own.

We could see that. We could see she was in trouble with Uncle. Where do you think you're going in that get-up, cover yourself up, keep your legs crossed, he shouted, forgetting our mother was in the house. But Merle's legs were as slippery as the satin my mother had bought for my dress, and after a few moments, they invariably slid apart. Merle had a way of looking at Uncle, one eyebrow cocked, her hand on her hip in just that same angle. He couldn't stand it.

"Wiseguy," he'd muttered. Merle was a real wiseguy. Knock it off, was what she told him.

"Wisenheimer, a genuine wisenheimer." She didn't know when to stop, did she?

"Wiseass," Merle called him back. She had to have the last word, didn't she? He couldn't win. He was drinking now even before he came to the table for breakfast.

On the day Merle had to take Joan in to have her cast sawed off, Uncle told her she better make damn sure that's all she did. Joan had tried all morning long to get the cast off herself. She'd stood in the bathtub pouring glasses of water down the cast to soften the plaster. She tore at the frayed edges near her toes, and above her knee, but to no avail. For Chrissakes, Merle said, leave that cast alone before I take the hacksaw and cut your goddamn leg off.

"She's just nervous," my mother soothed and pulled Joan to her. Merle seemed as nervous as Joan.

She was going to have to take Uncle's truck, the panel truck, because my father was going to Carl's right after work. She'd have to drop Uncle off at the stand so he could finish repairing a sideboard he'd found and then she'd pick him up on her way back. She was going to stop in Woolworth's and get a permanent, whether Uncle liked it or not. He didn't like it. Who was she getting all dolled up for? He didn't want to stand around the whole goddamned day waiting to be picked up.

Blah, blah, blah, was all Merle said, standing in the bathroom, admiring her face. "Not bad," she said, dropping the gold-lettered eyebrow pencil into her purse. "Not bad enough," she winked. She did look amazing sometimes, the way she could change her appearance by the shape of her eyebrows. She had gone from brown inverted vees to soft reddish brown half moons. Em stood in the hall watching her, Kevin on her hip. I was right beside her. Joan watched from across the hall. We'd seen Merle do her make-up a thousand times, but each new transformation drew us to her. Sometimes she didn't mind an audience and would ask our advice. This scarf? She'd hold up a pink nylon square. We shook our heads, not because we didn't agree with her that some pinks were made for redheads but because we didn't want to see anything cover her long white neck. Then she'd reach into her bag of natural beauty and pull out the opal on the silver length of chain that was just long enough so that the stone lay in the deep thumbprint of her neck. Before she left, she'd spray herself all over. She didn't believe in spraying her wrists. That was nonsense. A woman sprayed where she wanted to be kissed. Then she might or might not spray between her legs.

I had asked Joan to ask her mother if we could go with her, Em and me, but we needed to stay home and take care of our little brothers because when Merle was away, David was in charge of our mother. Anyway, Joan would have said no. She wanted to be alone with Merle. They drew together when Uncle was in one of his moods. Merle would send Joan into the kitchen to check on him, see if she could get some money from him. Joan would have to lie, say she owed book money at school. You're in cahoots, he'd say, but Joan persisted and sometimes wrung a dollar from him, which Merle claimed was harder than squeezing milk from a lemon.

They left together, the three of them, and the silence that ensued was more unsettling to me than their presence.

My mother called from the alcove. The silence made her uneasy, too. David went and sat beside her. They both stared out the window across the field where the year before Em and Toby had gotten stuck in mud. We'd gone to watch the wild geese feed in the stubbled fields before the Yetters plowed them. The farther we got from the house,

the deeper the mud got, and soon there was no turning back. No geese
either. Toby had started to cry and startled them. Em picked him up
and when she did, she sunk to her knees in the mud. She couldn't
move forward or backward. She'd told me to run and get our mother.
I ran as fast as I could, but when I reached the house, I looked back
and it looked like Em and Toby had sunk below ground. I started hol-
lering to my mother from the porch that Em and Toby were caught in
quicksand. "Where? Where, Rainey?" my mother yelled, her voice
coming back to me as she ran toward the field. But the fields spread
out before us empty handed. I started after her, though I was too
winded to keep up. Then David bolted out the door, running past me
and our mother. He seemed to know exactly where to head, and long
before I caught up to him, he was handing Toby to our mother and
pulling Em from the mud though her boots held fast. My mother was
laughing, holding on to David, marveling how fast he could run. He'd
lost a shoe himself, but still carried Toby all the way home. Afterwards
we sat in the kitchen and told the story again and again until it lost its
power over us. My mother made us cocoa and ladyfingers, buttered
bread sliced thin and sprinkled with sugar. She set the plate in front
of David first because she'd always been able to count on him. I had
been jealous of the attention that my mother gave to David, and to
Em who told how she knew to save Toby, and how she would have
held him above her own head even if she'd been sucked under the
mud. I started to point out that I had saved them both, but my
mother reminded me not to interrupt her while she spoke. She
reached over to touch Emily, telling her that she was small but she was
fierce. That was something my mother really admired. In light of this
I'd gone outside and gotten on David's old Schwinn bike. I had just
learned to ride it, but I hadn't mastered stopping it. I pedaled it up and

down our road as fast as I could, hoping that my mother would look out the window and tell me to stop, that she was afraid I'd hurt myself. But she didn't, and because of this, I really did hurt myself. I hit a patch of loose gravel and the bike skidded out from under me. The handlebars cocked under my rib cage when I hit the ground. I lay there until the pain caught up with me, then I sat up and lifted my shirt to examine my chest. Underneath my nipple a patch of skin was scraped raw. It wasn't bleeding, but it wanted to. Or I wanted it to. I stared at it a good long time. It looked like the skin under a blister looked like, shiny and raw. Angry. That's what my mother would say if she saw it. It didn't look as bad as it felt. And it didn't look like any injury I'd ever had. Because of this I ran to the house screaming that I'd been bitten by a snake. Then it was my mother who was screaming around in circles, swinging at me with the dishtowel, as though I was the snake itself. I was so startled by this I had to tell the truth. After this, I had to go to my room for making up a story. Later, when my mother called me down for dinner, she seemed to have forgotten about what I'd done. She smiled absently as she placed our plates on the table. When we began to eat, she lit a cigarette, inhaled, then set it down in the ashtray. She pressed her hand to her temple, held it there. She couldn't eat a thing. Instead, she sat watching the smoke from her cigarette, hypnotized by the length of it weaving rhythmically above the table. I watched her and I watched the smoke. It seemed every bit as real as the snake that had bitten me.

Looking at her now, a year later, as she sat with my brother, her hands trembly, her mouth twitching, I knew beyond a doubt that it was true what Merle had said. We had driven our mother crazy. Or I had.

I suddenly had an impulse to make amends for what I'd done. I wanted to give her something, a present so beautiful that it would make her forget the ugly things I'd done. I thought of the ring that Harold had given Joan. The diamond. If I could find the ring, it would replace the long ago lost sapphire, the one that she'd forgotten on the back of the sink when she graduated from eighth grade. By righting this wrong, I hoped to right my own. Beyond this, I didn't give any thought to what Joan would do to me when she found out.

I set about trying to find where Joan had hidden the jewelry. She was sly, I knew that, heard her father say it a hundred times, a thousand times. Hadn't he just said it earlier, after he handed her the wrinkled dollar bill. You're a sly lass.

I looked in the barn first. I could barely stand being inside it alone. It held so many secrets. It also held the sweet smell of hay, which when newly cut, smelled like cotton candy, or chocolate, even taffy, the smell that I would always associate with what had happened to me in the movie theater. The smell that even now made me want to rub my arms, the way the man in the theater had, or rub myself all over, the way Joan often did.

Our land spread out and covered nearly ten acres. To the east was the Zook farm, the foundation of the burned-out Birdseye place, the river, and the bridge. I couldn't see the bridge from where I stood, couldn't even see Zook's either, though I could if I stood in my bedroom. The roof at least and the telephone poles that lined the ridge, then swooped toward their farm, bringing the party line directly to their door. We were next in line for a phone, my father said. He promised. We were just waiting for the poles to be set. Sometimes my father made promises he could not keep and so he was very careful about making them. But we could count on the phone. Now that our mother was home, maybe home for good, she'd need one. The last thing he wanted was for her to feel completely alone in the country.

I had no idea how big ten acres were, but I believed that our land stretched for miles. In the face of that I gave up looking for Joan's hiding place outside. Since she'd moved into the summer kitchen, I headed for that, thinking, hoping, that she'd put the jewelry back under her mattress. But when I lifted the mattress there was nothing there but David's old pee stains. At the sight of them, I was somehow convinced that I'd never find the jewelry.

The one who did find it was Dr. Maybee when he cut off Joan's cast. The diamond ring, the locket, the silver bracelet embedded in the flesh near her knee.

Joan said the jewelry came from Harold. In a pig's ass, Merle said. Where would that boy ever get the money? Who would hire that freak? Joan insisted it had been Harold. Her mother didn't believe her. At least that's what Dr. Maybee told my father later that night when he came to tend to our mother. Merle had snatched it up and put it in her purse because she smelled a rat, and she knew exactly what rat hole to look in. *Easy, Mother*, Dr. Maybee said, but Merle had yanked Joan by the hair from his office.

Merle had left then with Joan in tow and headed for Eddie Birdseye's. She didn't stop for the permanent. She didn't stop for anything. Not even the one red light in Keansburg. The policeman who pulled her over gave her a ticket, told her to calm down, what was the rush? He made her sit by the side of the road and cool off. After he drove away, Merle said she needed a drink and stopped at the first bar she came to and bought a container of beer. By the time they got to Birdseye's, Merle had finished the quart of beer and was ready to take down Birdseye's house board by board to get at the truth. But no one was home and so she brought Joan home to us, pushed her through the door, and told her to get the hell upstairs and stay there until

Merle said she could come out. That might be when Joan was eighteen years old. Then Merle looked directly at me. I was stunned. I didn't know Merle had found the jewelry, but I did know she'd found out something, maybe that Joan didn't go to school anymore but posed for pictures for Mr. Birdseye instead. I starting shaking my head no even before Merle grabbed me by the arm. Don't you lie to me, too, she said.

Merle? My mother's voice, heavy with sleep, came from the alcove. Merle hesitated for a moment, dropped my arm, went in to my mother, gave her one of her pills. Then she fluffed the pillows, closed the blinds, and pulled the blankets over my mother's chest. Tucked her in. Before she left the room, she stopped for a moment, stood at the threshold, her chin raised but everything else on her sagging.

Then she turned to me, dragged me into the summer kitchen to have a private chat with me. I held my breath, terrified that she would pull the truth from me the way she'd threatened to pull my loose baby teeth from my head. The truth was written all over my face. She didn't need to be a frigging mind reader to figure out what was going on behind her back. But what she did need was a beer so that she could figure out how to make me talk.

What she was going to do was worm it out of me. I had had worms once. I caught them from playing in the sandbox before we knew cats dirtied in it. I remembered the horror I felt when I saw the worms in my underpants. Dr. Maybee had given me medicine for them, but even so, it was a long time before I could sleep at night. I felt my skin crawl just thinking about them and thinking about what Merle was going to do to me. She said she had all day. She'd sit there until I had calluses on my backside. Two could play the game as well as one. I thought of the way she played Slap Jack. Then I saw us sitting at the table for days to come, her hand slapping the face of the king, the queen, and the jack. She had slapped me across the face more than once, though we knew from our mother that was the worst place to hit a child. Outside the window, the wind took hold of the holly-hock bushes and shook the daylights out of them. When I was smaller, I used to hide underneath that bush and pull the buds off the stems, strip back the sepals until the pointed white heads emerged. At the base of the bud, where the petals were folded tight, there was a series of holes. One of these holes was big enough to fit the stem and flower of a bloom into it. I made flower dolls, this way. I had an entire fam-ily of them. It was under the hollyhock that Roger Smith ate the worm the summer before. It happened right before our mother went crazy.

"Well?" Merle asked. I didn't know what to tell. Sometimes when I set my flower dolls on the grass, the wind would blow, and they'd all tumble away. If I went after them, my mother might see me from the windows in the alcove. If she did, she'd mouth the words, *Don't sit on the wet ground.* I'd watch her mouth move, but pretend I didn't hear her, though I knew the worms could find me there, crawl into my openings.

I started to squirm. Merle said she didn't care if I peed my pants or passed out cold, I wasn't going anywhere until I gave her some answers. My bladder was full. I thought of peeing my pants, almost did, then tightened my legs. I was afraid if I released them, everything would pour from me. I felt my bladder give way a bit, felt the warm pee, then some relief. I decided I should tell some of the truth. I said that Harold had given Joan some jewelry, that he'd ridden to the fence every time he had something for Joan, and that I'd gone out and got-ten it. Receiving stolen property, Merle said raising her eyebrows. In my own defense, I said that I'd told Joan not to take the ring. Merle just snorted.

"I'll bet she didn't offer to share any of it with you," she smirked. It was true, she hadn't. I'd never even had one piece of candy from the Whitman Sampler, I said. Still, I was an accomplice. I'd had a hand in it. We'd both be sent to reform school. She'd sign the complaint herself if she had to. We'd both be sent away. I tried to remember the Justice Stories Merle had read to us. I thought that this could be true. We'd be sitting behind bars doing our homework. But not if Joan let me take the blame, Merle said. She was the one with the broken leg. For all anyone knew, I could have gone into Mr. Birdseye's house and stolen the jewelry myself. I told Merle that now Joan was the one who went to the fence, not me.

"Tell that to the sheriff," was all she said, then raised the beer bottle and took a long swallow. My own mouth was dry. "It's Joan's word against yours. Who do you think Mr. Birdseye is going to believe." Right then my heart sank. "Joan," I said.

"That's right. Believe me, sister, Joan's not going to come to your defense." I knew this was true. Still, I didn't want to tell about the pictures or that Joan didn't come to school ever since Harold went into the hospital.

I said that Harold would tell the truth. "Hah," Merle said. If he could. But his lips were sewn shut. The stitches wouldn't come out for another month. I closed my mouth, wished my own lips were sewn shut. Merle sat staring at me for a long moment.

"It'll break your mother's heart when she finds out what you've done," she said at last.

I felt my eyes fill with tears, tried to hold them back, tried to squeeze the pee back inside my body, and then it was out, the whole story. Merle sat there staring at me for a few minutes blinking her eyes, over and over again. Then she stood up, and very slowly collected her things, her keys, her cigarettes, and matches. She yanked her hairbrush from her purse and brushed her hair savagely, put it back in the purse. Then she straightened her skirt, lining up the back seam with the seams in her stockings, centering her cinch belt over the front seams. Strengthening her lines, she'd told us. Always make sure that when we made an appearance, all our seams were straight. Then we'd be taken seriously.

When Merle stood in front of me for the last time, I took her very seriously. I felt my face sting in anticipation of the slap I might get. Steeled myself for it. But she didn't need to slap me. All she needed to do was say three words to me, and I knew that I'd been tricked. *Hook, line, and sinker*, she said as she opened the door, slinging her purse over her shoulder, looking back at me a moment. *Sucker*. Then she was gone. I sat there for a few minutes, stunned, feeling like one of the baby guppies that had been swallowed whole.

After Joan heard her mother leave, she came down to me, her dress half unbuttoned and her sash untied. Her leg, her perfect leg, the one that was so strongly muscled she could ride Shadow bareback if she took a mind to it, was shriveled. It was all long blond hair and peeling skin. It stank. I was afraid that she knew what I'd done. But she was so bereft about her loss, she didn't notice. She told me about the jewelry, how Merle had taken it and stuck it in her purse. How she'd almost run away when Merle stopped for beer, but that her mother said that she'd be in a body cast from her Adam's apple to her asshole, if she moved one muscle. She shook her head, opened both her hands, and though nothing was in them, we saw the jewels fall away. Out the western window, the sky turned a brilliant gold, but within minutes that was gone, too, like the ring, the bracelet, and the heart. Gone for good.

We sat in the kitchen for a long time, both of us in the parlor chair. I knew this was a temporary situation. When Joan found out that I had told about the pictures, she would never speak to me again. I was sure she'd tell Eddie, and he'd never speak to me either. We were still sitting together when my father came home from work. We looked like partners in crime, he said. We were.

"How's your mother?" he asked. We didn't know. We'd forgotten all about her. We stared at him. "Sleeping?" We nodded. He stuck his head into the alcove. "Dead to the world," he said. But he was smiling. The more rest she got, the quicker she'd recover. He was going to head over to Carl's to do some studying, but he wanted to check on us first. Merle was all worked up about something, he said. She and Uncle were at the roadhouse drinking themselves blind, and he was afraid of a scene. Then he noticed Joan's leg. "Oh, honey," he said, "that leg's going to be good as new."

We had breakfast for dinner. Wheaties, the Breakfast of Champions. There was a picture of a football player on the front of the box, leaping through the air to make a catch. I thought he looked just like David. There was a mask on the back of the box, a mask of the Cisco Kid that we were waiting to cut out when the cereal box was empty. We'd seen his show at Willy's Garage, on his eight-inch screen when our father stopped to get a tire fixed. Even my father had seen it, had sat on the hood of the car and watched Pancho and Cisco, had laughed as hard as we did, his belly laugh that my mother loved.

My father stood and watched us eat our cereal after he'd gathered his books. He still wanted to go to Carl's. It was important that he not lose his momentum he told us. I had no idea what he meant, but I didn't want anyone else to suffer a loss. We told him to go. We'd be fine. But he hesitated. We looked like a bunch of sad sacks. He couldn't stand it. He had a cure for sadness, he told us. Did we want to try it? I did, believing that it was important to keep Joan's attention off me, so that she wouldn't see that I'd told on her. Em did because our father's cures were sometimes amazing. His headache cure really was.

He'd heard that the way to stop headaches was to hold the person's wrists under cold water for at least two minutes, so when my mother came into the kitchen one morning complaining of a headache he pulled her right over to the sink and held her wrists under the icy water. She'd tried to struggle free, but he held her fast. Then she fainted dead away. He was terrified and ran with her in his arms through all the rooms, but after he revived her, he came back to us and said confidently that our mother's headache was gone.

Another cure was the charcoal cure for stomach aches. He'd burn some toast, hold it over the fire until it was in flames and make us eat the blackened bread. He said that the charcoal was medicinal. If we vomited after we ate the bread, he said that that was a sign that it was working. If we didn't vomit, he said the same thing.

The Cisco Kid Cure did not cure our sadness as it turned out. My father cut out the mask on the back of the box and went inside the living room to find some string. We waited for him in the kitchen. Toby was upstairs in the bathroom. Kevin was in the playpen in the living room. I guess our father wanted to try the cure on him first because we heard him screech. *Shh*, my father whispered. If we weren't quiet he couldn't cure us. Not any of us. But Kevin laughed so hard we heard him plop to his bottom. We were smiling despite ourselves. Next our father crept upstairs to cure Toby. We heard him running from room to room shooting at my father who was talking like the Cisco Kid. But Toby was cranky. He wanted my father to stop. And he did stop. We waited for him to come downstairs to us. Even Kevin who'd pulled himself up again stood trembling in anticipation. Our father waited until we couldn't stand it anymore, then peered over the banister where Joan, Em, and I stood. I could see why Toby was scared. The face of Cisco sneered down at us. I knew it was our father but nonetheless I was terrified. I pulled back from the stairwell. Joan and Em were a little bolder. They stood along the wall ready to spring out at my father all the while listening with increasing horror as he crept stealthily down the steps. Joan's face, for all her scorn of our games, was as excited as Kevin's. Kevin looked as though he might throw the plastic crucifix he was chewing on right at my father. Anything seemed possible. I moved over to Em and Joan's side of the room, but we didn't leap out when we saw him in the doorway.

Instead we moved closer to one another. Emily's eyes hollowed. I needed to pee. I looked up at the china closet. My father's reflection in the glass was grotesque. He was poised to leap. We moved just as he did. He leapt first onto a kitchen chair and then to the center of the table. Emily and I ran around it. Joan stood in the corner, her face twisted with laughter. But not a sound from her. Not a sound. My father whispered that he was Cisco.

"*Ees Ceesco,*" he hissed, "*and nobody hescape Ceesco.*" No matter where we ran he had us blocked. His shoes were clattering on the table. The glasses were ringing in the cabinet. He held the fly swatter and used it like a whip. At one point Emily and I turned in opposite directions only to collide when we ran wildly toward the same corner. We stood absolutely mute. We didn't want to wake our mother. Our father was twirling madly on the table. Toby was running back and forth upstairs. Kevin was jumping. Joan was doubled over, her face wild with glee.

My father couldn't stop scaring us. Em, in a moment of desperation, grabbed the crucifix from Kevin's mouth. He stood still, not sure if he should laugh or cry. Our father waited. We could hear the heave of his breath. We both stood perfectly still staring up at him. Our father. Em held the crucifix toward him. And he, as if coming out of a trance, said, "*Aw, Jesus,*" and dropped the flyswatter. He jumped down from the table and came toward us with open arms telling us he was sorry, that he was only kidding, he was only having some fun with us. Did we believe for a minute that he'd ever harm a hair on our heads?

I did. I most certainly did. But even so, even though he still wore the mask of Cisco, I went straight into his arms with Em.

My father was ashamed of himself. We could see that. He made us cocoa and got Kevin ready for bed. He couldn't find a pair of clean pajamas and so put him in one of his own T-shirts. Kevin looked beautiful. His hair was golden, his eyes dark brown. We loved the way the T-shirt draped on him. Toby finished his cocoa and fell sound asleep in the highchair. He was famous for that. My father carried him up and laid him down in his crib. He would need a bed soon. My father said that by the time summer came Toby would be too long for the crib. He was nearly four years old. It was about time the boy had a bed. Then our father peeked in at our mother. She hadn't moved. We all could see that.

My father estimated that if he left right then for Carl's that the longest we'd be home without a responsible adult would be an hour. David was serving evening Mass but would be home by six. My father would stop at the bar and tell Merle and Uncle that we'd had dinner but he'd feel better if they made it an early night. Christ, he didn't care if they stayed out until midnight the next night. It was his day off. We told our father to go, we'd be fine.

Joan said she didn't care if her parents stayed out until midnight every night as long as they gave her the jewelry back. Then she told us what had happened when Dr. Maybee cut her cast off. "You should have seen Merle's face," Joan said, falling backward onto the parlor chair, as though shoved there by the memory of it. She pulled me close to her, made me promise that I would tell Merle that the jewelry was hers. She was determined to get it back, though I knew that would never happen now.

There was something thrilling about being home alone. It made us reckless, made Joan go into the bathroom and slip Merle's chenille robe from the hook and put it on. The coral one, the one impossible for anyone but a redhead to wear. It made her wrap her head in a towel, a turban, made her take the eyebrow pencil and put a mole above her lip. She fingered her own throat the way her mother often did. There's more where that came from, she said to me, knowing that I had seen the silver locket hang from her neck. Em and I stripped to our slips, put Merle's sweater on, her see-through blouse. I tied the pink silk scarf around my neck. We moved around the kitchen, glided really, made popcorn, looked at the dark windows giving us back our own reflections. Joan opened her robe, slid it off her shoulder until one pink round of nipple showed. Get a load of this, Wayne, she said to the glass. We stared into the dark. He could be anywhere.

We didn't save any popcorn for David, but he said he didn't care, though he looked in the bowl when he came home. Joan was still trying to be wild. She held up a hardened kernel of corn, one of the dozen that didn't pop. You know what these are called, she asked him. He shook his head.

Old maids, Joan laughed. David smiled uncertainly. They haven't been popped, Joan said. David turned his back on this news then turned on the radio. We played cards, Slap Jack, War, Memory.

David sat with us at the table, his seriousness settled us down. He said that he was going to serve my Communion Mass. Father Leary had asked him and he said yes. That was the following week. I didn't know if I wanted my brother to look down my throat. I guessed it was better than Roger Smith. I told Joan the story of the worm. David said that Roger was showing off, then he picked up my catechism and drilled me on the questions. *Who made you? God made me. Who is God? God is the Supreme Being, the Maker of Heaven and Earth.*

"The supreme bean," Joan yelled, slapping down her hand. We had to smile. All of us. Then David tightened his face and repeated the question. The Supreme Being, I began.

"The string bean?" Joan blurted out before I could finish, and even though we knew it was a sacrilege we couldn't keep from laughing, couldn't keep from collapsing against each other, falling off the chairs, holding onto our sides.

Why did God make us? To Know, Love, and Serve Him in this world, and be happy with Him in the next.

We were in bed by the time we heard Merle and Uncle downstairs. Half asleep, the three of us. We'd cleaned the kitchen though we knew that didn't cut any ice with Merle. If she was mad, she'd stay mad. Joan decided to sleep with Em and me. Safety in numbers, I thought. David stayed downstairs with our mother, just in case she woke up. He'd come to bed when our father came home.

Joan, her thin leg thrown over the covers, mumbled something in her sleep. She had her two middle fingers in her mouth, her pinky and her index finger on each cheek. The light from the hall flickered, the bulb was bad. It made a hum, flickered again, but held.

I heard Merle downstairs. She and Uncle laughing about something. I thought for a moment Merle might come up and tell Joan what I'd said, but she didn't. Her voice rose, then Uncle's. They were having fun. Having a nightcap. Two beers. I could hear the *chiff, chiff* of the caps as they came free of the bottle. I could hear them break into laughter over something that happened at the bar, a story about one of the Yetter boys. He stank so bad that the men he worked with brought a goat to the shop and tied it to his chair. *Jeez eez,* Uncle's laugh, more a wheeze than anything. Merle loud, full of herself.

I noticed something about the stars that night. I had never realized how the earth moved, though David had explained it to me again and again. The earth in its orbit took three hundred sixty-five days to circle the sun. But it seemed impossible that it was the earth and our own bodies that moved through space. And what about the moon? The moon seemed to follow the earth along. There'd been nights on our river rides to get Kevin to fall asleep that the moon seemed a balloon tied to the bumper of our car. But that night before I went to sleep, I went to the window and I saw that the Big Dipper was nearly straight overhead, yet, when I awoke later, the Dipper was on its side, like a chair toppled.

I drifted in and out of sleep. Woke again to some sound. Thunder? An argument going on in another room? If Uncle wanted a cigarette, he should get off his ass and get the pack from Merle's purse. I had no idea what time it was, if my father had come home. I woke to *slap, slap,* that sound, and thought Merle and Uncle were playing cards. Merle winning. I knew the sting of that hand. Later we all woke to yelling, terrific yelling, stumbling, chairs tipping, then silence. It flared from time to time, their voices, Uncle's trembling with anger. *You better watch that mouth of yours, that mouth is going to get you in trouble one of these days.* Merle's threatening, daring. *Go ahead and try it.* My father's voice, *"Keep it down, for Chrissakes,"* settling Kevin again. My father wanted no more trouble. Any more trouble and he was throwing them both out. *"For God's sake, think of your sister."* And that seemed the end of it.

I believed that anger could stop like that. Knock it off. It stopped. Cut it out. For crying out loud. Hadn't that worked on us? Merle snapped her fingers, we sat down.

Across the hall David opened his door. We could see right over to him and he to us. He smiled. I was sure that this was a signal that everything was all right. He wouldn't open his door and risk waking Toby if the fight wasn't over. He closed his eyes a breath at a time. I watched him, watched as the door made its nightly progress too, closed in small exhalations. Everything out of whack, our father said about the house. We could place a ball on the floor and it would roll to the other side. Nothing plumb in the whole damn place. But marveling about that all the while. He and Uncle hands crossed over their bellies, too much to drink that night as well, taking bets on the ball, which corner it would roll to. Pocket, that's what Uncle called it. Eight ball in the side pocket. Merle's head thrown back like a whistling swan. Her long white throat.

Soon we were all sleeping again. Soundly. Stars cart-wheeling overhead. I dreamed of cartwheels. Em and I on the front lawn, twirling and twirling across the grass until the day turned black and we lay reeling on our backs. Our hearts exploding in our ears.

It was the door slung open. The latch hard against the wall. The ticking of plaster, that woke us. Uncle's face, large, thrust into our room. Merle by the hair.

To each of us later there would come an image. For Em it would be of the carp she'd found along the riverbank, dead and stinking. She dragged it home through the dirt by its mouth. She wanted our mother to cook it for dinner. It was a family story, one that made us laugh. That carp was as big as my sister. For me it was the worm, the worm that was inside of me, that made me tell on Joan. Uncle was screaming, shaking Merle by the throat, her eyes split green and blue, cracked like the opal around her neck. *The worm, the worm.* It's what Merle had inside her, a worm that ate away at her. Her lips were the dusky purple of the night crawler Roger Smith lay on his tongue. Uncle, black with rage, pointing to his daughter, threw the jewelry he'd found in Merle's purse across at us. He pounded and pounded the door.

Sneaking around, the stinking whore. The whore, the whore. Sonofabitchingwhore, bought by Birdseye. We knelt on the bed, the three of us, clutching one another, our faces twisted. David was gone. His bed empty. I could see my face given back to me in the glass. I looked like my mother in the Crying Room. And then there was my mother, our mother. Her face was as hideous as the ones that came to me in my dreams. Deep purple veins pounded at her temples. Her eyes swelled, rose from her sockets. She was directly underneath the single light bulb. We could see her clearly. And so we could see it happen. Every blood vessel in her face breaking, as though it was she and not Merle who was being choked to death. Her mouth was open. So was mine. She looked straight at me. She tried to speak, but no words came. But even so, I heard her. I swear I heard her call her sister's name before she fell.

My father was behind Uncle, pulling at him, trying to get Uncle free from Merle. "Let her go. Let her go, for Chrissakes you're killing her." But when he saw my mother he let go of Uncle and cradled her head in his arms, pulled her into his chest.

Kevin wailed from below. Clover, running, nipping at Uncle,

barking. Toby silent across the hall. We could be next, any one of us.

David had run to the Yetters to get the men from the Bible, the five brothers. Gideon, Ezekiel, Jonah, Jacob, Seth. I heard their cars in the driveway, heard them on the stairs, the crack of a shotgun cocked. That sound stopped Uncle. He knew it. He dropped Merle.

Gideon held the gun on him, told him, *Easy, easy, Mac.* Take it easy. Uncle looked to the floor, to Merle, then to us, back to the men. We didn't know what he might do next. He didn't either. He was capable of anything. We could see that, see where the blood had rushed to his face, throbbed wildly in the pulse at his throat. Merle lay unconscious, her lips still purple. Uncle looked down at her, heaving, he reached down to grab Clover who was licking Merle's face. He picked the dog up by the scruff of her neck. Held her out for all to see, then with a look of pure hatred, dropped her to the floor. The worm, he said once more, looking directly at Joan. Two of a kind.

Joan was still in her mother's robe, the mole over her lip shifted, like the stars overhead, in that inexplicable way, the way that laughing shifted to tears, love to hatred. It was something I would never forget.

Gideon drove Toby and Kevin to Moe's, then he took David back to his own house. Jonah took Em and Joan and me to the Zooks. He made three trips, carrying each one of us gently to his car. Seth and Ezekiel carried our mother downstairs. The yard was full of light, full of men in cars.

The bridge, when we passed under the trestle, was bathed red then blue, red then blue. We'd had to wait until the ambulance went through, the one with Merle, the one with our mother. We had no idea what had happened to her, whether she'd had a stroke or whether the way we saw her, the last image we had of her, was how she looked when she went crazy. *Careful, car full,* I whispered as she went over the bridge.

CHAPTER FIFTEEN

Mrs. Zook was up when we arrived, the whole town was. She had two lambs in a wooden crate in the kitchen. Lambs whose mother wouldn't feed them. *Sheepies,* she called them. She called us lambs. We were lambs. She opened her robe and we buried ourselves in it. She would not let us go. We moved as one creature to the chair by the fire. She sat with us, not daring to move, her large and kind face turned toward the door, where the day was just forming, just coming into being, like a figure emerging from clay. We were trembling. Mrs. Zook said not to worry. No one would hurt us, we had nothing to worry about. Mr. Zook would keep watch if that's what it took to settle us. We had nothing to worry about, nothing at all.

What about our mother? Our mother was in good hands, she said. I saw again the way my father held her, the way his hands had rubbed her face. I wanted to ask about Merle for Joan's sake, but I was afraid of what Joan might see if I did.

Em and I sank into Mrs. Zook's kindness, but not Joan. Her body hardened. We tried to hug her, hold her to us but she wouldn't bend. Mrs. Zook knew to leave her be, knew her shock to be greater than ours. She'd nearly lost her mother.

Merle's voice box was crushed and her jaw was broken. It had to be wired shut. She might never be able to speak another word. This news, when I heard it from my father, brought me enormous relief. She would never be able to tell Joan that I'd told on her. Our own mother had suffered a seizure. Grand Mal. We had no idea what that meant except that she was in the nuthouse again.

The Yetters came to see us, Jonah stopping by with ice cream for us after work. Dixie Cups, vanilla-chocolate split down the middle, hard as rocks, with flat wooden spoons that tasted like the tongue depressors Dr. Maybee used. He came as well, to check on us. Our father asked him to. We certainly had more than our share of troubles hadn't we? He hoped this was the end to it. Our mother had had a setback, he told us, but she'd pull through. She'd suffered a seizure, a pretty severe one, he said. Dr. Maybee believed in telling children the truth. If I had any more questions I should ask my father. But my father wouldn't tell us anything more. We only knew that our mother was back in the nuthouse again. The sheriff also came to visit. He wanted to talk to Joan about the jewelry, where she'd gotten it from. From Eddie or from Harold?

Harold, she said. I nodded that this was true. We all did, we all knew it was from him.

"Of course it was from Harold," my father said. Good Lord, he'd known Eddie Birdseye for two years. He was a decent man. My father was proud to have him for a neighbor. Still, the sheriff wanted to know if there was anything else we knew about Mr. Birdseye's relationship with Joan. Emily and I shook our heads, no. The sheriff kneeled down to our size when he spoke. Was there anything we wanted to tell him in private?

"There's nothing else to know, for God's sake. Let's not make Eddie the scapegoat." My father said Uncle was a jealous man and a drinker. Merle, well, she didn't know when to leave well enough alone. What had happened was an accumulation of things. But the responsibility lay with Uncle. Jesus Christ, he didn't want to see Eddie Birdseye dragged into this. My father would vouch for his character.

We'd be all right. Em and I. We had each other. But Joan. Dr.

Maybee was worried about Joan. She might need to see her mother, be convinced that she was okay. Joan shook her head, no. Leave her alone. When the Doctor left she took a paper clip and carved that word in the soft underskin of her arm. ALONE.

When Monday came, Joan refused to go to school. She refused to eat. Our father came to talk with her. She sat slumped in a chair trying to pick the flowers that grew in the pattern of the fabric. My father said that she was going to be made a ward of the state. The sheriff recommended it for her own sake. Uncle was threatening to beat her bloody if he made bail. And my father couldn't put the Zooks at risk. No. He'd imposed on them enough. She'd be in foster care temporarily. Not permanently. There was nothing he could do about it, not for now, but someday he hoped we could make a home for her. Joan yawned. Lice were all I could think about. Joan's head shaved bald.

Jay stood with his arms akimbo, shaking his head. He was afraid of Joan's anger. All right, all right, he said until his father grew exasperated and made him go to bed.

When we first came to the Zooks, Mrs. Zook said we could all sleep in one bed if we wanted. But Joan refused. She said let the sisters sleep together, dragging her spit across the word *sisters*. She hated us now. We could feel it. Mrs. Zook gave her the bedroom over the kitchen, the warmest room in the house.

Easter Sunday was six days later. We woke to baskets filled with chocolate rabbits, dyed eggs, and marshmallow chicks. It was the third Sunday in April, the eighteenth. Mrs. Zook said she liked it when Easter came late. Nothing made her sadder than seeing everyone in linen coats and straw hats digging out from under a foot of snow when it came too early. She worried about everyone it seemed and would have had us all wrapped in wool if she could. Bless us and save us said our Mrs. Davis while jumping over a peck of potatoes, she said when one of us sneezed.

Mrs. Zook seemed ready to keep us for good. She'd always wanted little girls. Jay nodded. He'd wanted sisters. Now he had a houseful of them. The Zooks' house was like nothing we'd ever seen. Dumplings soft as pillows, chicken sliding off the bone. Feather beds so deep we were afraid we'd suffocate in our sleep. A fireplace in every room. Tea cozy, rag rugs and seat cushions, everything soft as the Zooks' laps. Mr. Zook sat in his chair after Easter dinner and filled his pipe from a humidor. Ivanhoe tobacco, flecked like blood against his Sunday shirt. He listened to music from the homeland, made us birds from his pipe cleaners, let us help him with his jigsaw puzzle. Still, he'd killed the Easter lamb and so we made sure that everything we said was please and thank you. Except for Joan, who stayed in her room, off to herself. Mostly she sat in her window waiting for the State to come for her.

But the only person who came for her was Eddie Birdseye. It was fine with him if she kept some of the jewelry. Not the ring, of course, but the necklace and matching bracelet. Even the earrings. But Joan shook her head. She didn't want anything. The crusted brown threads still hung in her ears. He tried everything he could to cheer her up. He talked about Shadow, how he'd be happy to teach her how to ride, now that her leg and Shadow's were healed. It would mean a lot to Harold. To both of them, because he knew it would mean a lot to her. Did she want to give it a try, take her mind off her troubles?

Go, I prayed. But she wouldn't. I felt sorry for Joan, but I felt sorry for Eddie Birdseye, too, because he was being so kind to Joan and she didn't care. He looked at me so beseechingly, I shrugged. I would ride Shadow if he asked me, I knew I would, even though I was scared to death of that horse. But when he looked back at Joan, she just stood up and left the room.

Mrs. Zook said to leave her be. But Eddie Birdseye said that he couldn't. He felt that responsible for what had happened to Joan. That's why he came. He wanted Joan to leave with some good memories at least. I thought of all the days she'd spent with Eddie Birdseye while Harold was in the hospital and we were in school. I was sure those were some good memories for her. Mrs. Zook said he needn't feel responsible for Joan because she was responsible for us now, and she wasn't letting any one of us out of her sight. Then she showed him to the door and closed it firmly behind him.

On Monday after Easter the weather changed. The light rain that had been falling seemed to freeze in place as the wind brought on the cold. We were close enough to Canada to still get snow in April, but it was rare for the temperatures to drop so low. We stayed indoors for two days while low and high fronts struggled overhead. It was perfect weather for pneumonia, and Mrs. Zook would have none of that. She showed us how to tie rags for rugs. She taught us to crochet. She let us feed the baby lambs. We peeled apples for pie and threw the peels over our left shoulders to see who'd we marry. It had worked for her. When she was twelve years old she'd thrown a Z. She smiled over at her husband, his hands over his belly fit together as neatly as the puzzle pieces he worked.

Whatever she had to do, we were incorporated into it. So when she went out to check her garden — she'd put her peas in on St. Patrick's Day — we followed along with burlap sacks hoping to save what was most surely lost. We stayed so close to her she said we reminded her of the ducklings that had just recently hatched. We could see them over at the Sucker Hole behind the barn waddling gingerly over the thin layer of ice that had formed overnight. There was only a small place for them to swim and they huddled there, determined to feed. In the afternoon Mrs. Zook let us take some chicken scratch and bread crusts out to them. Don't follow the ducklings the way we followed her. Just throw the scraps onto the ice.

Across the frozen pond, the freshly plowed fields were stiff and webbed with new snow. The old snow that lay in the spring woods looked like the gray in Mr. Zook's beard. The trees, many fallen under the weight of ice and gusts of wind, looked like someone had stepped on them, squashed them under foot. Beyond all of this, our house stood alone on the ridge. Despite everything that had happened to me, to us, I was drawn to it, wanting to reclaim it as the winter had reclaimed spring. My father stayed there with David, but we hadn't been back.

Sometimes when Mrs. Zook went out to feed the sheep, I'd pick up the party line. It hummed with the news that Merle and Uncle were always trouble. Come up from the Bronx. City slickers. Uncle was a drunk, Merle was no good. A tramp. She had it coming. She still wasn't out of the woods. She had to have police protection twenty-four hours a day, in case Uncle made bail and came to finish her off.

West of us in Buffalo, where the people from the State resided, snow had been falling since Easter. The roads were impassable. It would be several days before any one could come for Joan. Mrs. Zook was happy to have Joan for as long as she could. We could look over our shoulders when we were out by the pond and see her sitting in the window. Even when we waved, she didn't move. She seemed as frozen in place as the world around us had become.

Of all of us, she had the least. A small suitcase bound with clothesline held her possessions, her wine-colored sweater, her white skates, her slip and dresses. Mrs. Zook remedied this. She knitted her two pairs of mittens and a hat, a festive blue beret. Crocheting was faster, but knitting made a sturdier mitten, she said. She could knit and read, and at night after dinner that's what she did. While we slept she made Joan a jumper out of black watch plaid and one made out of red wool. When Joan saw the red jumper her eyes flared a bit. We all knew it was her mother's color.

Merle was going to be all right, though she had to remain in the hospital for a while. She wasn't going to come back to us. She was going back to the Bronx. My father was shipping her there.

On Thursday Mrs. Zook got the call from the State. We were in the kitchen making cookies. Mrs. Zook was afraid of the phone. Whenever it rang she jumped. Two long and three short meant the call was for her. Most of the calls were two long and two short, and that meant it was for Moe's, thank heavens, she said. We'd held our breath whenever the phone began to ring, we felt that loyal to Mrs. Zook. When the third short ring sounded we turned to her, Em and I. She picked up the phone and listened, then very carefully and quietly, put the phone back in its cradle and walked up the stairs to Joan. When she came back downstairs, she called my father at the bar. He came to see Joan at lunchtime. She refused to come down, so he went up to her room. We followed him, but he waved us back. Her door was shut and my father knocked softly, but Joan didn't answer. He stood with his forehead against the door, his hand lightly on the knob, but he was too much of a gentleman to walk in uninvited. In the end he left her a note, which we slid under her door. She wouldn't open it to us either.

Dinner was served at six o'clock sharp. Pork and sauerkraut, cinnamon baked apples. Mrs. Zook tried to coax Joan to eat with us, to have a good meal before her trip, but she refused. Since our arrival we ate in the dining room, which was in the front of the house. The kitchen was in the back, facing the barn, and like our house, had steps that led upstairs. That stairway was closed off by doors at the top and bottom to conserve heat. Despite the fact that the kitchen door was known to stick, we didn't hear Joan open it.

I had wanted to go in to Joan, even though she wouldn't answer my knocks. I knew from past experience that she could change her mind any second. After dinner I went up and sat by her door. The State was coming in the morning, then it was going to be gruel in wooden bowls, straw mattresses and schoolmasters with hickory switches that stung your legs. I didn't understand why we couldn't keep Joan with us. I blamed my father for it and when he came that night to tuck us in, to see if Joan would say good-bye to him, I turned away from him. He was as stricken as if I'd taken a hickory switch to his bare legs.

Good Lord, he hoped I didn't think he wanted Joan to leave. His hands were tied. I looked at my father's hands. They were broad hands, with tufts of dark hair on each finger. I'd seen him arm wrestle with Uncle and though Uncle was the bigger man, my father, his hand clasped in Uncle's, bent his arm over, effortlessly, gently, with the same tenderness that he used when he dipped my mother, in the days when they danced for us through the rooms, showing us how they could do the fox trot, the tango, the swing.

My father knelt by our bed, Em's and mine, as though we were saints that he prayed to. Saint Jude, the patron saint of hopeless cases, Saint Gerard, the patron saint of all mothers, new and old, Saint Anthony the patron saint of the lost. He had done his best to keep us together. He'd done all that was humanly possible. We knew that, didn't we? We nodded that we did, Em's tears ruffling just the edge of her chin. We knew that, but still it was not enough. Not for me. When my father left, when the Zooks had turned off all the lights, when Jay was sent to bed, when even the lambs curled quiet in the kitchen, I took up my post beside Joan's door. She could come out and strangle me for all I cared, because after she did she'd lie down beside me. She'd wait while my ears stopped ringing, my throat opened, my breath filled my chest one rib at a time, she'd watch over me and bring me slowly back to her, slowly back to life.

I never felt Mr. Zook pick me up and bring me back to bed. He'd found me asleep on the rag rug in front of Joan's door. When I awoke, I was back in bed alone. The day had gotten off to a start without me. I dressed quickly and made my way to Joan's room. The door was open. I was more shocked by this than by the fact that Joan was gone. The State had come and gotten her, I was sure, come and gotten everyone it seemed. The Zooks were gone, Jay was gone, and my sister Em was gone. I was almost afraid to leave the house in the face of this, feeling as I did that everything would collapse if one more person left.

I put on my coat, forcing the black buttons through the closed lid of each buttonhole. Outside the air was cold, the wind was strong, strong enough to bend the trees. I thought again of my father's hands bending Uncle's arm. I could hear voices behind the barn, see cars in the drive, one very new, sleek, shiny as patent leather. If it was the State's car then they hadn't taken Joan yet. I followed the sound of voices. I could see Jay standing with his hands on his hips. Mrs. Zook was in her gray wool sweater, arms up her sleeves hugging herself, the way she'd held us the night we came. The men, my father, the sheriff, Mr. Zook, the Yetters' boys, were looking across the pond. As I drew near, Mrs. Zook, sensing me before seeing me, put her hand out, drew me next to her. *Oh, lamb,* she whispered. On the ice were Joan's skates, thrown there or left there, it was impossible to tell. The ice was too unstable for anyone to walk on it, too unstable for anyone to check to see if Joan had. The world around us seemed unstable too. There was no way to know when Joan had left, whether late at night or while we were at dinner.

The land was as grim and tight-lipped as the sheriff. My father stood staring out at the pond, shaking his head. Why Mrs. Zook hadn't considered that Joan might leave, she'd never know. It was not as though the child had anything to stay for. She looked over at the people from the State, a man and a woman, both in thick gray overcoats. The woman pulled a muffler over her mouth and nose, but I could still see her eyes, impatient and unforgiving. The man stood helpless. The wind worried his hat, fluttered it against his brow as though something under it longed to escape. Em sat in my father's car, getting warm. She looked like a lone dog in the back seat.

I didn't think that my cousin was in the pond though her footprints ended at its edge. She knew how to retrace her steps, we'd practiced often enough whenever we went back into the woods in case Wayne was following us. Besides, I knew the pond could never hold Joan, not when the river had tried and failed. I'd seen her rise from that water, but I'd also seen her rise from this pond as well. It was a week before she'd broken her leg. She'd wanted to practice by herself, when none of the girls from town would be there. It was evening, and she had the pond to herself. I'd come across the field to get her. Dinner was on the table, and I didn't want her to get into trouble, didn't want anyone to get into trouble. Trouble followed us, that's what my father sometimes said, and I believed it.

When I arrived, Joan was out in the middle of the pond. It was almost dark enough for me to be scared, but the memory of light still hung on in places. Joan's skates seemed incredibly white as they went through the eights she was trying to perfect. She almost had them down. I stood watching her. If I broke her concentration, she might break my neck. If I didn't, Merle was sure to break both our necks. I hesitated. Joan might have sensed me there. She came out of the top half of the eight and went immediately into a squat. She had some speed but wanted more. She moved out toward the center again, gained speed, turned, came back straight toward me, and dropped again into a squat. It was very cold, the moon bobbed up like a skull. I waved her in. She came toward me, stood up once more, and when she did, there was just the softest bending sound, a heave, and she was gone, gone through the ice.

For a moment I thought I was dreaming, that she hadn't been there at all. Then my legs began to shake. I felt like I was underwater with Joan, that the heavy sky above me was as vast and as unyielding as the ice above Joan. I tried to remember what my mother had said to us, to Joan too. We were to look for the light because if we went through the ice, we might come up under it and be confused, but the place where we went through would be lighter. Float. We were to float. I felt my own skirt begin to lift. But it was only the wind. Only the wind. Then a sudden *ho*, and Joan popped through the ice. Light. That's all I could think of. She must have seen the light. Joan was not far from where I stood. She could stand and she did, she'd walked through that ice to me. Then she walked home through the white fields, her pants in frozen folds, her heavy sweater, stretched, the sleeves hanging inches below her hands. We walked to the house in silence, Joan's skates slicing through the snow. I brought her in through the cellar door, went back outside, came up the steps and stood on the porch and watched my brothers and sister eating dinner. Merle had taken her plate and a plate for my mother and gone into her. They sat in the alcove eating, Merle using her fork to encourage my mother to pick up hers. I slipped inside, unlatched the cellar door and motioned to Joan. She came up the steps, through the kitchen, past Toby and Em and Wayne, sodden and shaking, her face deeply red. They stopped and stared at her, then bent to their plates, as though everyday someone half-drowned, half-dead, wandered through their midst.

There'd be no dogs chasing Joan down, this day, said Mrs. Zook looking over to the Yetters' dogs. Joan had suffered enough pain and humiliation at the hands of adults as it was.

Jay had put on his favorite hat, a duplicate of his Dad's hunting cap, the red ear flaps that normally covered his ears, were turned up, expectant as the hounds pacing their cage, now that the wind had softened, now that spring had come back to us just as suddenly as Joan had left us.

Jesus, my father said. Jesus Christ Almighty. It was how we all felt. We bowed our heads.

Jay's hat blew off just then, kited and looped across the mud. But the man from the State's hat held. Clouds moved overhead, blocked the sun, then framed it. The morning was both light and dark. I thought about that. How a day could hold both winter and spring, light and shadow, moisture and dryness. How one hat could blow off and one hat remain. How my cousin Joan could be so far away from me but feel so close. Jay broke from us then, running after his hat. He was clumsy, his man's body at odds with the boy he'd always be. My father, his eyes raw with tears, said, Rainey, be a good girl, help him catch his cap. And I was.

But the sheriff was not so cooperative. He signaled for the dogs, asked for an article of Joan's clothes. Mrs. Zook shook her head. She wouldn't be a party to this, she said, turning, taking my hand, and looking round for Emily and bringing us back into the house. It was Mr. Zook who finally brought something of Joan's to the men. We didn't know what it was, we only heard him overhead, his boots heavy as our hearts, as he searched her room for some memory of her.

The dogs sounded both urgent and mournful. Sometimes we'd hear them from a distance as they ran back and forth across the field to our house. Other times it seemed they were under the very windows we sat behind. Once the people from the State came to the door and asked to use the phone, but Mrs. Zook wouldn't let them in. The day warmed, Joan's footprints melted, the ground wept. Emily and I went to the window each time we heard a car or truck arrive, thinking that Joan had been found. Mrs. Zook didn't try to stop us, though she had set herself the task of teaching us how to embroider. Men gathered in small groups, tight as the French knots we were working on. An occasional woman handed a thermos of coffee and sandwich from her car to her husband, but finding Joan was the business of men, not women.

Whenever Mrs. Zook left the room, I'd pick up the party line. Though I knew it was wrong, I couldn't help myself. Em would stand across the room watching, but she never tried to stop me. Once I heard a woman say, directly to me it seemed, that Joan was loose, just like her mother. She was brazen. That she'd stolen the jewelry, that everyone knew she was a little thief. Mr. Moe had caught her with a pack of cigarettes the week before. But because of Andy, he hadn't said anything. Andy Dougherty had the worst luck. But maybe that was changing now that he was rid of them all. Joan probably put her thumb up and hopped into the first car that stopped. The apple didn't fall far from the tree. From where I stood, I could see Zooks' apple tree, buds of ice on all the branches.

Sometimes when Mrs. Zook came back, I'd be crying. She didn't even care when I used my practice piece of linen to wipe my nose. You go ahead and cry, she'd say, and when I was through, she'd take me into the bathroom, wash my face and say, there, doesn't that make you feel better.

Even though the wind was mild, it was late afternoon before the clouds thinned and a ribbon of blue sky floated over our heads just like the one that I'd seen caught in the ice the day I'd taken Joan's skates. That ribbon had probably come loose by now. I thought of Joan, what the woman on the party line had said. I prayed that Joan was loose, that she had hitchhiked away. Even though some man had once pulled her into his car and made her touch his privates, she wasn't afraid to get into cars with them.

But the search for Joan always ended at the pond. That's where the men and the dogs gathered. Mr. Zook lit a fire, and the men, as they came in from the fields, held their hands to the heat. Someone had dragged a rowboat to the bank. There was a long pole balanced on top of it. It looked like the kind of pole tightrope walkers used. I could see the flames reflected in the water. Somehow I believed that if Joan was in the pond the flames might warm it up enough that she would surface, come walking out of the water to her skates, which lay folded against the logs, like small white wings. I couldn't leave that window, not even when the men left and the fire burned down, then burned out as the snow began to fall again. I stood behind the glass and waited until my limbs were as heavy as they were the night Wayne tied me to the tree. Mrs. Zook walked me up the stairs, pulled a chair to my bedroom window, and made me drink some warm milk. She checked on me several times, laying a blanket over my knees, tucking a pillow behind my back, but she never made me come away from the window.

Sometime during the night I heard a horse whinnying. Shadow, I thought. Harold riding out in the fields looking for Joan, calling her home. If anyone could bring her in, it would be Shadow. I pressed my forehead to the cold windowpane. The snow had stopped but I couldn't see past the pines nodding under the weight of it. I rested my cheek against the glass, felt the thin layer of ice that my own cousin's face might be resting against. The shock of this made me stumble back against the chair, pull the blanket all around me.

"Rainey?" Em said, from the bed. "Did you hear Shadow?"

"Did you?" I asked. She nodded. The Zooks didn't keep horses, just cows and sheep. I wondered if Mr. Zook had thought to search the barn for Joan. She could have been in there waiting until we all were asleep, waiting for Harold to come for her, take her to his house, where he and his father would never let the State take her.

But that is not what happened. I awoke wrapped around the warmth of my sister. She slept, mouth open, a circle of gray on the white pillow below her chin. Mrs. Zook was standing by the bed with a breakfast tray. Breakfast in bed though it was nearly lunchtime. We'd slept that long. The shade was drawn, the organdy curtains swagged like the fullness of her bosom. She had made us blueberry pancakes, the blueberries canned from last year's harvest. They bled like bruises beneath the golden cakes, matched the gray under Mrs. Zook's sad eyes. She told us that the first one to finish was in for a treat. She fluffed our pillows, set the tray over our knees, amazed that it bridged our four legs. We were such tiny girls, she said, busying herself with the down comforter. All of us, such little girls, she said, shaking her head. I looked toward the window. Mrs. Zook averted her eyes. Eat, she said, just take three bites, that's all we needed to do, get something warm in our bellies.

Between Em and me, we finished one pancake. Because of this, Mrs. Zook said we both earned the treat. We were going to the movies to see *The Golden Slipper*. A matinee. What about Joan, we asked. Mrs. Zook said that she was sure that by the time we got back, we'd have some news. With so many people looking for her, it wouldn't be long before she was found. Would Joan still have to go to the State? Mrs. Zook shook her head, she thought other arrangements would be made. Then she lifted the tray from the bed, sat down beside us, gathered us to her as she had the first night we came. She didn't know about us, she said, kissing the tops of our heads, but she certainly needed a change of scene.

The scene, when I went to the window after Mrs. Zook had bathed us and washed our hair, was eerily still and this frightened me more than if the searchers had been there. The pond was a dark hole in the completely white day. I could hear the muted honk of geese, could feel their buried movement behind the falling snow, imagine their long necks black as the telephone receiver that was just then beckoning me to lift it once more.

"Oh, lamb," Mrs. Zook said, when she saw the telephone in my hand, my stricken face. "Oh, lamb, no."

CHAPTER SIXTEEN

Sundays we drove out to see our mother. It was the only time we were together, the five of us. Em and I still stayed with the Zooks during the week. David was at the house with our father. Mrs. Douglass, who lived in town, boarded Toby and Kevin. She called them bairns. Wee bairns. Even though we went home on the weekends, we rarely saw our father. He was spread too thin. He *had* lost weight. Anyone could see that.

Despite this, he made sure that he gathered us all together to visit our mother. It took us hours to get used to one another again. We'd wait in the car. Kevin was walking, Toby tried to kick him whenever he did. David would sit in the driver's seat, his arm on the window's ledge. Em could still fit in the way back, in the slender window space above the backseat. She read there, lost in her books, waiting for a call. Waiting to be called by Christ, she said. It was entirely possible, I thought. We had the party line at Zooks'.

At last my father would bring our mother down to us. It was like a park, the nuthouse, everybody waltzing along paths, the stairways, the lobby, the way we had the night we tried on Merle's clothes. The night when she almost had her lights put out for good. My mother didn't know about Joan. Dr. Maybee wouldn't allow it. Not yet. Maybe when she was stronger. Even so, even if I had been allowed to tell her, I wouldn't have, I felt that possessive of her memory.

Mrs. Peterson was our mother's personal nurse. She stayed with her all the while she was with us. This didn't bother me at all, though normally I didn't like to share my mother with anyone. Mrs. Peterson never said a word. Sometimes she bent to check my mother's pulse, or simply stepped forward if my mother started to cry. Just that movement was enough to make my mother stop.

And only once was Mrs. Peterson not there. Then our mother told us why she couldn't speak. She'd suffered a terrible trauma when she was younger which left her mute. It wasn't a physical ailment. Nothing of the sort. No. It was all in her mind. In fact, Mrs. Peterson had been a patient in this very same hospital years before.

"She's all right now," my father reminded our mother, "she's pulled through." My mother stared at him for a long moment. The nuthouse, in the soft fading light of the summer evenings, beckoned us. We knew that there were mothers in those very rooms who had tried to murder their children, tried to throw them in the fire, tried to feed them poison, crushed glass. We knew that there was a woman in there who tricked a nurse, got the scissors from behind her back when the nurse bent to untie the ropes that restrained her, and plunged the scissors through the nurse's heart. Hadn't Merle told us this? Hadn't she told us all their stories?

I moved closer to my mother. She looked at all of us. Her children. "She pulled through," my mother repeated to us.

"Merle, too. Merle's going to be fine," my father said, moving quickly to ward off what we knew was coming.

"He crushed her voice box," my mother told us, sadly. She was shaking her head. Our father was shaking his as well.

"Merle loved to sing, but Grandma D. forbade it in the house. Dancing too. Grandma D. and her daughters tried to squelch Merle's spirit. So, she packed up her things and left for good. She lied about her age and got a job in St. Pat's. Not St. Pat's the church. The bar. That's where she met Uncle. She was barely sixteen years old at the time, but she managed just fine. She rented a room on Jerome Avenue. It was a little dollhouse, the way she fixed it up. She was underage when she married Uncle," my mother said. She wished that someone had caught this, had had the marriage annulled. But the aunts were glad she was out of their hair.

"She had a twenty-inch waist. Uncle could span it with two hands," my mother said. I tried to picture this, but all I could see was his hands around Merle's throat.

"She had the better voice, but she gave it up for him. She wanted him to shine. But he knew she was the singer in the family. That's the one thing he hated." *Ca-li-forn-ya, here I come, right back where I started from* was all I could hear.

"A twenty-inch waist," my mother repeated, shaking her head, "and a heart of gold."

The cool arms of the dark firs lining the drive enclosed us, kept us out of Uncle's reach. He was cooling his heels in jail, my father said. We had nothing to worry about anymore. Neither did Merle.

"I'll never hear her voice again. Never," my mother said. "Not if I live to be a hundred years old. I'll never hear my sister's beautiful voice again." I took my mother's wrist in my hand, turned it over, fingered the lightning strike of veins.

"I'll never forget it. I'll never forget the sound of her voice." We were all silent then, even Kevin who didn't really know how to be. Even Toby who stood stock still for once. David smiled his practiced smile at Em, but her head was cocked, as though still hearing Merle threaten to tie us to trees, stick socks in our mouths, glue our asses to chairs, and beat the bejeezus out of us if we didn't sit down and shut up.

I was thinking about the worm, again. The one that got into people. The worm inside of me. Inside us all. I pressed my thumb lightly on my mother's wrist, but her blood continued to flow. She turned to look at me, to ask me what it was I wanted, but I couldn't speak. "You're awfully quiet anymore," she said, suddenly anxious. I looked up at her, at the attendant just now coming to take her back inside, at the sure hold the night had on us all. Above our heads, a deep summer night sky was forming. Though it was perfectly dry, the night seemed moist, in full bloom, the Milky Way a swirl of star pollen sprinkling the heavens the way Father Leary sprinkled holy water over our heads. "Tell me again," I said to my mother, "tell me how you will never hear your sister's voice."

The day of my Communion, my mother came home for good. She wasn't able to see me receive the sacrament, but that didn't matter to me. Not at all. Em and I sat waiting for her on Zooks' front porch, swinging on their glider. It was a latticework of metal, painted white, the color of my dress. I'd had to go to confession the day before and receive absolution for my sins. I hadn't wanted to go because I knew that I would have to confess to Father Leary that I had lied when the sheriff asked me about Joan and Mr. Birdseye. I couldn't do this because I didn't want to get Mr. Birdseye in trouble. As it was, my father said, the entire episode had tarnished Mr. Birdseye's reputation.

It was really my second confession if I counted the practice one the winter before, and I knew that I'd have to recount my lies, my curses, my meanness to my brothers. I thought of my own reputation being tarnished. As I stood in line, I looked at the altar, the gleaming silver candleholders, the starched altar linens as white as a pure soul. The flames from red votive candles licked the feet of the Virgin Mary and St. Francis with an *i*, not an *e,* the one Merle used to call birdbrain because she'd seen a statue of him with a bird on his head. Thinking of this made me smile, though I knew it was a sacrilege and that I'd

have to add it to my list of sins. I also added the sin of not telling when
Joan had taken money from the poor box. I was an accomplice to that,
too. The weight of all my sins began to make me tired, and as I bent
to the kneeler, they pushed me down, held me in place. There were a
few dark moments in the confessional where I thought to reflect on
my sins. Actually, I was sick of them and had the urge to stand up and
walk right out of the confessional, away from them and Father Leary,
but just then Father slid the screen open to me. I began to recite my
sins in great detail, the many times I hit my brothers, the days when I
said curses under my breath, the seven lies that I had told, and the cir-
cumstances around each one. I had three more to tell, including the
one about Mr. Birdseye and Joan, when Father stopped me. "How
many more child?" he asked. I said three. "Are you truly sorry for
them?" Father asked. I whispered that I was. I truly was. "Then make
a good Act of Contrition," he said. As I prayed, Father made the sign
of the cross and absolved me. I made my way very carefully to the altar
rail and knelt to do my penance. Within the interior of the church I
felt cleansed, as though I glowed in the dark like the crucifix Em hung
above our bed. As long as I stayed in church, I would remain in a state
of grace, so I took my time saying my penance because I loved the way
I felt.

Though my mother was coming home, we wouldn't be going
home right away. She and my father needed some time alone. This
meant that my father would have to tell her about Joan's disappearance. Dr. Maybee said she was finally ready to hear the truth. My
father told us this but added that in the future, we weren't to run to
our mother with every little scrape or bruise. If we needed someone to
share our troubles with, we were to wait until he got home. No problems were that urgent that they couldn't wait. And we were to stop

looking so sad. Nothing was worth all that sadness. Nothing.

Mrs. Zook had bathed us, set our hair, polished our shoes. We only had to sit still and wait. We watched for my father's car for hours. He'd promised to bring my mother over to see me in my dress and veil. Emily was reading out loud from *Lives of the Saints*. Mrs. Zook said Em was on the road to sainthood. The week before my sister had told me about St. Sebastian, who'd been shot through with arrows. She practiced putting pins into her fingers to see if she could bear the pain. She lit candles and passed her hands through the flames, some of the very things Joan had done to me. Because of Joan, I could have easily made it to sainthood.

Emily was holding the kitten she'd gotten for her birthday in her lap. She was trying to find a name for it. Finally she decided on Aloysius. I asked her if he was one of the saints that was roasted on live coals or had his skin pulled off with hot pincers. She said neither, that he had come to his vocation when he was young, just as she had. Aloysius the kitten yawned lazily and curled tighter against her. Aloysius the saint died when he was twenty-five years old. Em said that he died of consumption after helping the sick. He wasn't a martyr, though like the martyrs he suffered with joy. She said some of the saints were never called to prove their faith. Some seemed to die simply from goodness.

A truck bore down on us from the ridge. We watched it come on. It slowed as it drew closer to us. It was Eddie Birdseye. He was already a saint according to my father. Eddie Birdseye had put in a word for him at Morse Chain, the machine shop where his brother-in-law worked, and now my father would be able to spend more time with his family. Sometimes Harold was in the truck with his father. He was learning how to drive and didn't ride Shadow anymore. He'd had another operation on his face, and now the outline of how he'd once looked was taking form. The first time I saw Eddie and Harold in the truck together, I thought it might be Joan, that Harold had found her in the barn that night and had taken her to his house. Each time since, I'd held my breath just in case.

Em turned the kitten upside down to check its privates. We still weren't sure if it was a boy or a girl. Aloysius Agnes Melissa, Em decided. I liked the sound of that.

Eddie Birdseye was alone. He was coming to take a picture of me for my mother. We watched him make the turn into Zooks' driveway. I felt sorry for Mr. Birdseye because he rarely smiled anymore. On the weekends, when David, Em and I were home, Eddie and my father sat outside on the Adirondack chairs drinking beer the color of the stagnant water that remained in the milk bottles long after the bouquets of lilacs had died. Many of our neighbors wouldn't drink with Eddie anymore, wouldn't sit next to him during Mass. But I would sit with him if I had the chance because I knew that he missed Joan as much as I did. Sometimes it was on my mind to ask him for one of the pictures he'd taken of Joan, though I never did. David wouldn't pose for pictures anymore because some of his friends were making fun of him in school. Posing wasn't one of the seven virtues so Em wouldn't do it though she was exquisitely beautiful, *a china doll*, my mother called her whenever we went to visit her. Emily was very photogenic, David too, but I wasn't. None of the pictures she had taken of me looked a thing like me, my mother had said on our last visit to the nuthouse. My father said that if anyone could do me justice, it was Eddie Birdseye. He was opening a photography studio on the empty corner opposite Moe's Store. My father liked this idea, the symmetry, the last of the four corners occupied. For some reason I thought of the kaleidoscope the

Yetters had given me, the colors shifting, the way the shards fell into place. My mother had smiled then. *All my geese are swan,* she said.

Mrs. Zook had made my Communion dress. She'd let me choose the fabric and I'd chosen satin again. I loved the way it felt against my skin. The piece my mother had bought for me had disappeared. I thought maybe Joan had taken it because sometimes when she sucked her fingers, she'd rub the silky blanket binding against her lips. After my dress was made, Mrs. Zook washed it in case other shoppers had handled the fabric. Then she turned it inside out and pressed it, put her hand inside the capped sleeves, spread her fingers, and ironed. But the sleeves wouldn't stay puffed up until she put tissue paper inside them. Then they stood up like dandelions gone to seed. When I put on the dress, I'd felt that light, that expectant, that ready to float away.

When we got home from church, Mrs. Zook said it might be a good idea to take the dress off until Mr. Birdseye arrived, but I couldn't bear to. In that case, I had to sit on the glider and promise not to move a muscle until he pulled into the driveway. I kept my promise, standing only when I saw him drive up.

As I walked down the steps to his truck, my heart began to beat faster. I could feel my legs tremble just a little, but my steps were sure. In the distance I could hear the sudden unease of a dog's complaint. Above Mr. Birdseye's truck a crow, black as the tar on the new telephone pole in front of our house, ratcheted a sudden outrage, then quieted. The wind flared, caught my veil and blew it across my face. I lifted my hand and pulled it free. Eddie Birdseye put his elbow on the window ledge, rested his chin on his hand, then he smiled down at me. I smiled back.

"What a picture," he said, raising his camera and aiming it at me. I was ready. I turned on my heel and spun. My dress flared wide for a moment, held, then slowly settled down around my legs. Eddie Birdseye was looking at me carefully. Then he winked.

Right then, I knew I would be next.

ACKNOWLEDGMENTS

It has taken me ten years to complete this book and many, many people, beloved to me, essential to me and my journey to a writing life, often held my future in their hands. When they did, they cupped their palms around the flame that was my life and made sure that it didn't go out. Thank you to my parents, married sixty-four years, orphans both, who forged for their six children a history of generosity and love that we have hoarded against the lean times. Thank you especially to my brother, Michael Freund, for the years before the blossoming and his faith, a tender bloom, that was his greatest gift to me. Thank you to my sister Patti Morrison and her husband Neal, who, when I had no one else to turn to, turned to me and called me home. And thank you to my children for the long nights they waited up for me to give what they themselves sorely needed, and when they couldn't wait up any longer, left for me a steeping tea kettle whose comfort warms me still.

Thank you to my teachers, especially Angela Bodino who, twenty years ago, put her finger on my calling and her heart into my work. To Cori Jones, Myrna Smith, Alicia Ostriker, and Mary Elsie Robertson, teachers who shaped my creative life and nurtured my teaching life.

Thank you to Gerald Stern who saw the story I would write long before I did and whose poetry gave me mine.

Mary Ann Taylor Hall and James Baker Hall, dearest hearts, had so much practice reading drafts of this novel that they can sing it by heart, and unlike me, never sound off-key.

To Connie Zdenek whose magic transforms me, whose writing

inspires me, and whose friendship sustains me. Thank you for your many careful readings of my work.

I need to thank Gail Hochman for years of effort on my behalf.

Central to my development as a writer are two prizes. In 1992 I received an Arizona Council of the Arts Grant for the first two chapters of this book, and in 1999 I received the Faulkner/Pirate's Alley prize for the completed manuscript. These prizes, though seven years apart, came at crucial times in my writing life and have made all the difference. Joe DeSalvo and Rosemary James, founders of the Faulkner/Pirate's Alley Society, have made all the difference in many writers' lives. Jayne Ann Phillips selected my novel for this prize and wrote of it so beautifully I was worried there would be no gorgeous language left for any of us.

My deepest gratitude goes to Pat Walsh, my editor who has the instincts of a writer and wisdom of a reader, to David Poindexter, my publisher for his intuitive and rare understanding of the importance of nurturing a relationship between editors and writers. Thank you as well to Leslie Koffler who found my misplaced manuscript, read it hurriedly, and ensured its safe passage.

Finally, Deborah Grosvenor, my agent, who, finding me at the end of my journey to a writing life, showed me it was just the beginning.